"I decided not to push trying to remember. If I relax, maybe more will come to me."

"That's true. There are some things you can't push."

She took a sip of hot, rich and creamy coffee. Oh, hot damn, full fat was the way to go. "Please don't let me stop you from anything you have to do today. I don't want to get in your way."

"Well, I'm supposed to be taking it easy, though that hasn't been going well so far." He set his mug down.

"And I haven't been much help in that pursuit."

He shrugged. "You've been a *great* help. I discovered fishing isn't for me."

"I wouldn't say that. You fished me out, didn't you? But please, go do something fun. Don't worry about me. I'll just...stay here and...and..." Her voice trailed off.

"You could watch the news or read. Take it easy and maybe something more will come to you."

"That's a good idea."

She hated the thought of him leaving her again. He'd had to at the hospital, and she all too well remembered the panic it had induced. She felt safe with him.

Dear Reader,

Welcome to the holidays in Charming, Texas!

This is my first amnesia story and I had a lot of fun imagining what it might be like to feel so vulnerable and lost at such a festive time of the year. Our poor heroine falls off a yacht, hits her head and forgets who she is. One thing she does know: It's Christmas, and she's alone.

Ronan Sheridan is fishing in the bay, trying to remember who he was before he joined the service, when he accidentally catches a whole lot more than he ever expected.

In her drive to prove she was worthy, Lauren Montez lost sight of her values. This Christmas, a big Irish family and the kind folks in Charming are going to help her find her way back to who she was all along. Somebody to love.

I hope you enjoy the journey Lauren and Ronan take to their own happily-ever-after.

Merry Christmas!

Heatherly Bell

OVERBOARD FOR THE HOLIDAYS

HEATHERLY BELL

SPECIAL EDITION

If you purchased this book without a cover you should be aware that this book is stolen property. It was reported as "unsold and destroyed" to the publisher, and neither the author nor the publisher has received any payment for this "stripped book."

MIX
Paper | Supporting responsible forestry
FSC® C021394

Harlequin®
SPECIAL EDITION™

Recycling programs for this product may not exist in your area.

ISBN-13: 978-1-335-18018-6

Overboard for the Holidays

Copyright © 2025 by Heatherly Bell

All rights reserved. No part of this book may be used or reproduced in any manner whatsoever without written permission.

Without limiting the author's and publisher's exclusive rights, any unauthorized use of this publication to train generative artificial intelligence (AI) technologies is expressly prohibited.

This is a work of fiction. Names, characters, places and incidents are either the product of the author's imagination or are used fictitiously. Any resemblance to actual persons, living or dead, businesses, companies, events or locales is entirely coincidental.

For questions and comments about the quality of this book, please contact us at CustomerService@Harlequin.com.

TM and ® are trademarks of Harlequin Enterprises ULC.

Harlequin Enterprises ULC
22 Adelaide St. West, 41st Floor
Toronto, Ontario M5H 4E3, Canada
www.Harlequin.com

HarperCollins Publishers
Macken House, 39/40 Mayor Street Upper,
Dublin 1, D01 C9W8, Ireland
www.HarperCollins.com

Printed in Lithuania

Bestselling author **Heatherly Bell** was born in Tuscaloosa, Alabama, but lost her accent by the time she was two. After leaving Alabama, Heatherly lived with her family in Puerto Rico and Maryland before being transplanted kicking and screaming to the California Bay Area. She now loves it here, she swears. Except the traffic.

Books by Heatherly Bell

Montana Mavericks: The Trail to Tenacity

The Maverick's Christmas Countdown

Harlequin Special Edition

Charming, Texas

Winning Mr. Charming
The Charming Checklist
A Charming Christmas Arrangement
A Charming Single Dad
A Charming Doorstep Baby
Once Upon a Charming Bookshop
Her Fake Boyfriend
The Ex Next Door
Overboard for the Holidays

The Fortunes of Texas: Hitting the Jackpot

Winning Her Fortune

Montana Mavericks:
The Real Cowboys of Bronco Heights

Grand-Prize Cowboy

Visit the Author Profile page
at Harlequin.com for more titles.

This is another book for Aliyah

Chapter One

When it came to parties, Lauren Montez thought the Raven Advertising Company's holiday extravaganza had reached a new standard for excellence.

The December night on the Gulf Coast was cool and calm as the party on the hundred-foot luxury yacht kicked into overdrive. This had been the best year on record for Raven, a full-service ad agency located in Dallas, and their CEO had gone all out for the celebration. They'd been pulled into platinum territory this year by Lauren's account with a winery in Napa Valley, which credited her campaign with their best sales year on record. And all she'd done was remind folks why they loved wine. It was almost too easy. Lauren expected a hefty bonus to round out the year, which would easily pull her income into the mid six figures.

It would more than justify the price of the sparkly red-and-white Valentino dress she wore tonight, paired with matching Manolo pumps. Under the slinky dress, which accentuated every curve, she wore a black Victoria's Secret thong and plunging demi bra she hoped someone would be skillfully removing later tonight. Someone by the name of Drew Poindexter, the CEO's son and a gorgeous dark-haired man who was wearing a double-breasted Italian suit. Great taste. Even greater stock portfolio.

They'd been dancing around each other for months in a sexually charged cat-and-mouse game. Unfortunately, he'd brought along a date, though given the smoldering looks he kept sending Lauren, he didn't intend to go home with said woman. Lauren avoided messy romantic entanglements, but Drew was a different story. They seemed well suited for each other, or maybe that was the champagne talking. Either way, they were both workaholics with ruthless ambition.

And face it, it would be nice, since she'd imagine not too many girls raised by poor grandparents wound up with the son of a CEO. If only her earliest detractors could see her now. All those mean kids who made fun of her for living on a farm. They were probably all working their nine-to-five ordinary jobs, living on a tight budget, in misery.

Laughter and clinking glasses merged with the string quartet hired to play Christmas music. Her assistant, Katrina, was with a dark-haired man who wouldn't leave her side, like a lovesick puppy. Good for her. She was a beautiful twenty-six-year-old woman in the prime of her life and should be playing the field. Their receptionist, Priscilla, was dressed in a ridiculous Mrs. Santa dress, wearing a reindeer headband. Her constant cheer was almost too much for Lauren. She was not a big fan of celebrating Christmas since her grandparents had died years ago, but she had to come to this party every year anyway.

"No, thank you," Lauren said when offered duck confit for the umpteenth time.

She'd been offered truffled canapes and oysters on the half shell, too, but she was sticking to a steady diet of champagne. It took hard work and quite a bit of sacrifice to fit her five-foot-nine frame into this dress, thank you very much. Tonight, she looked and felt like she'd been poured into it.

Harry Poindexter approached, handing her another flute of champagne. A waiter skillfully took the half-full one out of her hands and placed it on a tray.

"Another banner year, thanks to you." Harry cocked his head and flashed a grin. "I never want to lose you to another firm, so just say the word. Whatever you want, you get. Corner office? Yours. Hefty expense account? Done."

She already had all of those things. Her eyes briefly flitted to Drew, who'd loosened his tie and was puffing on a cigar. She smiled, finding a man who'd loosened his tie the sexiest thing on the planet. Drew's date caught Lauren looking and glared.

Drew, oblivious, caught Lauren's eyes and winked.

Lauren smiled at Harry. "I'm very happy here. If that ever changes, you'll be the first to know."

"See that I am!" He waggled his index finger.

What Harry didn't know wouldn't hurt him. She'd arranged to have a week off after tonight, rare vacation time, because she had an interview with a headhunter agency in Denver that had been actively trying to recruit her. She couldn't ever leave her native Texas, but fact was that having another firm competing for her would only add to her net worth. It meant another significant raise and more of Poindexter's utter devotion when she chose to stay. Win-win.

"I want you to have a great vacation, enjoy yourself, and be ready to kill it when you get back!"

"Oh, I will. I plan to lounge poolside and chill."

Please. She'd never lounged poolside a day in her life. And chill? That was for wine.

A waiter came by with a tray of half oysters and Harry took one. A good-looking man in his sixties, he had a soft stomach and a dad bod, unlike his built son. One could still see the hint of the handsome man he must have been at one time. He and Drew had the same patrician nose and full head of hair, though Harry's had gone all silver.

No sooner had Harry been whisked away than Drew appeared at her elbow. "What are you doing later?"

"Last minute packing. I'm leaving on my vacation tomorrow."

He tugged on a lock of her hair. "Can I see you tonight?"

Lauren quirked a brow and slid a look in the direction of his date. "Aren't you busy enough?"

"It's not serious," Drew said. "She's an old fling and comes with me to these things just to meet new people."

"You're wrong, Drew. She's into you."

Ironic the way some men refused to see what was right in front of them.

"It's not mutual."

"Pictures!" The cry came from Harry's wife of forty years, a sweet woman who either didn't realize Harry cheated on her on a regular basis, or didn't care. "Let's all line up here in front of the grand piano."

Photos were taken, and Lauren wound up in a row in front of Drew. Moments later, his warm hand slid down her back to her behind. It didn't move until several shots were taken. Oh, the boldness. So attractive. She turned to him, and he lowered his head with a wicked grin.

"Sorry, but not sorry. It was as wonderful as I imagined."

"Hmm. Do you want to get out of here?"

His eyebrows quirked in surprise. "Yes. I just have to… do something first. I'll take care of her…um, that situation and then we can go somewhere with a bit more…privacy."

Lauren wouldn't ever be a party to cheating if the woman was a girlfriend but Drew made it clear this wasn't serious. Even if Lauren believed the woman felt differently, it was better she find out about Drew's intentions now. Lauren certainly wished she'd learned a man's true colors before she fell for him. It had happened more than once. Lauren used to dissolve into tears when a man cast her aside but crying didn't change a thing. She couldn't remember the last time she'd cried over anything, much less a man.

At one point, she'd realized that being happy with her life would be entirely up to her and not on any man satisfying her needs, sexual or otherwise. That day, she'd declared her freedom and independence from men and all the hopes of forever love. Since then, she'd controlled the things she could and left the rest open to chance. Tonight, she would have her first night with a sexy man she'd been thinking about for weeks. It might lead to something. Or not. She was too smart to expect loyalty from a man who would get rid of his date just so he could have a new sexual conquest.

Drew headed to the woman, took her arm, and led her to another room. Once, that young and confused woman had been her. Wondering why she wasn't *enough*. Some people said she was pretty. Certainly, she was tall, and now (thanks to yoga and a strict Paleo diet) lean. But most men didn't really appreciate her attention to detail and need to impress. She'd even dated a celebrity once, who told her that she should really learn how to Netflix and relax. Lauren didn't *relax*. She achieved. She slayed her goals.

Lauren wandered up the steps to the upper deck and strolled, enjoying the cool evening breeze when it ruffled her hair and the solitude of the night as it seeped into her soul. There wasn't anyone else out here, since below deck, they were serving a celebratory cake baked by the winner of the *Great British Baking Show*. All that sugar and excess. Definitely not her style.

Reaching the stern, she pictured the scene from *Titanic*,

when Kate Winslet stood, a handsome Leonardo DiCaprio behind, his arms wrapped tightly around her waist. She and Drew would look great together, envisioning a possible future. Well, she didn't need him for this Instagram moment. Her future would be forged on her own. A good statement to make for the end the year. Kicking off her heels, she climbed closer to get a selfie. She held up her phone and tried to get a good shot of the shimmering stars behind her, the bay at her back. The wind kicked up, tousling her hair. Good thing these extensions were weaved in by the best celebrity hairdresser in Dallas. She tried again, climbing up higher to get the perfect shot. A wave rocked the boat, and Lauren lost her balance. She tried to recover, employing her valuable core strength, but she still fell overboard, losing her phone in the process.

She floated to the surface, her wet hair and extensions covering her face, one of her eyelashes coming off when she rubbed her eyes. Unbelievable! What a way to end this fantastic year. Literally tossed into the drink. She was so annoyed she almost laughed. Almost. But she'd have time to tell the ridiculous story later. Now she had to get back on the yacht before it sailed any farther away. She swam for it, heart racing, shouting for help. The party boat kept sailing as the music of Taylor Swift pulsed through the speakers, loud and inspiring on a normal night. Tonight, it simply made Lauren feisty and angry.

"Hey! Help! Drew! Harry! Help me! I fell in the water! Hellooooo!"

Nothing. They probably couldn't hear her at all.

Lauren got winded as she tried to keep up with the yacht while it continued to cruise away. Eventually, she realized she wasn't going to be able to catch up to them as another waved tossed her farther away.

"If you think you can get rid of me that easy, you're mistaken! I'm stronger than you know!"

Well, they'd figure out she was missing soon and turn back for her. All she had to do was tread water long enough to outlast the cake feasting. She could do that. Her legs were strong. It would take more than this mishap to keep Lauren Montez down! She pictured Drew right now, telling that lovely young woman who obviously cared about him that he had a business meeting, or whatever lie he'd decided to give her. Deep regret pulsed through her. If Drew were here right now to pull her out of the water, she'd tell him to forget about tonight. That young woman would love him in a way Lauren never could. She just didn't have it in her anymore.

But Drew wasn't here. No one was with her now except perhaps a seagull or two, and whatever type of sea life filled Galveston Bay. Preferably, no sharks nearby, looking for fresh meat. No one to save her, as usual, so she'd save herself. Giving up on the yacht she could no longer see in the distance, Lauren turned to the lights in the other direction, hoping to get to shore. Once she got there, she'd borrow a phone. She'd call Drew, or his father, and read them both the riot act for leaving her behind. Hell, maybe she'd even threaten resigning and really give them a scare. They certainly deserved it after the way they'd sailed off without even noticing she was gone.

Lauren turned in a circle wondering which way to go next. Her only option left was the shore.

She spied the silhouettes of people night fishing in the near distance, so she had to be close. Just a few more strokes. She was already so tired she wanted to sleep for twenty-four hours. By her calculations, she'd been treading water for hours, though she'd lost track.

She'd spent enough time in this bay to review every mistake she'd made after her mother died when Lauren was ten. The best memories, the ones she eventually came to, were of the safety she'd felt at the only one time in her life when someone truly loved her. Held close in her mother's arms, she had a home. Later, her maternal grandparents gave her a home in a farmhouse in San Antonio. A place in the world. She'd had a dog, on the farm too, named Nugget.

Lauren loved her mother so much that for a long time she didn't speak after her death. Eventually, with therapy, she spoke again, and when a beloved math teacher encouraged Lauren, she'd never looked back.

Her memories hadn't disappointed. She'd been scrappy for three decades. She'd survive this, too.

"I'm going to make it, and you'll all be very sorry you left me behind!"

Never let it be said she couldn't rise to a challenge. She was close to getting help, because she could see them all now. Four fishermen in their boats, lines cast in the water, their flashlights attracting the fish.

Then something hit her head. Hard. It felt like a rock, or a plank. She brushed her hand on her temple and came back with fresh blood. Great. The sharks would be circling next. She should call out for help again because these fishermen were so close that they might actually hear her. But she couldn't seem to formulate anything over a whisper. It felt like the old days, when tragedy took her voice until someone taught her how to roar.

"Help."

Her head ached and spun, the world coming off its axis. It was over. She was too tired for this. No more swimming. Done.

Her next word was also not above a whisper. "Mama."

Closing her eyes, she gave in to the darkness.

Chapter Two

After hooking his live bait on the hook for the tenth time of the night, Ronan Sheridan cast his line from the steel fishing boat he'd rented, sat back, and waited for some action. Little fish, big fish. Trout, black drum, or redfish, anything would do. He could be at the gym he'd joined instead of here performing this exercise in futility. He'd like something to show for all this "relaxation," as foreign to him as fish in the Mojave Desert. The irony was not lost on him. He was a sailor who couldn't fish worth a damn.

Fishing was the biggest waiting game of all.

Uncle Dan claimed if Ronan could master the art of fishing, he would conquer life. Well, Ronan did not know about *that,* but after his last deployment overseas with the US Navy SEALs, he had some life-changing decisions to make. If he did what his uncle wanted him to do, he'd consider transferring his leadership skills into the civilian world. Ronan appreciated that Uncle Dan worried about him during combat times, having already lost his only brother. But the Navy had always been Ronan's first love. It was how he'd obtained his education and training, and eventually, excelled by joining the elite SEALs. He was an adrenaline junkie who lived for slaying goals. Leaving a path he'd followed from the age of eighteen would not be easy. His accomplishments might not translate into civilian life but there was only one way to find out.

The facts were that he'd lost a relationship which meant a lot to him because of his commitment to the Navy. Ronan had been in love with his own high school sweetheart, but on his last deployment of six years, she found someone else. Unfortunately, that someone else had been Ronan's best friend. Correction: *ex*–best friend. He hoped Paul would rot in hell. He could almost excuse Belinda for not wanting to wait six more long years for him, in addition to all the time she'd already been waiting. But Paul had moved in with zero respect for loyalty or boundaries. To Ronan, people who cheated were despicable, but he understood that his standards were higher than most. In the military, cheating could mean a court-martial. It was taken seriously, unlike in the civilian world, where it seemed to be the norm and easily forgiven.

If his mind went in this direction when empty of other thoughts, he did not like this outcome so far.

His line tugged for the first time that night. Other boats nearby had been reeling in catch after catch since he'd been here, and he'd been about to ask what kind of bait they were using. Finally, he *had* something. By the feel of it as he pulled, he had a big one. This might be the large trout or redfish common for this area. He reeled in, heart pounding, wondering if his cousins Finn or Declan had ever caught anything this big. The three of them were forever locked in competition with each other, since the time they were kids. Okay, so maybe Ronan had been competing with *them*. Either way.

Wait. What the hell.

His line broke, and when he picked up his lantern to get

a closer look, he saw the distinctive shape of a body floating in the water. *A body.*

"Call 9-1-1!" he shouted to the other men, pulled off his boots and jacket and plunged into the bay.

Some vacation. Here he was, minding his own business, *trying* to relax, and his fishing line caught a damn body. Trouble seemed to attract him. Maybe, with any luck, the person was among the living and had just fallen in somehow. Because who in the hell went for a swim at this time of the night? He reached the person, and noticed she was a woman, skin so pale she looked frozen. Something dark disengaged and floated away. It looked like hair, possibly a wig.

"Don't you dare die on me."

At least his stellar swimming skills and all the tactical rescues he'd been involved with over more than a decade were working in his favor now. Her body felt light in his arms, and she seemed to be wearing little clothing. He, on the other hand, was swimming in his clothes, which made him about ten pounds heavier and far less agile. Finally, he reached his boat, and not wanting to waste another second, braced against it and tilted her head to breathe into her lungs. By now, the other men had surrounded him and they helped him lift her into his boat.

"I called 9-1-1," one of them said. "They're on their way."

Ronan went to work performing CPR while the others around him murmured and cursed. He understood the sentiment because Ronan wanted to curse, too.

It's not fair. She's too young. Too beautiful.

He heard sirens in the distance and challenged himself, that by the time they arrived, he'd have a response from the woman. Signs of life. That's all he wanted.

Just one sign.

"Come on, come on," he muttered before giving her another one of his breaths. "Don't do this to me. Please."

Then the most amazing sound came when she turned, coughed, and spit up water. For a moment, her eyes widened, then narrowed. Her hands came up against his chest and she gave him a surprisingly strong shove. Ronan turned her onto her side where she continued to gag and hack. The men around him cheered and Ronan decided he could relax. He sat back, wet and cold, watching her. She had on some kind of a red-and-white dress, which appeared to be stuck to every inch of her skin except in the places where it was torn. That was probably their fault when they'd heaved her into the boat. Her dark hair was shoulder length, and those long bare legs were shivering.

He settled a blanket on her. With signs of life, he now motored back to the shore to wait for the paramedics.

On the way back, she started to talk. "Where am I?"

"You're in the bay near Charming, Texas. Do you know what happened to you?"

"I think... I think I hit my head." She rubbed it, wincing.

"Okay, don't touch it. We're getting you help. You're going to be alright."

"You saved me," she said, barely above a whisper. He'd had to strain to hear her. "Thank you."

"What's your name?"

"I'm, um, I... Oh, I'm a little dizzy." She cradled her head.

He noticed some blood in her hair. "Did someone hurt you?"

"I don't think so, but I don't remember."

"You'll think of more later. Don't worry." He'd seen enough combat trauma to know what shock could do to a person. "My name's Ronan Sheridan, and here are the paramedics now."

He pulled up to the dock and lifted her out of the boat, carrying her to the stretcher. From there, the paramedics and EMTs sprang into action. They dried her, then covered her in a thermal blanket and tended to her head wound.

"What exactly happened?" one of the EMTs asked Ronan.

He explained how she was unconscious when he reached her, and he'd performed CPR. Told them her dress might have been caught in his line, skipping the part where he stupidly tried to reel her in until the line snapped.

"I'm not much of a fisherman." He shook his head. "Just out here for some R & R with my family."

"He saved my life," the woman said. "But... I still don't know what happened to me."

"You'll have to get checked out," one of the men said. "I assume no ID with you?"

"No," Ronan said, then quietly told the man, "It was almost as if someone threw her overboard. Or, I guess, she could have fallen in."

"True. There were lots of boats around here tonight, a cruise liner was even late taking off." He turned to the woman. "Do you think you might have missed your ship?"

"No..." She shook her head. "I... I don't remember."

"She's in shock," Ronan said. "Didn't even tell me her name yet."

"It's...something with an *l*," she added helpfully. "I can *almost* remember."

"See? You'll get there," Ronan said to encourage her.

"I'll just write her up as a Jane Doe for now," the paramedic said.

They lifted the stretcher into the back of the ambulance and prepared to take off.

"Ronan," she called to him. "I don't think I can afford this. It's funny that I can't think of my name or anything else, but I don't have much money."

He quirked a brow, because that dress looked like it may have once been expensive. He'd seen something similar in catalogs at his cousin Declan's house. He and his fiancée were planning a wedding next summer.

"Really? That dress is pretty spendy, I'd say."

She looked under the blanket. "I don't think it could be *mine*."

"Maybe you borrowed it?"

"Probably. I must have." She tugged on Declan's hand. "I'm worried about a hospital bill I can't pay."

"Don't even think about it. It's going to be fine." He moved away from the stretcher, not wanting to intervene with their work.

"Wait!" She didn't let go of his hand. "Can't you come with me?"

"Why don't you meet us there?" the paramedic said to Ronan. "You'll be fine, lady."

Lady. It seemed like such an impersonal thing to call her, and yet *Jane Doe* wasn't much better when it likely wasn't her name. Especially if her name started with an *l*.

"No, that's not it." She shook her head. "My name isn't Lady."

The paramedic snorted. "What do you want to be called?"

"I don't know." She burst into tears. "How can I not know my own name?"

Something tightened in Ronan's chest. This poor woman. She'd just been through a traumatic event, and she was all alone. He figured it wouldn't be for long, as someone would be looking for her. They'd hear from a cruise liner missing a passenger, or somebody would be searching. She belonged to someone, no doubt, someone who likely loved her very much. Everything about her carefully manicured nails and smooth creamy skin showed care and attention.

"I'll go. I'm a former medic with the Navy," he said, hating to press his advantage in that way. But she needed him.

The doors to the ambulance closed and Ronan sat on one side of her. She continued to hold his hand like a talisman, like she'd fastened her affection and sense of security to him. This was not uncommon at all in the context of a rescue like this one.

"Do you think I'll remember everything soon?" she asked Ronan.

"Yes, but first we're going to worry about checking out your lungs and that head injury. You're very lucky. You almost drowned out there."

"Without you, I might be dead."

"Thank you for not dying on me. You would have ruined my day." He tried a smile.

"Mine, too."

He got to see her smile for the first time and damn if she didn't also have perfectly straight and white teeth. This woman was definitely not *poor*. Also, the way she'd pushed him off her led him to believe she possessed a quiet kind of strength. She was not even close to helpless. Except, of course, in this unique situation. It made sense she would rely on him right now.

"Tell you what. How about if I call you Elsa until you remember your real name? Because I honestly thought you might be frozen when I found you."

"Do you like that name? *Elsa?*"

"From the children's movie."

"Oh yes! I know that movie! Elsa is a princess, the oldest sister." She squeezed his hand. "I probably have children, and a husband. I bet we watch that movie all the time."

They arrived at the emergency room, Elsa still holding his hand. A memory came back to him, sharp and swift, of the last time he'd held a woman's hand while rushing through the entrance of the hospital. His mother fought hard to beat cancer, but in the end, she'd lost the battle. He was grateful he'd been with her on that last trip.

Just before the went through the double doors, a doctor gave Ronan the once-over. "Husband?"

"No," he said. "I'm the one who found her in the bay."

"Sorry. Only family from this point forward."

There wasn't even time for Elsa to protest before the doors slammed shut in Ronan's face.

Chapter Three

Since she'd been admitted to the hospital, at least five people had asked for her name and she still couldn't remember it. Even if everyone, starting with Ronan, told her not to worry about this, her sense of panic grew with every moment she couldn't recall. How could she not know her own *name*? She couldn't summon up how she'd fallen in the water, either, or anything else. It was the strangest out-of-body experience to be a person without a past. Without memories. It wasn't possible. They were in there…somewhere.

Her earliest memory was of waking up to find a behemoth of a man hovering over her. Her first instinct—anger that he'd taken such liberties with her. She didn't *know* this man and she pushed him off. Then she realized he was trying to *save* her. His name was Ronan Sheridan, which sounded like the name of a soap opera hero. Or possibly the name of a swashbuckling character in a historical romance novel. *Shanna*. Suddenly she remembered she loved that book. Wait. *Rourke* was the hero, not Ronan. Okay, she could recall things, so she wasn't a total zero. Maybe she'd drank too much and fell off a pier, though that didn't sound feasible.

She'd realized quickly she was half naked in front of this handsome man named Ronan. She tried to cover her legs with what was left of the dress. The slinky red dress was unlike anything she'd ever wear. It might have been superexpensive before it was ripped. She could never afford this on her salary as a…as a… Wait a second. Something *else* she didn't recall. Whatever she did for a living eluded her. Also, she was in Charming, a town she'd never heard about. Who named a town *Charming*? It sounded way too cutesy. Well, at least she was in Texas, because that felt right. She was a Texan!

"Thank God, I remembered something," she told the nurse taking her blood pressure for the one hundredth time.

"Wonderful, dear! And what's that?"

"I'm from Texas. That's for sure."

"Oh, *good*. I do hear a little twang," she said, but her level of enthusiasm was that of praising a five-year-old who'd mastered tying his shoelaces for the first time.

Not too impressive, she understood, but hey, considering they'd talked about a cruise ship tonight, it could be important. She was from Texas, not vacationing from some other state or country.

The police had come by to take a report and they would start an investigation into anyone with her description missing from the area. They left assuring her they'd be in touch with her through the hospital. It was another thing to worry about. Where would she go next? She couldn't stay in the hospital. With any luck, her family would find her soon. By tomorrow, she might be in her own bed, this whole experience a freaky one-time thing she'd laugh about later.

They were all referring to her as Jane, which didn't feel right. She preferred Elsa so much more and wondered if she'd ever see her rescuer again. It was strange but she already missed him. She didn't even know the man, but he inspired such safety and security in her that all she wanted was to see him again. He would help her find herself. She knew this like she knew she was from Texas.

The doctor said she'd had a concussion and required a few stitches, and they kept her overnight. After a battery of tests proved that there wasn't anything seriously wrong with her, the specialist came to see her in the morning.

"While highly rare and unusual, I believe you have a form of temporary amnesia."

"It's temporary?" Hope rose in her. This wouldn't last. She *would* remember.

"Almost always."

"How long will I be this way?" She had so many questions.

"No way to tell for certain. There's simply part of your brain having a slower recovery than the rest. But it will come."

Her next question wasn't for the doctor.

Where am I supposed to go when I leave here?

The nurses and staff were helpful, but so far, no one had invited to take her home. She completely understood. These people had families and lives. It was Christmastime, something she'd been able to deduce by the decorations of garland and tinsel hanging at the nurse's station.

It was Christmas and she apparently had *no one* looking for her.

"Has no one come for me yet?" she asked the nurse while they waited for the wheelchair that would take her downstairs.

"Not yet, sugar, but give them time."

The nurse's words were soft, and she could feel tears well in her eyes. She was going to miss these kind people.

She tried not to cry as the elevator doors opened and a group of nurses came to see her off. Apparently she was somewhat of a sensation in the small hospital. They'd never tended to an amnesiac before, certainly not one who'd been fished out of the bay by a local fisherman.

"Merry Christmas, Jane." The nurse named Cassie handed her a bag full of red-and-green-frosted cookies. "Eat them in good health."

"Thank you," she said, holding them tight.

"You're going to be okay. Come back and see us when you remember." Another nurse winked.

"And you will," the third one said, waving one last time before the doors shut closed.

"Where am I supposed to go?" She wiped away a tear.

She clutched her bag of cookies and a change of clothes the nurses had given her. The scrubs were roomy but the shoes a size too small.

"You *really* don't know who you are?" The attendant pushing her wheelchair said. "I thought that was just in the movies."

He wheeled her to the curb where she figured he'd drop her off and wish her luck. She had no idea where to go or what to do but figured she'd just wander around or find a bench to sit on until she figured something out.

"Here he is now," the attendant said as a truck pulled up near the entrance.

"Have they found me? Is it my husband?" She didn't know why the thought occurred, but it felt like she should be a wife, even though she wasn't wearing a ring.

She might not be married but could be committed to a partner, or perhaps she was a single mom. The whole *Elsa* thing felt very familiar and comforting, like a movie she'd seen more than once. And the doctors estimated she was in her thirties, which meant she would probably have a husband and maybe even have children. Just the thought of being separated from them, even for one more day, filled her with indescribable fear.

The man who emerged from the truck was not her husband but someone she recognized.

Ronan.

"Hey, Elsa."

She was so relieved to see a familiar face that without much thinking she went right into his arms and pressed her face against his neck. "You came back."

"Did you think I could forget you?"

He held her tightly, his arms around her waist, and the welcome human contact made her feel she hadn't been truly hugged in a long while.

Pulling back, he cupped her face. "Listen, I've talked to the police and the staff at the hospital, and we've worked it all out. For now, you're staying with me. I've got an extra bedroom and it's not a problem."

"Oh my God, thank you. Thank you." Elsa grabbed on to his T-shirt. "I promise you, it won't be long before my family comes for me. They're probably going to be so grateful to you, and so am I."

"I'm sure that's true, and until then, you'll be safe with me."

And for the first time since she'd been fished out of the bay, Elsa relaxed.

The moment he'd driven home the night of the rescue, memories of the fear in Elsa's eyes piercing him, Ronan knew he couldn't walk away from her. So he'd made some phone calls. First, to his Uncle Dan, because without his input he'd have never been fishing in the first place. Next, his cousins Declan and Finn. The entire Sheridan family agreed. Ronan had to help this poor woman. His next calls had been to the hospital to make the arrangements and to the police to find out if they'd been any developments. Nothing yet, and he advised them to contact Elsa at his residence.

Ronan drove Elsa to his rental home, previously occupied by his cousin Declan. He'd moved in the house next door with his fiancée, Amy, and her twins from a previous marriage. Ronan slid in to pay the rent on the vacant house until he decided what to do with the rest of his life.

"You'll see my house is nothing fancy, but I've cleaned out the spare bedroom. You have fresh sheets and you'll be comfortable while you're here."

"I didn't know where I was going to go. This is the nicest thing anyone has ever done for me," Elsa said.

"That you can remember," he joked, hoping she'd appreciate some comic relief. "Don't worry. We've got photos of you on the police website and they're reaching out to surrounding law enforcement. I'm sure it won't be long before you're back to your old life."

"It's the strangest thing," Elsa said. "I feel like there's something niggling at my brain, but it won't come to me. Every time I get close, it slips away. It's just out of reach."

"Like when I can't find my wallet. I can think of when I last had it, but in between there and the moment I realize I've lost it, there's nothing but dead space."

"It's a little bit like that. I remember some things, like I'm from Texas. I'm certain of this."

"See? Great. You're getting there."

Uncle Dan had suggested that Ronan be encouraging, like Elsa's own cheerleading section. No one knew more about coaching and self-improvement than his uncle.

"That's what they told me at the hospital. I'm getting there."

"Be patient. Most people can't imagine what you're going through."

"No, I guess not. I felt like an oddity at the hospital. They treated me a little like a celebrity. A few nurses wanted their photo with me, and I let them."

"No kidding. You were okay with that?"

"I figure if they tell people or put it on social media, someone might eventually recognize me."

"Good plan. You were in a fancy dress so maybe you were out celebrating and something happened. Who knows? Maybe some others were injured. If that's the case, we'll find out soon enough."

She splayed her hands in front of her. "This is, well, *was* a nice manicure. It looked like it might have been expensive."

"My cousin's wife, Michelle, does her own nails, and they look kind of like that. So, you never know."

"Maybe I'm a manicurist by trade." She glanced at him. "Have you been a fisherman for long?"

He laughed for the first time in hours. "Who, me? No, I'm no fisherman."

"Oh, I thought…"

"I could see why you would think that, but it was my Uncle Dan's idea I learn how to fish so I could relax." He snorted.

Bad idea, Uncle Dan. Bad idea.

"And then I came along. Not very relaxing, was it?"

"That's okay. It's not in my nature to relax. I should have never even tried."

"So, what *do* you do for a living?"

"That's a good question. I've been a Navy man for years, just like my father was, but I'm thinking of becoming a civilian again. It's a big decision to make. For now, it's R & R. Not easy for me."

"No wonder you were such a good swimmer. Imagine my luck, being rescued from the bay by a sailor. I think somebody out there is looking out for me." She glanced out the window again, which she'd been doing almost the entire time.

Ronan pulled into his driveway and tried to see the house through a stranger's eyes. It was a bit much for some people. Those people included his Aunt Lorna and his cousin Finn. *Overkill* was the word they'd used, but they didn't live next door to *Declan*.

They couldn't understand.

"Wow," Elsa whispered. "You must really love Christmas."

Chapter Four

Another memory swiftly came to Elsa. Long ago, her mother had taken her to homes like these around the holidays, belonging to extravagant and wealthy people who decorated them to the nines for Christmas. She and Mama would walk hand in hand down the street and enjoy the shimmering display of lights and sounds.

I can only imagine what their electricity bill must be like, Mama had said.

Elsa was only five or so, but she understood Mama had trouble paying bills and one of the bills kept the lights on.

Ronan's house was in a decidedly middle-class neighborhood, which felt familiar to Elsa. The house next door was similar, an explosion of holiday cheer. There were strings of lights hanging from every bough and tree. There even seemed to be some lights on the lawn itself, meaning at night, the very grass would be glowing and blinking. There was a Nativity scene, a Santa Claus and his reindeer, several gigantic, wrapped presents, pine trees, inflatable elves, a Grinch, stars… Oh boy.

"I know it's a little bit much." Ronan winced, perhaps due to her silence and gaping jaw. "But you need a lot of wattage to be seen from outer space."

"And the house next door." Elsa pointed between the homes. "Are you two in some sort of a competition?"

"Eternally. My cousin lives there. It's all in good fun. He's got a couple of stepchildren to impress, and I've never been able to back down from a challenge."

Ronan came around to open her door and Elsa snapped out of it. She'd been staring straight ahead but she was now in her new temporary home, where at least she'd never forget it was December. Carrying her cookies and spare scrubs, her only possessions in the world, she followed Ronan to the front door. It was humbling to realize this was all she had of her own. Somehow, it felt wrong, but she shouldn't be surprised. Everything would feel off from this point forward. She was operating purely on instinct, dropped into her life with no memories.

"So… I've never been here before?" Elsa asked.

"Not to my knowledge." He opened the front door and motioned her inside. "But you'll soon meet my family and friends, and if anyone recognizes you, this will be a whole lot easier."

"I'd like to believe if I've been here before, something would look familiar."

"Nothing so far?"

She shook her head. She'd looked out the window on the drive, but nothing jogged a single memory. Not one sight, sound, or scent triggered anything, until the Christmas decorations, and even that was an old memory.

Ronan had driven down a coastal highway where in the near distance she spotted a lighthouse. They passed a boardwalk near the seawall and sandy beaches filled with umbrellas. Several sailboats dotted the bay. So far, this bucolic town had come by its name honestly. Charming, indeed. She rather liked this area, and if circumstances were different, she might feel happy to be here.

Inside, she discovered that other than a little Christmas tree in a corner, Ronan's home was small and modest but uncluttered. There was a leather couch in the living room and a large flat-screen hung on the wall. The open-floor design was connected to the kitchen.

"Down the hallway are the bedrooms." Ronan led the way and she followed him into a room with a twin bed, nightstand, and lamp. Very functional. Everything served a purpose. There were only a few framed photos displayed, baseball insignias and multiple trophies on a bookcase.

She turned to Ronan. "You played baseball?"

"My cousin did. Some of his stuff is still here, and I don't mind, since it's just me. He's gone from living alone in this house to living in one next door, the same size, but with three other people. His stuff will slowly migrate over." He shrugged.

Elsa was still clutching her cookies and the extra pair of blue hospital scrubs. They also didn't feel natural or familiar, so she probably wasn't in the health field.

She sat on the bed, feet aching, and kicked off the tight shoes, which were donated.

"It feels strange not to have any clothes, or any money to get them. In a lot of ways, I feel like a child. Helpless. The nurses took up a collection for me and gave me these shoes, which are too small, and some scrubs to change into when I got tired of these." She took a cookie out of the bag and offered it to him. "Cookie?"

All she had to give, all she had to offer him. A cookie. Ronan simply smiled at her, his gaze filled with such warmth and compassion that she burst into tears.

"Oh hey, hey." In an instant he was beside her, taking

her into his arms. "You don't have to cry, okay? This is all going to be fine. I promise."

"I'm so scared."

The emotions were too strong to hold back, as if maybe she was a person who didn't cry often and had years of angst pent up inside. This didn't feel at all familiar or natural as her body heaved and shook. She cried uncontrollably until she'd wet Ronan's shirt and still he didn't let go. One hand slid up and down her back in smooth and gentle strokes, and he whispered sweet and calming words.

You're okay. I'm here. Please don't cry.

"I'm s-sorry," Elsa said, her sobs finally ebbing.

"Anyone would be upset in your situation."

"You must regret going fishing. Now you're stuck with me." She wiped away her tears with the backs of her hands.

"I'm not *stuck* with you."

She waved her hands dismissively. "Please don't let me intervene any more than I already have. I'm sure you have a life, and plans and people to see. Maybe even a girlfriend?"

Someone like Ronan Sheridan probably had more than *one* girlfriend. Even if she had a lot more on her mind than a good-looking guy, she couldn't help but notice the obvious. Tall and built, his sun-kissed, light brown hair was cut short, and he had distracting beard stubble. His eyes were the most interesting shade of midnight blue.

"No girlfriend. Don't worry about me. We're focusing on you. You need help."

"However long I'm here, and I hope it isn't long, I want to pull my weight. I want to do my part and help in any way."

Guilt spliced through her when a strong surge of desire hit her. Ronan smelled delicious, and she couldn't help but be attracted to him. Any woman would be, so it was nice to know that in this way she was normal. Yet she didn't know if she'd actually be cheating on someone if she kissed him. Not that she was going to kiss him. That would be wrong. He was a stranger, and she didn't *kiss* strangers. Probably not.

Of course, right now everyone was technically a stranger...

Ronan was gazing at her like he might be hearing her thoughts, which unnerved her.

The doorbell rang and he let go of her and stood. "I'll bet that's Amy."

Elsa wanted to ask who Amy was, but he was already halfway down the hall. She didn't know what else to do but follow him. He opened the door to a pretty brunette with long curly hair and a sweet smile.

"Hey." Ronan turned to Elsa, who had come up right behind him. "This is Elsa, or at least, that's what I'm calling her. Elsa, this is Amy Holloway, soon to be Sheridan. She's my cousin Declan's fiancée and lives next door."

"Nice to meet you." Amy walked inside carrying a bag with her, throwing a teasing smile Ronan's way. "Did you actually name her after your favorite Disney character?"

Ronan shrugged. "Hey, she looked frozen when I found her."

"I like the name," Elsa said. "It's more creative than Jane Doe."

"It's certainly a unique set of circumstances," Amy said, walking toward the couch where she set the bag down. "I brought you some clothes and shoes. But Ronan didn't tell me how *tall* you are."

"Sorry."

"Nothing to be sorry about, honey. I think some of my dresses might fit you, because they're not short on me, and the tops should be fine, but these jeans definitely won't do. I'll go shopping tomorrow."

"Thanks, Ames." Ronan pulled out his wallet and handed her a card. "I know y'all are planning a wedding."

Oh my God. He was *paying* for her. A knot formed in Elsa's stomach. Instinctively, she didn't like being indebted to someone else. She didn't know why, but it felt completely foreign to rely on a man in this way. But if not for Ronan, she'd have to depend on Amy, who was saving for a *wedding*.

Amy rolled her eyes. "True, but you wouldn't know it the way Declan keeps buying Christmas decorations. Pretty sure you can see our house from the Space Station."

"Well, that's the idea," Ronan chuckled.

"What you have to know, Elsa, is that these two geniuses are in constant competition with each other. If Ronan buys a lawn decoration, Declan has to buy a bigger one."

Ronan shrugged. "It's all in good fun. My uncle used to encourage our competition."

"You may not feel that way when you see your electricity bill," Elsa said. "I want you both to know that I'll pay you back for these clothes. For everything."

"No worries, it's my pleasure to help." Amy waved a hand dismissively. "I have to warn you. My children are fascinated by your situation. You can pay me back by being patient with their questions, and please tell them when something isn't any of their business. I encourage a healthy curiosity, but there are boundaries."

"Aw, they're good kids," Ronan said.

"I'm lucky." Amy smiled.

"I doubt luck has much to do with it," Ronan said. "Amy is a first grade teacher at the local elementary school."

"And Declan teaches calculus and is the head baseball coach at the high school," Amy said.

"Wow. That's impressive." Elsa didn't have any idea why, but she thought athletes weren't necessarily also smart.

Maybe, somehow, that had been her experience.

"They're a match made in heaven, or so Aunt Lorna says," Ronan said with a wink. "High school sweethearts."

"We had a little detour but made it back to each other." Amy reached for Elsa's hand and squeezed it. "And that's all this is for you. A little detour you didn't expect, but thank God you survived. Think of all this as an adventure you're having."

"You're right. Ronan saved my life."

The perspective was exactly what Elsa needed. She had to remember that if not for Ronan, they might be fishing her cold and lifeless body out of the bay and her family would eventually have to identify her by checking *dental* records. Elsa shivered. At least now she had a chance to live the rest of her life. Wherever it might be and whoever she might be. She had a chance.

"Well, I'll see y'all later." Amy moved to the front door. "I'm going to get the kids and go do that shopping, then I hope to see you two later at the Snowflake Float Boat Parade."

The...what?

Ronan shut the door and turned to Elsa. "We don't have to go."

"I don't want to stop you from doing the stuff you normally would."

"Actually, it might help jog a memory if you think you're up for it. But I don't want to push you. There's no rush." He took her hand and led her to the kitchen. "Are you hungry?"

"Yes, actually."

She hadn't touched the breakfast they'd offered her at the hospital, too scared about where she'd go when discharged.

"I've got stuff for sandwiches." He got busy taking out sliced meats, cheese, and lettuce.

"Let me help."

It didn't feel right for him to do everything, which meant she must be a self-sufficient woman in her real life. She didn't feel at ease with someone else taking care of her. Ronan pulled out plates and the bread and they formed an assembly line. They worked well in tandem and she marveled at how much came by way of instinct.

Elsa slathered on mayonnaise and added lettuce leaves on two slices of bread. "What's the Snowflake Float Boat Parade?"

"It's another Charming Christmas tradition. Granted, it's been a few years for me but my cousin Finn, Declan's brother, is heavily involved. He co-owns Nacho Boat Adventures, and they decorate a sailboat or two every year, tricked out with lights and holiday decorations. A lot of the town residents come out to support the display. The kids love it."

"And it's by the bay where you found me?"

"Not far from there." Ronan sliced tomatoes and layered them on the bread, adding the cuts of meat and cheese.

"Maybe it will trigger a memory of how I wound up in the bay."

"That's what I'm thinking. But I also don't want to press you because…you never know. Maybe it's not a good memory."

She tried not to picture the idea of someone pushing her off a boat, but she had to consider the possibility. It was an ugly thought and spoke to the kind of people she might have associated with in her recent past.

She didn't want it to be true.

"I think I can handle it, as long as I'm with you."

"Good. Believe me, I won't let anyone hurt you."

Elsa had no doubt. "I can't lie. It's scary to think someone might have thrown me overboard."

"Think positive. You don't look like the kind of woman who has enemies, so I doubt it. We may find out this was all an accident."

Accidental or intentional, it was hard to understand why someone hadn't noticed a woman falling overboard.

Chapter Five

Ronan would be lying to say he wasn't worried that tonight's holiday event might be a little too much stimulation for Elsa just a day after her near drowning. However, it might help to get her a bit closer to recalling her past. He *wanted* her to remember because it killed him to witness her complete state of confusion and most of all, the tears. She cried like someone had ripped her heart out.

He could only imagine the state of emotional chaos he'd be in if his wife or significant other was *missing*. Then again, he couldn't get past the idea that if his woman had fallen into the bay, he'd either be right behind her, or drowned while trying to save her. For this reason alone, it was difficult to picture that she had a relationship or a family looking for her. He was reserving judgement because it had only been a day, but in his mind, if someone loved her they would *find* her. It was what he'd do.

Families had come out early and already staked the best places to view, setting folding chairs out hours in advance. He had great memories of this time of the year, coming out with Belinda when they were in high school. The thought of running into her or Paul tonight set him on edge, but he was here for Elsa. If not for her, he'd have stayed home.

He'd been here with his mother when he was a kid, and

occasionally, his father when he wasn't deployed on a mission. His mom had been one of those people who loved Christmas and started planning and shopping in July. She'd get a kick out of Ronan's front-lawn Christmas competition with Declan, which was one of the main reasons Ronan had joined in. She was gone, and someone had to honor her love for the season.

"Over here!" Declan called out from the area where he'd staked out chairs.

Ronan steered Elsa in their direction, hand on her back. "There's my cousin and his family."

He called it the way he saw it, because Declan had definitely slipped into the role of stepfather-to-be with an ease Ronan almost envied. He was passing out cups of hot chocolate to Amy and the kids. Being a father suited him, but then again he was Uncle Dan's son, so no surprise there.

"Hey." Ronan fist-bumped with Declan. "This is Elsa. And this is my cousin Declan."

"It's nice to meet you, but sorry about the circumstances," Declan said. "All that being said, you're with the right person to get you through this. If I were ever in serious trouble, Ronan is the first man I'd call."

Despite their occasional one-upmanship, both of his cousins were more like brothers. Uncle Dan made sure of this when his only brother, Ronan's father, died in an IED explosion when Ronan was twelve. They'd always been a close family, with both Lorna and Dan reaching out every time his father was on a long deployment. This was often, and they'd spent many holidays and summers together. When Declan's mother died of cancer a couple of years ago, Ronan became even closer to Uncle Dan.

"You already know Amy, and those are her kids, David

and Naomi." Ronan pointed. "And that's Michelle sitting next to Amy. My cousin Finn's wife."

"Hi!" David came up to Declan, who ruffled his hair. "Is it true you can't remember *who you are*?"

Instinctively, Ronan moved closer to Elsa, as if he might somehow emotionally shield her from probing questions. They were bound to come up, but at least, David was simply filled with the natural curiosity of a child.

"It's true," Elsa said. "I fell and hurt my head, and now I've forgotten a few things."

"Wow," David said, mouth hanging open.

"David," Amy called out from one of the chairs where she sat. "I know you're curious, honey, but let's not be rude."

"I'm sorry, ma'am," David said to Elsa. "But it's really *weird*!"

"You're right," Elsa said. "I think so, too."

She spoke with ease to David, and Ronan noted the way she'd censored her situation for the kid. It was possible she did have children, and a stone slid over Ronan's throat. He understood far too well what it was like to miss a parent.

"Okay," Declan said. "Let's take a seat, buddy. The parade is about to begin."

The evening was cool by Gulf Coast standards, so good thing Amy had returned from her shopping trip with several jeans that fit Elsa's long legs. Still, when he caught Elsa shivering, he slipped out of his hoodie and set it on her shoulders.

"Thank you." She snuggled into it, then cupped her hands to her lips and blew into them.

He chuckled and took one of her hands, rubbing it between his own. "You're cold."

"I'm fine."

She turned to stare at a yacht that sailed by, decorated with a brightly shining Texas flag, making him wonder if something about it seemed familiar. Maybe her shivering wasn't entirely due to the weather. However, that yacht was owned by the mayor, Tippy, and her husband, and he'd no more suspect them of nefarious activity than he would Santa Claus himself.

The boats continued to glide by, decorated with colorful bright lights shimmering against the dark sky. First came the "Santa" boat hosted by the Salty Dog Bar & Grill, with a chubby Santa dressed in full regalia, waving to the crowds. Other boats had blinking patterns of fairy lights, flashing stars, and carried wrapped presents, a tiny sleigh with plastic reindeer, and artificial trees galore.

One boat sailed by, with characters from *The Nightmare Before Christmas*.

"You don't have that one." Elsa pointed.

"Something to remedy." Ronan chuckled. "I'll go see if they have any left at the store."

There seemed to be a float for everyone, and all glided slowly by to waves and cheers from the audience. Bringing up the rear came Finn and his business partner Noah's sailboat, decorated with wreaths, trees, and plenty of twinkling multicolored lights. Nacho Boat Adventures, the neon sign read. They received the biggest cheers of the evening as Finn and Noah waved to the crowds.

"Mommy! It's Uncle Finn!" Amy's little girl, Naomi, squealed. "I *know* him!"

"That's right," Amy said. "Wave!"

"Woo-hoo, baby!" Michelle jumped up and down. "Yours is the best one!"

After the parade, those with young children were the ones to pack up first. Declan and Amy said their goodbyes, hauling the kids away from the direction of the boardwalk's carnival ride section. Michelle waved and rushed off to meet up with Finn.

Vendors had set up small kiosks and were giving away free samples. There was kettle corn, hot chocolate, peppermint cupcakes, and more.

"Do you like hot chocolate?" In his own experience, smells and tastes could pull back strong memories.

"I think I do," Elsa said.

"Let's find out." He led her to the hot-chocolate kiosk, where a pretty and very pregnant blonde was handing them out.

"Hi, y'all!" she said. "I hope you enjoyed the Snowflake Float Boat Parade. I'm Ava Del Toro, owner of The Green Bean Coffeeshop."

Ronan had frequented the shop since he'd returned home. It was one of the newer establishments in town and he loved the strong and stout coffee they served there.

"What? No coffee?" Ronan joked.

"Sorry, just hot chocolate tonight. But it's my special brand of Mexican chocolate and very rich. And goes better with candy canes." She handed a plastic cup to Elsa. "I'm sorry, have we met? You look familiar."

"I do?" Elsa said.

The hope in her voice just about slayed Ronan.

"Well, I used to be the Charming Chamber of Commerce president, so I came across a lot of people," she said, cocking her head. "Maybe we met at a conference somewhere?"

"Maybe," Elsa said. "I don't know."

"Elsa has a unique situation." Ronan took over and explained, watching as Ava's eyes went wide and her hand flew over her mouth.

He didn't blame her, or anyone else. It was the most bizarre situation he'd ever been in, and he'd been in some crazy scenarios.

"So, you see," Elsa said. "I would appreciate any and all information."

"You can count on me to help," Ava said. "I know a lot of people in Charming, and all of Texas, in fact."

"Great," Elsa aid. "I know for sure I'm from Texas."

It would help if she remembered which *city*, since searching for her particular city in Texas was like searching for one needle in a stack of needles.

Ava held up her phone. "Let me take your photo and I'll see what I can do."

When Elsa nodded, Ava took several, then took Ronan's contact information. By the time they walked away, Elsa's spirits seemed higher, and she smiled at Ronan. It was only the second time she'd smiled since he'd met her, and it nearly knocked him over. She was beautiful, but her smile was nothing less than mesmerizing.

"I'm sorry if all this was too much for you tonight," Declan said as they walked along the seawall drinking their hot chocolate.

"No, it was fine. I wanted to come. If I want to find out what happened to me, I can't be afraid to get out there and let people see me. Someone might recognize me." She sighed. "I can't tell you how weird it feels to say that."

"None of us can imagine what you're going through, but I'm probably the closest to someone who might understand."

"How so?"

He'd been thinking about this earlier, not sure he wanted to share it, but this felt like the right moment.

"On one of my deployments overseas..." he said. "Let's see. How best to put this? I had a serious concussion, and for several interminable minutes, I couldn't tell you *who* I was or *where* I was. It was as if everything was just... gone. So, I understand how frightened you are. It all came back to me, though."

"Lucky you." Then, as if realizing what she'd said, she shook her head. "I didn't mean that. You're not *lucky* you got a concussion."

Good thing he hadn't relayed that the same IED had killed several men. He'd learned the hard way not to overshare.

"I know what you meant." He took her free hand in his and squeezed it once before he let it go. "Let's just say I can identify with what you're going through, but on a microlevel."

"I wouldn't even be here without you. You *saved* me. I owe you everything."

"Stop saying that. You don't *owe* me."

"Take it easy, sailor. I'm grateful, okay? You'll just have to *deal* with that."

"Okay, boss," he chuckled.

There was a bite to her words, and she took charge, which both pleased and surprised him. She'd been so lost and helpless until then, but in that moment, he saw a self-possessed woman who had her own mind. Interesting. Being with Elsa was a bit like watching a movie with some twists and turns. He only hoped the ending wouldn't disappoint.

"What's the verdict?" He jerked his chin toward her cocoa. "Are you a fan?"

She gave him a smirk, tipping the empty cup toward him. "What do *you* think?"

Chapter Six

When Elsa woke the next morning, she didn't recognize her surroundings. She went up on her elbows, and sharp panic and fear pulsed through her in waves. Then she recognized the navy-blue curtains, the digital clock on the nightstand, and plaid comforter. She was in the spare bedroom at Ronan's house. Her rescuer. The man she'd never stop thanking, no matter what he said. Yes, she *owed* him. For her life, and for allowing her, a perfect stranger, to stay in his home free of charge because she literally had *nothing*. Except, of course, for the fancy ripped-off and destroyed party dress the hospital incinerated. It seemed criminal, but the thing was unsalvageable.

Too bad the rest of her memories couldn't surface as easily as remembering Ronan. Maybe she was trying too hard to force them back.

Obviously, her short-term memory remained intact, which had to be a good thing. The long-term memory would come sooner or later. She had to relax and let it happen gradually, because the stress wasn't helping. Maybe something pursued with too much enthusiasm tended to resist. Ronan had been so encouraging, and no wonder, since he could at least be partly empathetic to her situation. She hadn't even wanted to ask what event had caused *his* concussion. The images that came to mind were too frightening.

She found that she could recall random things, like while brushing her teeth last night, the best brand of toothpaste. Not the kind Ronan had. She also knew she loved shoes, and was a bit disappointed by the choices she now had. Two pairs of boots, thanks to Amy's friend, Valerie, another schoolteacher, who happened to be the same size. Shoes, however, were the least of her problems. But she was surprised by the unhelpful stuff she remembered. Things like the 1,000 thread count of the sheets she preferred. Weird.

Rolling out of bed, she stretched. While not a fashion statement, the soft and worn-in scrubs made adequate pj's. She shuffled out the door and found Ronan making noises in the kitchen.

"Coffee?" he said.

"Um, sure." She rubbed her eyes.

Nope, damn, he was *still* handsome. Her memory hadn't failed her there, and she hadn't imagined, or unrealistically hyped, his looks to be more than they were. His morning appearance was probably even better than the one the previous evening. Maybe he'd never be rumpled and tousled the way she was at the moment. She supposed that was the military man in him. She admired people like him, people who had it all together. Maybe once she'd been one of them.

"Cream? Sugar?"

"Um, do you have skim milk?" Funny how some things came to her easily.

"Sorry, no. Full-fat house."

He could afford the calories, of course, being as he appeared to be 50 percent muscle.

"That's fine. I can't be picky."

"Yes, you can. I'll stop by the market today and get

some." He handed her a steaming mug. "It's interesting how you know that's the way you take your coffee. I have a good feeling about this."

"You're right." Her spirits lifted, like when Ava said she'd help get the word out. "I decided I need to stop trying so hard to remember. If I relax, maybe more will come to me."

"That's true. There are some things you can't push."

She took a sip of hot, rich, and creamy coffee. Oh, hot damn, full fat was the way to go. "Please don't let me stop you from anything you have to do today. I don't want to get in your way."

"Well, I'm supposed to be taking it easy, though that hasn't been going well so far." He set his mug down.

"And I haven't been much help in that pursuit."

He shrugged. "You've been a *great* help. I discovered fishing isn't for me."

"I wouldn't say that. You fished me out, didn't you? But please go do something fun. Don't worry about me. I'll just…stay here and…and…" Her voice trailed off.

"You could watch the news or read. Take it easy and maybe something more will come to you."

"That's a good idea."

She hated the thought of him leaving her again. He'd had to at the hospital, and she all too well remembered the panic it had induced. She felt safe with him. On the other hand, she didn't particularly think she'd be attractive as Ronan's appendage. She had no idea how long she'd be here. Maybe she should make herself useful and not further complicate his life.

"I have to confess," Ronan said. "It's difficult for me to relax."

"I don't think I'm good at relaxing, either."

On the other hand, who could possibly relax in *her* situation? She had an important job to do: recollect her entire life!

"Something we have in common." Ronan pulled a carton of eggs out of the refrigerator. "I like to keep busy, and I've always been an overachiever. That's probably why the whole lawn-decoration competition suits me. I also know my mother would get a kick out of it because she loved Christmas. But eventually, I'm going to have to decide one way or another."

"Decide?"

He cracked an egg into a bowl. "Whether I'll re-up for another six years. The thing is, I'm only a few years away from twenty years of service and retiring with full benefits. But my uncle would consider it a personal favor if I don't go back."

"Why? He doesn't support your service?"

"He's definitely proud. Uncle Dan has been like a father to me. My own father passed away when I was twelve. He was in the Navy, too, and needless to say losing a brother hit Uncle Dan hard. He'd rather not lose a nephew, too."

"I'm so sorry, and that makes a lot of sense. I don't blame your uncle."

"It feels like a long time ago now, though losing my mother was more recent. She died of cancer a couple of years ago. I think my uncle worries about me too much."

Inexplicably, Elsa's eyes welled up with tears at the mention of Ronan's mother. She didn't remember her mother past the time when she was a small child, but the love she had for her, even now, linked them forever.

It took her a few moments before she could speak.

"I'm sorry about your mother."

"Thanks, that was a rough time. That's probably why

I'm so close to my uncle, aunt, and cousins. I was an only child and they're my family now."

"It's a major change in your life. Do you have any idea what you're going to do?"

"Not yet, but don't worry about me." He stirred eggs in the pan. "Damn, I forgot to ask if you like eggs this way."

"I do like scrambled eggs."

Some things were instinctive, she'd found, such as whether you were attracted to a man or not. If she had a significant other somewhere in the world, she now felt guilty about the feelings she was having for Ronan. She'd like to believe she'd remember someone important to her, but she had no idea how amnesia worked.

"You don't have a phone, so you can use my tablet over there for now." Ronan nudged his chin in the direction of a device on the counter. "You can look stuff up if you want. Maybe something you see will jog a memory."

"I want to look up amnesia, possible outcomes, that kind of thing."

"All right, but just remember you can't trust everything you read on the internet. Check the source."

She smirked. "Right. Well, brain tumor has already been ruled out."

"It's not a tumor," Ronan said in an exaggerated Austrian accent.

"Hey, that was pretty good!" Elsa snapped her fingers. "Arnold Schwarzenegger, *Kindergarten Cop*."

"Amazing," he said with a huge smile that did funny things to Elsa. Her heart fluttered at that smile.

"I must like movies, or Arnold Schwarzenegger," she said with a shrug. "And it's frustrating the little insignificant stuff I do drum up."

"The big stuff will come next."

He said this with such confidence, and she desperately wanted to believe him.

Ronan served eggs and toast with the coffee, and Elsa determined she'd cook for him next if she wound up staying here much longer. She wanted to help. He'd done enough simply by saving her life. When he tried to take her dishes and wash hers, too, she intervened, sidling next to him at the sink. This put her in close proximity, and he smelled like soap and some kind of light-scented delicious cologne.

"Let me," she said.

If being close affected him the way it had her, he didn't show it. "I'm going to run to the store and get a few things."

After Ronan left, Elsa cleaned their dishes and dried them, too, even if he had a dishwasher. She hunted for the right cupboards, which took a while. Then she took a quick shower, lamenting at the choice of hair products. Granted, maybe most men were not particularly attuned to the best brands, which suddenly came to Elsa like a missing piece of the puzzle. She owned all the best in products, she realized, though she had no idea why. It still seemed unlikely she had money.

Finally, she hit the search engines for *amnesia*. The number of responses was baffling. This happened more than she would have ever imagined. She read about amnesia from dementia, chemically induced substances, and dissociative trauma. There was transient global amnesia, which caused a temporary loss of memory and sounded like Declan's situation. Most people recovered their memory in twenty-four hours or less. There was amnesia from a head injury, which sounded closest to her situation. Loss of memory could last up to a week, and in rare cases, months. *Months*. What was she supposed to do for months? Get on with it, get a job, and start a brand-new life?

Cases like hers were unusual. There were a handful of people who never regained memories, which sounded incredibly discouraging, but those people were surrounded by family members who could remind them of their past, with photos to show them. She had to admit, she would rather have the memories than photos.

She came across a headline from several years ago, which made her stomach drop. "Man Believed to Have Amnesia is a Fugitive from the Law."

What if she was such a terrible person someone had tried to get rid of her? What if she'd done something horrible to someone else and fell off the boat by accident? She was almost afraid to call the police and ask for an update. Instead of agonizing anymore over something she couldn't change, Elsa got busy with something she could control.

She found the cleaning supplies under the sink where they would normally be and got busy cleaning Ronan's house.

Chapter Seven

Ronan's first stop was to the local department store. He had to find one of those *Nightmare Before Christmas* lawn decorations before they were all gone. In their small town, with only one big box store, the merchandise was picked over this close to the holiday. He'd had to drive to Houston for much of his inventory. Declan had the advantage of a fiancée who already had some decorations and the fact he'd started sooner. It didn't quite seem fair.

"Aha! The last one."

Damn. That was the unmistakable voice of Declan. When Ronan got to the Christmas aisle, there he was with a salesclerk, taking a box down of precisely what Ronan wanted.

"Hey, I was going to buy that," Ronan said. "It's the reason I'm here."

"But I got here first." Declan flashed the smile that earned him the title Prom King in his senior year.

He forgot that Ronan was not at all affected by his cousin's charm.

"How did you get here first? I came here right after breakfast. Don't you have a job where you should be?"

"Christmas break, dude." He lowered the box into his cart. "Amy and the kids are making a wish list, and I'm doing my thing, making sure our house is seen from the space shuttle."

Ronan groaned. "I'll give you twenty dollars if you let me buy it."

"Twenty bucks?" Declan laughed. "You're kidding, right?"

"It's twenty more than you came in with, plus you don't have to buy the thing. So, I'm saving you even more money. Twenty plus whatever that costs." Ronan pointed to the box.

"Try again. Remember, I'm a teacher and soon-to-be stepfather to twins who like to eat. Plus, Amy and I will be having some of our own kids eventually."

"Fifty dollars and that's my *final* offer!" Ronan pulled out his wallet and fished a bill out of it.

"Gotta admit I'm tempted."

"Amy would rather you spend this fifty on something for her and not another lawn ornament."

As if she'd been conjured, Amy came walking down the aisle in Declan's direction.

She frowned when she saw what Declan had in the cart. "I thought you were getting your mother's gift."

"I did. The perfume she likes." Declan fished it out of his cart and waved it.

Amy came up to Ronan and gave him a hug, then sighed. "I see you two are still continuing with this madness."

"Please talk your fiancé into letting me have this ornament. It's the last one. He's obsessed." Ronan crossed his arms.

"*Who's* obsessed?" Declan laughed then draped his arm around Amy. "Baby, the kids are going to love this. Didn't you see them pointing to it last night during the parade?"

"I'm not sure who loves it more," Amy said.

"You're forgetting I'm right next door," Ronan argued.

"They're still enjoying the lights display, but I'm footing the electricity bill on one of the houses."

Some days, Ronan half wondered if Declan had tricked him into this competition. It wouldn't surprise him. Two houses for the price of one.

"Therefore, if I let *you* buy it, we're still enjoying it." Declan tapped his chin. "Food for thought."

"Don't think too long." Amy rolled her eyes. "We promised the kids pizza tonight."

Ronan prepared to move in for the kill. "And, if you don't let me buy it, instead I'll have to buy another one of those displays with 'O Holy Night' playing nonstop. With two of those playing at night, correction, *three*, since you also have one, well, it might get a little loud."

"Let your cousin have it," Amy said, tipping up on her toes to kiss Declan's cheek. "Please."

"Because I'm such a great guy, and this is the last one, you can have it." He pulled the perfume out of the cart and rolled the cart to Ronan.

When he waved and turned to go, arm around Amy, he held his palm out behind him. Ronan slipped the cash in his hand because a deal was a deal, and at least, he'd won this latest round. Although the jury was still out on who'd won and who'd lost when Ronan spied the price and his eyes widened.

He'd saved his cousin a whole lot more than fifty dollars.

On the way back from the market, where he'd discovered that there was indeed something called "skim" milk, his cell phone rang with the theme from *Rocky*.

He pressed the button to answer through the truck's speaker. "Hey, Uncle Dan."

"Lorna and I missed the parade because we were wasting another year of my life looking at wood floor samples. How are things going with the young lady you saved?"

"I've got it under control. Don't worry."

"Why would I *worry*? That young lady is blessed you were there when it happened. You saved her life! Everyone in town is talking about it."

That was probably because by now his uncle had informed everyone he knew. Ronan had simply done what anyone else in his position would do. This sounded like Super Proud Uncle all over again.

"Did you tell everyone about the part where my fishing line literally got caught in her dress? It was the first thing I'd caught that night. Fishing is not for me."

"You'll just have to try something else," Uncle Dan chuckled. "The sport always helped me unwind but it's not for everybody."

"I'm going to be busy helping Elsa for now, so I don't think I have time to relax." Ronan turned on the residential street leading to Bluebird Lane. "Needless to say, she's feeling a little lost."

"I can only imagine. Maybe some distraction would help. Be sure to invite her to the Sheridan family Christmas dinner."

"Well, that would do it. Are you sure?"

"Of course. It's Christmas, a time for reaching out to strangers. We want to meet this poor woman."

"Well, first don't refer to her as a *poor woman*. She's young, beautiful, and very capable."

"I'm sure she is."

"Also, who knows if she'll still be here? I imagine someone has to be looking for her, and it probably won't be long before she remembers everything."

He'd miss her, and that was with only one day of knowing her. But when her family or significant other came for her, he'd know it was what she wanted. He wouldn't even *attempt* to intervene if she didn't recognize them. Besides, he was already uncomfortable with the way he'd noticed her, and how the air crackled between them with chemistry. She was the type of woman he'd have asked on a date, if he'd met her any other way. Now, he had no idea whether she already belonged to someone. Neither did she, for that matter.

"Sounds like she needs a little cheering up. If she's still around, be sure to bring her along. We'll have a full house. Lorna's thrilled. Our home is finally ready to entertain."

Dan had been working on the house he and his wife retired to since the moment they moved in. It would seem everything should be done by now, but his uncle always found a new project. The latest was replacing all the floors in the entire house, which they'd decided should be done after the holidays.

It was true that his uncle was a one-man cheering squad for anyone he'd ever met and Elsa could certainly use one. Just before pulling into the driveway, Ronan hung up with his uncle, promising to bring Elsa to dinner. Then his phone alerted again, this time the Charming PD.

He froze for a moment, then answered. "Ronan Sheridan here."

"This is the only number we have to contact Jane Doe," a man said.

"Yes, that's right. I'm her contact person. Any news?" This could already be over, and if so, Ronan would simply have a fond memory of a mysterious woman for many years to come.

Something to tell his grandchildren.

"Nothing yet. Just wanted to update y'all that we heard

back from everyone who'd launched a boat that night, and no one has reported a missing person. Same for the cruise liner, which unfortunately for us, is one of the larger ones, but they still have to issue us a head count for all four thousand on board, which they're happy to do. But you can imagine that may take a while. Only two reported missing in the last few days in the greater metropolitan area of Houston or Galveston, and those were men."

"Thanks. I'm sure everything will come back to her before long."

"That would certainly help," the officer said. "We're obviously checking surrounding cities, but that will take longer."

Ronan hung up, then juggled the bags of groceries he'd purchased, mostly for Elsa, and headed for the front door. He walked inside, and for a moment, wondered if he'd entered the wrong house. To be fair, he wasn't a neat freak, but he kept his living quarters tidy. Now every appliance in his kitchen gleamed, the wood floor shined, and some of the furniture had been rearranged.

"Hi!" Elsa's head popped up from where she'd been crouched near the oven. "You're back."

"Um, yeah." He glanced around the room. "You've been busy."

"We can change everything back if you don't like it this way." She pointed to the attached family room. "But it's more functional this way, and you might even be able to see the TV better. There was a glare on the screen from the sunlight pouring in through the front, paned window."

He'd been meaning to address that. "Thanks, but you didn't have to do all this."

"Like I said, I like to keep busy." She took a grocery bag from his arms. "I'll just put this away for you."

Ronan didn't want her to stress, but on the other hand, if cleaning and rearranging his house kept her mind off her problems, it wouldn't hurt. He helped put away the groceries, occasionally bumping into her like two people who hadn't yet learned the rhythm of living together and sharing personal space.

"I heard back from the police." Ronan hated to bring something unpleasant up when she seemed to be happily distracted, but he couldn't keep this from her.

She stopped in the middle of putting away cans of soup in the cupboard, holding a chicken-noodle soup in each hand, giving him her rapt attention.

He continued. "And there are no reports of anyone missing from boats that evening, or from the cruise liner that had been taking off that afternoon. No reports of missing women in the greater metropolitan area."

"It makes no sense. What was I doing there that night?" Her shoulders slumped. "There's something missing."

"There is, and with more time, we'll either figure this out, or you'll remember."

"Right." She nodded and put the cans away. "I just have to keep a positive attitude."

"And, if you're still here in a few days, you're invited to the big Irish Sheridan family dinner."

"Irish?"

Ronan sighed. "We're Irish-American, though we don't like to talk about it."

"What? Why not?" Elsa laughed.

"Well, you've heard the luck of the Irish?"

She nodded.

"We don't have it."

"None?"

"We stay far away from Vegas and never gamble. It's safest that way."

She frowned. "I don't think anyone should gamble. It's irresponsible."

"You're right, and the house always wins."

"Surely you've had some luck in your life."

"I'm telling you, should I buy stock in Apple, the next day the market will crash. I don't think it's fair to do that to the economy."

"You're exaggerating."

"Not really. I updated my smart phone and the very next day the new one dropped. It was too soon to upgrade for another year."

"That could happen to anyone." She smirked.

"I once bought ten pounds of coffee to save money and the next day my aunt gifted me with a Keurig. I then had to buy those little cups."

"That's ironic, not bad luck." But she was starting to laugh.

He shrugged but bit back a chuckle. "Maybe you're right.

Date your high school sweetheart for years but then lose her to your best friend.

Meet a beautiful woman you'd like to get to know better but she can't even remember who she is much less if she's already committed to someone else.

He could already hear Alanis Morissette singing. Face it, without bad luck he'd have no luck at all.

"This family dinner. Are you *sure* it's not an imposition?"

He shook his head. "The more the merrier. They've already heard about you and would like to meet you."

"I'm kind of an oddity so I understand the interest."

"That's not why. There are no strangers when it comes

to the Sheridans. Everyone is welcome. If you're ever uncomfortable with all the attention that night, let me know. I'll do something to make everyone forget about you."

"Like what?" She smiled and cocked her head.

"So many options. Tell an off-color joke so my aunt will blush and scold me, start singing 'The Star-Spangled Banner' off-key and, at last resort, dance. That makes everybody laugh so hard they almost can't breathe."

Elsa laughed out loud. "You're *that* bad?"

He nodded, fighting a smile. "It's tragic."

"I might have to see proof of this at some point."

He'd succeeded in distracting her, at least, and he wasn't done yet. She insisted on fixing lunch, which was sandwiches with the sliced turkey he'd bought from the deli. But if there was any hint to him that she didn't do this often, it was in the fact she forgot mayonnaise and condiments. Not wanting to embarrass her, he ate the driest turkey sandwich ever.

She chewed, swallowing water after every bite. "This isn't very good, is it?"

It was his chance. "You forgot the mayonnaise."

She shot up in her chair and face palmed. "Why didn't you tell me?"

When she brought him the jar, he slathered on some on his sandwich while she did on hers.

"Oh wow, so much better," she said, taking a bite. "I wonder why I forgot that."

"Considering you drink skim milk, maybe you don't normally use mayo. It makes sense."

"Or maybe...someone in my life doesn't like mayonnaise," she mused. "God, I hope I'm not allergic."

That made Ronan pull out of his smartphone and look it up. "It's not likely, especially if you did okay with the eggs."

"I didn't even think about any of this."

"From now on, I guess we should be more careful. Let's just have you stay away from peanuts as a precaution."

There was a knock on his front door, and he opened it to find Declan with both kids.

"We're here to help you put up the new display."

Chapter Eight

Elsa thought David and Naomi were the cutest kids she'd ever seen. It turned out they were twins even if they didn't look any more like each other than most brothers and sisters. In fact, she thought Declan and Ronan looked more like twins that the actual twins did. But the more time she spent around them, the less she believed she might have children of her own.

"Is your name Elsa like in the movie?" Naomi, Amy's mini-me, who had the sweetest smile, piped up.

"You know that movie?" Elsa said.

"*Everybody* knows that movie," David said.

"I guess they do," Elsa said. "But that's not my real name. They were calling me Jane Doe at the hospital, but Ronan called me Elsa because I looked frozen that night."

"But does the cold *bother* you?" Naomi said.

It very much did, as Elsa believed herself to be a dyed in the wool Texan. But she didn't want to ruin it for the little girl, whose sparkling brown eyes were wide and hopeful that she'd found a real life Elsa.

"Not really." Elsa winked.

"Okay, kids!" Ronan called out once he and Declan unboxed the display. "Where should we put this one? Next to the Nativity Scene, or next to the Santa Claus and his reindeer, or next to—"

"You're running out of lawn." Declan stood back, arms crossed, surveying the yard for the perfect place.

"What about right here?" Amy pointed to a spot between their shared lawn.

Ronan, Declan, and the kids all agreed she'd found the only available space left on the yard. After it had been set up, extension and power cord included, they all watched it light up along with the rest of the twinkling lights and music. Then Amy invited them all inside their home for cookies she and the children had made.

When Elsa walked into the house next door, she found an indoor layout similar to Ronan's and yet different in every way. This was truly a home, filled with framed photos of the children as they were growing up, pictures of Amy and Declan, both when they were teenagers and more recently. Toys were strewn about, a general sense of controlled chaos. It took everything in Elsa not to start straightening up the place. This must be what it was like to live with children. It didn't feel familiar, not in the slightest. She'd go nuts living here. Either she didn't have children, or she was a bad mother who spent little time with her children.

She hoped it was the former.

Declan flipped the flat-screen on to a football game and Ronan joined him. When Amy went into the kitchen, Elsa followed to make herself useful.

"We didn't get to talk much last night," Amy said, pulling out plates and cups. "How are you feeling?"

"I'm doing my best," Elsa said. "Some things are instinctive, like the fact that I'm particular about my shampoo and hair products. I'm not sure why, but I am."

"You, too, huh? It might be a girl thing." She closed a

cabinet and turned around. "I'll get you some of mine. I know Ronan must have only functional stuff. A girl needs her product."

"It's the least of my problems."

"Even so, you can be comfortable while you wait for news."

Amy stacked a variety of frosted cookies in shapes of stars, Christmas trees, and candy canes on a plate, not bothered when Elsa intervened to help.

"Um, so how long have you and Declan been together?" Elsa made polite conversation, even if this didn't really matter in the grand scheme of things.

These people were being so kind, and she should be interested in their lives.

"That depends on if you mean the first or the second time. We were high school sweethearts. We went to different colleges, then I married someone else, and Declan went off to play pro baseball. *This* time we've been together for a little over a year. We'll get it right this time."

Elsa wondered if she, too, had a high school sweetheart. Too bad if she did, because she couldn't remember him anyway.

"Congratulations on your upcoming marriage."

"Thank you. It's a long time coming." She sighed, glancing into the attached family room and all but drooling over Declan. "I fell in love with him when I was sixteen years old and I don't think I ever stopped loving him all these years."

Elsa didn't think she could ever be that patient. Doing the math, she figured Amy had waited close to fifteen *years* to be with Declan. Elsa wanted what she wanted and wanted it yesterday, but too bad for her. As usual she'd have to figure this out on her own, because apparently nobody was looking for her. Whenever she did get home, she was going to have words with whomever didn't even *realize* she'd gone missing. If it was a significant other, like a fiancé, that relationship would be on life support afterward. If someone she loved was missing, she'd know it. And she'd never stop looking for them.

"Never let it be said that good things don't come to those who wait." Amy poured milk into several cups. "Not that I was always waiting for Declan. I lived my life, got married, and had my children. But I always had a special spot for my first love. I never forgot him. When the timing was right, we got to live our happily-ever-after. And that's just how it will be for you, too, I bet. Don't worry, you *will* get back to your life eventually. Even if you can't remember, someone will be looking for you soon. They're probably looking for you as we speak."

"I hope so. It's a weird feeling, like I've left something undone. Like there's something I should be doing right now."

"Is it that odd sensation when a word is on the tip of your tongue but you just can't get it?"

"That's a close comparison."

"Frustrating." Amy gathered the plate of cookies and a cup and gestured to Elsa. "Can you bring the rest of those? There's one for everybody."

Food in the family room? Amy must like to live dangerously. Against her better judgement, Elsa handed out cups filled with milk. They joined Declan, Ronan, and the kids in front of the TV as they all watched the 49ers play the Seahawks. The cookies were delicious with cold milk.

"Do you like the cookies?" Naomi said, sitting next to Elsa. "I helped Mommy make them."

"They're very good," Elsa said.

She listened as Naomi described in detail how she'd mixed the colors, then piped icing in perfect rows.

"First I put in the yellow, see?" Naomi pointed. "Then, some green and red right here."

"You did a wonderful job," Elsa said.

"So did I!" David piped up. "I did most of the stars in yellow."

"You both did a great job," Declan said, taking his eyes off the screen for a second.

"Mommy, why aren't you eating my cookies?" Naomi said.

"I think I had too many of them when we were baking." Amy laughed and patted her stomach. "Mommy had way too much sugar."

"You can never have too much sugar," David said as he grabbed yet another one.

"Ronan," Amy said. "I've been meaning to invite you to the Once Upon a Book's literary character contest. A new Charming tradition."

"I don't know if I'll be able to make it," Ronan said, seemingly distracted by the game.

"You don't even know when it is." Amy chuckled.

It occurred to Elsa that Ronan didn't want to commit when he had caretaking duties with her to consider. He was her landlord, driver, provider, her everything.

"You should go," Elsa said. "It sounds like fun. It's exactly what I'd do if I owned a bookstore at Christmastime. You have to find a way to bring people inside, and dressing like literary characters sounds ingenious."

She wasn't sure where that thought came from, except it made good business sense.

"That's exactly what Twyla said," Amy said. "And, of course, you're invited, too."

Ronan turned to give his full attention to Elsa. "You want to go?"

"Sure, yes. If I'm still here, I'd like to go."

"Okay, we'll go." Ronan shrugged.

Amy gave Elsa a conspiratorial smile. "Well, that was easy."

A commercial rolled across the screen of a winery in Napa Valley. The video... It was a memory somehow. The gorgeous, lush California valley filled with rows and rows of vines. It was all so *familiar*. She'd obviously somehow been there at one time. Maybe for a visit, or maybe...they were all looking in the wrong place.

Dear God, *what if she was from California?*

"I'm telling you, Ronan. It was all so *familiar*."

For the past hour, since they'd returned from Declan's place, Elsa had been trying to convince him she might actually be from California. He just didn't buy it, though anything was possible. First, there was the distinctive twang in her voice. Even *he* didn't sound as native to Texas as she did, and he'd lived here on and off since he was a kid. Second...

"It still doesn't explain what you were doing, um, floating in Galveston Bay."

"That's true." She deflated. "I could have been on vacation, or simply attending a party with friends. What a mystery."

"I know you want to get back to your life, but while you're here, I'll make everything the best I can for you."

"You're already doing so much. I'm forever grateful. I feel like I'm cramping your style. I've taken over your life."

"You're not cramping anything. I'm not complaining."

She elbowed him. "Hey, wouldn't it be funny if I wind

up being a lost princess from some obscure kingdom and my family doesn't even realize I'm missing?"

"Hilarious."

Honestly, he'd hate it. A princess would be as far removed from his reach as possible. For sure, he'd never see Elsa, or whatever her name was, again. Believing she could be from Texas meant he could lie to himself that, even after all this, she might still somehow be a part of his life. This time, both of them knowing who they were and what they wanted. In at least one part of his life, Ronan knew what he wanted. He wanted what Declan had found with Amy, and not just because he was competitive. Declan was already ahead of him in that department, but Ronan was happy for him. Amy and Declan were perfect for each other, with an unconditional kind of love and loyalty everyone should have.

Either way, tomorrow he'd call the police department and give them the latest update. They might consider widening the scope to missing women in California. Yeah, that ought to be easy. First Texas, then California. Maybe next they could try *Alaska* and throw another hugely populated state into the mix.

"I mean, if I'm a princess I'd be able to give you a big reward."

"While I'm sure the king and queen would be grateful, I don't need a reward for doing the right thing."

"But one would be nice. That way, maybe you could take even more time to decide what you're going to do with the rest of your life."

She was not wrong. His experience with Elsa had led him to one fundamental conclusion: He thrived on helping and protecting people, in whatever capacity. Clearly, his uncle had been correct in that he could also do so as a civilian. This time, he could help people not caught in a war zone. Maybe not as exciting or adrenaline producing, but important, nevertheless. Rescuing near-drowning victims would not happen often, thank goodness, but he could help anyway.

He definitely hadn't been *relaxing* enough, which is why the next morning, he found himself writing Elsa a note explaining that he'd gone to run errands. He'd be gardening today. Yes, him. *Gardening*. When he'd researched "ways to relax," spending time in nature was at the top of the list. The others were less attractive to him, like meditating and *yoga*. Maybe he'd get there, someday, but the idea of sitting still and making his mind a blank space sounded horrible.

Back in the day, his mother had a small vegetable garden at the side of their home, so the way Ronan looked at it, he was continuing his mother's family tradition in her memory. So, he would plant a garden and at least all these efforts would *accomplish* something. Then he would have fresh vegetables and save money on groceries. Win-win.

He drove to Back to the Fuchsia, the garden center owned by Amy's mother, Moonbeam. Getting busy, he chose plants without much discretion.

"Ronan?"

He turned to the woman's voice, while holding a tomato starter plant, and probably wearing a scowl. That voice sent a sharp slice of pain through him. Damn it. *Belinda*. Should he say hello, or ignore her? She definitely deserved the ignoring. His mind was blank. Apparently he didn't need yoga.

He went for calm, distant, and aloof. "Hello."

"I'm glad I ran into you."

"Sorry, but I'm busy right now." He moved away, but she followed him into the tomato aisle.

"I feel like we have unfinished business. We should talk."

"There's nothing to say. I wish you and Paul well." The fact he said this between gritted teeth was probably not convincing. "What's done is done and all that. I've moved on."

"What are you doing here?" She picked up a plant from the displays as if she were also shopping, so he moved to give her space.

"Parasailing. What do you think I'm doing? Starting a garden so I can learn how to relax."

"I heard you were back, this time to stay."

"The jury is still out on that. Still considering all my options."

"Is there anything I can do to convince you?"

"To stay?"

She was still achingly pretty, with long straight blond hair and green eyes. Ronan's mind flashed back to simpler times and how great life could be with the right woman. He missed her, but he'd also never be able to forgive her.

"Stay for Dan and Lorna. It would mean so much to them, and I want us to be friends again."

"*We* were never friends. You must be thinking of Paul. He was my friend. Past tense."

She reached to stay his hand, just before he picked up a tomato plant. "Please, Ronan. You were such a huge part of my life, for years. If we are all going to move on, we have to get past this resentment you have for us."

"I already *said* I'm past it."

"But that's not true. You can't even look at me."

"I can look at you fine."

With that, he turned and gave her the full weight of his stare down. She wanted him to look, he'd *look*. He watched with a sense of satisfaction when she wilted under his glare.

He had no time for people who didn't understand the basics of loyalty. The last time he'd seen her, she'd said she loved him. Three months later, she was with Paul. That wasn't love.

Her smile was shaky as she moved away, finally getting the message. "Maybe I'll see you around. After all, it's a small town."

Unfortunately, she was right. He'd probably run into her again. Paul, at least, knew better than to try to approach or ask for forgiveness he didn't deserve. But Ronan should really consider dating again if he wanted Belinda to believe and accept he'd moved on. And he wanted what Declan had. Women weren't just going to throw themselves in his path. Except for Elsa, but she was an exception in every way. When Belinda left, he pulled his thoughts back to vegetables and away from faithless ex-girlfriends.

Moonbeam came by a moment later to water some of the plants, and Ronan grabbed her attention.

"I'm starting a vegetable garden," he said, holding up the starter plants. "Which of these would be best?"

"Good for you! 'To plant a garden is to believe in tomorrow.'" She pointed. "Of course, spring is the best time, but it's possible to start a small garden with a few winter vegetables. Root ones work best, like carrots, beets, radishes, and broccoli. Leafy greens like kale and spinach are a good choice. But starters like those are for people who want it easy. Not much of a challenge unless you start from seeds."

"Seeds?" He didn't think his *mother* had planted seeds. "Won't that take longer?"

Moonbeam shrugged. "Sure, but anything worth doing is worth taking your time and doing it right."

Ronan couldn't have said it better himself. She was speaking his language.

"Where can I find seeds?"

An hour later, he was in the backyard. He removed all the weeds standing in the way of progress. As far as he could tell, all Declan had ever done out here was keep the lawn mowed and the bushes trimmed. Ronan would show *him*. He used the new rake to plow lines in the dirt. Seeds. He would start with seeds. Much more of a challenge and he was up to the task.

Can you see me, Instagram? I'm touching grass.

Elsa came outside when he'd just finished the last plow line. "What are you up to?"

She'd probably cleaned the house again. A woman who didn't know how to relax, either. What a pair they made.

"I'm starting a vegetable garden." He leaned on the rake.

"Cool! Can I help?"

Before he could answer, she was walking toward him. For the next two hours, they worked in tandem. Elsa ran inside to grab his tablet and looked up advice. She sat on the back step and read tips to him from the master gardeners. It was like being able to do two things at once with her help. For the first time, they were learning a natural rhythm around each other. She seemed to anticipate his every move, too, and handed him whatever he needed before he could ask for it. When they were done, she bent to stick the seed packet at the end of each row so they'd be able to identify them as they began to sprout and grow.

"Have you done this before?" he finally asked her.

"I don't remember."

"You seem like a natural. I'm using seeds because it's more of a challenge."

"That makes sense. It's going to be incredible to watch those little seeds sprout and grow into plants and later actual vegetables." From the ground where she was patting a tiny mound of a tomato seed, she glanced up at him. "Does this mean you've decided to stay?"

Damn, he hadn't even thought of that. These seeds would take weeks to grow into saplings, or sprouts or whatever they called it, and by the time he had vegetables...he didn't know where he'd be. The only thing he truly knew for certain was that he had become a little too fixated on watching Elsa bend over and on the sweet curve of her behind. He blamed Belinda for reminding him of a whole other part of his life. He'd been behaving like a monk because they had no idea if Elsa was in a relationship with someone. He would never do to someone else what had been done to him. Attraction was one thing, but acting on it was another. Elsa might have someone at home, desperately wondering how he could find her. He knew too well what it felt like when someone made his move on your girl in your absence.

It struck him that Elsa had just been dropped into his life and they were cohabitating like they'd been together for years. This was exactly how he'd pictured his life with a woman. Someone like him, who understood his need to be the best at whatever he attempted. Elsa didn't even question him, because she always seemed to be on the same page. She'd jumped into this gardening project without a second thought.

But she couldn't even remember who she was, and for all he knew, she'd leave tomorrow with her husband or lover.

All of a sudden, he broke out in a cold sweat.

This wasn't at all relaxing.

Chapter Nine

For the next two days, Elsa got up every morning, showered, had coffee, then checked patterns for rain on Ronan's tablet. If no rain was expected, she watered the garden. Ronan was right. This *was* relaxing and it gave her a purpose. When she'd first spotted him digging in the dirt outside, she thought maybe a pipe had burst or he might be installing a sprinkler system. Then he raked the tough Texas dirt, the muscles in his arms bunching under his T-shirt. It seemed a little voyeuristic to simply stare at all that male attractiveness, so she jumped in to help. When she was outside, her mind wandered, free of all the worries. She was just…here and nothing else mattered. For a few minutes, anyway.

Gardening took her mind off the fact that it had been almost a week and not a single person had come to find her. Every day, she checked in with the police. Nothing. Was she really that much of a loner? It was disheartening to think she meant so little to those people in her previous world. Perhaps it was for the best that no one was waiting for her to read them a bedtime story or crying for their mother. No one was waiting for her to come home and hang out. If she had a job, and every intuitive sense in her said that she did, her coworkers didn't care that she hadn't shown up to work for days.

In fact, it was the people she'd just met who had demonstrated they cared. Yesterday, Amy had dropped by with Michelle, Finn's wife, carrying more clothes and shoes for Elsa. They'd actually taken up a collection. They'd bought her sexy underwear, too, and a few other new things, like a red dress she would wear to the Sheridan family dinner. She'd become a *charity* case. If something didn't change soon, she was going to have to move out, move on, and make a new life for herself. She wouldn't wait forever to live the rest of her life. Michelle, a family law attorney, promised to do some investigating as to what actions Elsa might need to take next if she had to start over. She'd need a birth certificate. A social security card. All things most people took for granted.

If she was forced to start a brand-new life, she'd want everyone she'd met to continue to be a part of it. Ronan especially. Well, he probably wouldn't be interested in dating her, but maybe they could stay friends. Really, really good friends. Maybe even friends with benefits. And hey, excuse her for little flights of fancy if she belonged to someone else. Because whoever he was, he didn't seem to care enough to *find* her. And it sure felt like more than a week since Elsa had been with a man. Funny enough, she hadn't forgotten sex. If her instincts were right, she was pretty good at it, too. It would be nice to know she was free so she could figure the rest of it out with Ronan. She would love more than anything to kiss him. Just once. He'd sort of kissed her. Okay, so it was CPR, but still, it was a nice first memory.

Ronan popped his head out the back door. "Hey, Amy's here. Something about taking you shopping?"

Elsa squinted at him beneath the bright pool of sunshine. "I didn't know anything about it."

"Oh, look, you have a garden!" Amy squeezed past Ronan. "What a great idea."

"It's Ronan's garden. I'm just helping." She shut off the garden hose and walked toward them.

"We're going cosplay shopping today! Want to come?" Amy said.

She took a long look at her jeans, which were slightly damp from the leaky hose. "Do I have time to change?"

"Sure!" She turned to Ronan. "Do you want to come, too? I told you you're also going to need a costume."

"Yeah but I don't need to *buy* one. I'm going as a sailor."

"Oh c'mon! That's not cosplay for you," Amy said, and held a hand to her heart. "Declan and I are going as Romeo and Juliet."

"Of course you are." Ronan crossed his arms. "What if I get a pipe? I'll be Popeye the Sailor Man."

"I can see it," Elsa said, biting back a laugh.

"No way!" Amy shook her head. "Remember, it has to be *literary*. Do either of you have a favorite book that might work?"

Elsa had a suggestion, but she was afraid it might sound presumptuous. Still, she had an idea in her mind and Ronan would fit the bill quite nicely. Yesterday, bored out of her mind, she'd binged a few episodes of *Outlander*. She happened to know it had been a book first, so it counted.

"What about *Outlander*?" Elsa suggested. "I can be Claire and I think Ronan would make a great Jamie. He's got the whole Scottish vibe going on."

And Elsa would bet he looked great in a kilt. She would fight in the Anglo-Scottish war to see those bare legs.

"I'm *Irish*." Ronan cleared his throat. "There is a difference, however slight. And we Irish have kilts, too."

Elsa mentally face-palmed. She felt like a total idiot. A major faux pas. "Yes, I'm sorry. I know that. An Irishman without any luck."

Amy clapped a hand over her mouth, then lowered it. "I thought we had a good chance at winning with Romeo and Juliet, but if anyone can beat us it's Jamie and Claire."

"Winning?" Ronan quirked a brow. "Winning what?"

"I didn't tell you? The whole thing is a contest. There's one winner chosen. Last year it was Mr. Finch who came dressed as Sherlock Holmes."

"I had no idea there was a *winner*," Ronan said. "This changes things."

"I figured." Amy sighed. "*Please* don't tell Declan I told you."

"Ah, he's not afraid of a little competition. This makes it more fun for him, too."

"So, you'll do it?" Elsa said, hands clasped together in a prayer. "Be Jamie the Scottish Highlander?"

"Wear a kilt? Hell, yeah. For the chance to beat Declan, you better believe I'll do it."

After changing into another pair of jeans and a short-sleeved blouse, Elsa went with Amy to the local boutique in town. Glamtique was tucked away behind some other buildings not far from Once Upon a Book, where the contest would be held.

They were greeted at the door by a beautiful woman. Tall like Elsa, she had flawless latte skin and corkscrew curls falling over her shoulders. She looked like a model.

"Hey, y'all. I'm Zoey. Welcome in!"

"We're here for some ideas for Twyla's contest," Amy said. "We're going to put an outfit together."

"I've still got some gorgeous vintage pieces in the back. Normally I'd be picked over, but I got some unexpected inventory yesterday. Because of the costume contest, all will probably be gone tomorrow." Zoey led them to the back of the store, and Elsa passed rows and rows of gorgeous garments.

This was more like it. She would never complain about the clothes so kindly donated, but every day she put on a pair of jeans, a little something died inside. Glamtique was filled with cutting-edge fashion and, oh my Lord, the *shoes*. Shoes everywhere. Sexy high-heeled stilettos, and boots with cutouts and elaborate tooling. Shiny wedge sandals. She could die happy here.

"Are you coming?" Amy called back to Elsa, who'd gone almost catatonic admiring a pair of shoes.

They looked so familiar, but no way could she afford anything like these. She must have simply admired them at another time. Somewhere, in another life. Right. Despite her joking with Ronan, she didn't actually believe she could be royalty. Not with her twang.

She reluctantly set them down and joined Amy.

"Anything in particular you're looking for?" Zoey asked.

Everything. I'll take it all, Elsa wanted to say.

"We're looking for something that would work for *Outlander* cosplay," Amy said. "She'll be going as Claire."

"Ooooh." Zoey went hand to chest. "Be still my heart, I love that show! Leave it to me, this is my wheelhouse. I've got you."

She flipped through skirts and dresses and eventually came up with a vintage long dark flannel skirt with a dark paisley vest and a long-sleeved white button-down. With all the pieces put together, it looked just like the Scottish Highlands dress Claire wore in the first season of *Outlander*.

"You're a genius!" Amy said. "Damn, y'all might actually beat us, even though I have to confess Declan makes a *very* sexy Romeo. Hard to beat."

Zoey rang up the purchases. "And you're going to make a gorgeous Juliet."

"Good thing our story is not nearly as tragic." Amy handed over her card.

Elsa winced. "I'm going to pay you back for everything. I swear."

"Don't worry," Amy said. "I got you *into* this."

"Oh, you must be the woman Ronan rescued." Zoey's brown eyes widened.

Elsa nodded. "He saved my life. I would have drowned without him."

"And you honestly don't remember who you are?" Zoey handed Amy back her card.

"I know," Elsa said. "Pretty unbelievable, isn't it? I literally have nothing to my name. No ID, no money, no clothes except the ones Amy and Michelle have given me. Everyone here has been so kind. I hope I deserve it."

"Everyone deserves kindness," Zoey said. "Personally, I would bet you can't lose everything about yourself. I think if I lost all my memories, I would still love clothes and hamburgers and pizza. Even if I didn't know my own name."

Amy laughed. "Some things are intuitive. If I lost my memories, I'd still love books, my kids, macaroni and cheese, and, of course, Declan."

"And I'd bet he would never stop looking for you," Elsa said.

Amy squeezed Elsa's shoulder. "If you have someone, he's looking for you."

"Any luck finding out what happened to you?" Zoey asked Elsa.

"Not so far. The police here are investigating but no one has reported anyone that fits my description missing," Elsa said. "So far. And it's been almost a week now."

"How about Instagram?" Zoey said, pulling out her phone. "I have a ton of followers from all over the country because I have an online catalog and I drop-ship. Who knows? Maybe someone will recognize you."

"As long as we don't get any stalkers. I mean, Elsa is very pretty," Amy said. "I don't trust social media anymore."

It hadn't even occurred to Elsa that someone who simply wanted a girlfriend would claim to be her lover. She would have to ask for proof, in photos that hadn't been photoshopped. Besides, Ronan would never let her go if he suspected anything devious.

"That's a good point," Zoey said. "I'll be more nuanced and I won't mention any details. I'll just say you're a couple of my regular customers. Can I take your photo and upload it?"

Elsa didn't consider herself to be exactly photo-op ready, but she was so tired of being someone's problem. First, it was Ronan. Then he'd involved his cousin's family. Ava, the coffee shop owner said she'd help, and now Zoey. Still, Elsa wanted her life back so she could begin the process of paying everyone back. Even if it took years.

"Sure." She tried a smile and smoothed down her hair for the photo.

When she got back home with her purchases, Ronan was sitting in front of the TV, tablet in his hands.

She held up her bag. "Hello there, sir, nice to meet you. I'm Claire. Now, we just have to worry about your costume, Jamie."

"Done."

"When? I was only gone about an hour."

"I found it online."

He couldn't be serious. He'd just *found* it? Online?

"But if it ships, then it won't be here in time, will it?"

He glanced up at her from under hooded lids. "Tomorrow."

"Oh, you took all the fun out of it." She plopped down beside him. "You're supposed to look and look until finally you're rewarded with the perfect outfit."

"That's what I did, just cut the time in half. And the *fun* is going to be winning this contest." He held up air quotes around *fun*. "If I have to wear a kilt and embarrass my Irish heritage, then I better win."

"Wow. Okay, *please* explain to me why you and Declan are in such competition with everything. When did this all start?"

Ronan looked at the ceiling as if remembering. "We were probably pretty young. Six?"

"*Seriously?* This is silly."

"Not so silly. We were both on the same Little League team. My Uncle Dan was our coach."

"I'm beginning to see the issue."

She'd heard horror stories about Little League parents, shouting and cursing to the coaches from the stands.

"Look, there's no harm in it. The way I see it, Declan is constantly raising the bar for me. I try to do the same for him. It makes us both better men."

"So, this is a good thing?"

"Go big or go home."

"And how is this helping you relax?"

Ronan leaned back, crossed his arms behind his neck, and gave her an easy smile. "Winning is how *I* relax."

Chapter Ten

Ronan was going out of his flipping mind. Elsa had been walking around parading her new outfits as if on a personal mission to slowly torture him to death. This morning, she'd put on a pair of shorts and a tight top to *water the garden*. He was therefore teased by her long and toned legs and curvy behind. Even if *he* was no longer relaxing by gardening, he couldn't be sorry, because Elsa did a lot of bending in the garden, pulling out weeds as they encroached. She seemed completely unaware of the effect she had on him which meant he was hiding his attraction well. *Winning*.

Aunt Lorna always wanted him to dress up for the family shindig, so tonight he'd located his best dark slacks and blue button-down shirt. Even if he didn't always bother with shaving, he did so today, in honor of his aunt, who would consider it a personal affront if he didn't make the effort. Since he loved the woman like a second mother, out came the shaving kit. By five o'clock, he was ready and pacing the family room waiting for Elsa. He hated being late to anything.

"Elsa! We have to leave." He knocked on her bedroom door. "Now."

"Almost ready!" she called out. "Be with you in a jiffy."

Not like he hadn't been through this scenario before.

With anyone else, he'd leave without them and teach them a lesson. Not an option here. He wanted to tear the door off its hinges when she finally emerged a few minutes later, and he swallowed hard, feeling a kick to his heart.

"You look...nice," he said, choosing to censor his thoughts.

Nice was an understatement. Her shoulder-length dark hair was bouncy and wavy, falling around her shoulders. She wore makeup for the first time, courtesy of Amy's stash, no doubt. It gave her an entirely different appearance. Gone was the fresh-faced girl, replaced by the sexy siren.

"Thank you!"

More cheerful than he'd seen her since he'd agreed to dress in a kilt, she held her arms out and spun in a circle once. "The girls got me this dress, and though it's a little small, I love it."

Dear God, so did he. He was ready to *propose* to that dress.

"You look nice, too." Her gaze slid up and down him and landed on his face. "You *shaved*. Wow, you look somehow...younger."

He palmed his jawline. "My aunt would be insulted if I didn't go to the trouble. But I get by fine shaving every few days."

"Yes, well, the stubble is also attractive." She said this a bit shyly, not meeting his eyes.

Attractive. So, she found him attractive, even if he wasn't Scottish. Or a Highlander.

He cleared his throat to break this spell. "We ought to go, or we'll be late."

"I'm sorry to have taken so long," she said, going out the front door he held open for her. "I just want to make a good impression on your family."

"Don't worry, they're going to love you." He drove down the coastal highway again, but this time he kept going past town.

His aunt and uncle lived on the outskirts of Charming. Thirty minutes later, he pulled into the driveway that led to the Sheridan home. And damn, of course Declan had *beaten* him there. He also spied Finn and Michelle's luxury sedan parked a few houses down. The house sat on a small hill with a spectacular view from the newly refurbished deck. In the distance, one could view the lighthouse and the sandy beaches of the coastline.

"According to my uncle, better than living on the water is having a good view of the coastline."

"Oh my, it looks like something out of *Architectural Digest*," Elsa said. "Like one of those jewel showplaces. But they are not as nearly into Christmas as you are."

They had a solitary string of fairy lights across the eaves, and an animated reindeer, who bowed his head every few seconds as if grazing.

"Not nearly. A lot of work has gone into the house," Ronan said. "My uncle retired from the post office and he's not the type to sit still. So, he started renovating the place. He's still not done, because apparently they're now replacing the floors. It's always something. Funny, he's the one who told me I have to learn how to unwind. The way he does it is fishing."

"Ah, he's the one I have to thank for the night you caught me." Elsa flashed a smile.

That wicked smile of hers *did* things to him. "Yeah. He's the one."

He took her hand, warm and soft, and led her up the stone-paved walkway to the front door. "You ready for this? Brace yourself."

She laughed. "Why? Can it be worse than what I've been through?"

"You have a point. It's just…a lot. Like a rogue wave of love, I call it."

"And you don't *like* love?" She gave him a questioning look.

Well, she had him there. His little family unit had never been particularly demonstrative, which his military-man father had called the "Irish way." His mother was far more affectionate but even she wasn't like Lorna Sheridan. During the pandemic, when family get-togethers were almost nonexistent and virtual hugs became the norm, Aunt Lorna behaved as if she'd been placed on life support. By now, he was accustomed to it, but he understood levels of comfort varied.

"Of course I like love." He rang the doorbell, to warn everyone, and opened the unlocked door for Elsa.

"Ronan!" Here came Aunt Lorna, arms outstretched, and he folded her into his arms, bussing her cheek. "What's it been? Over a week since you came to see me. Way too long."

Then she caught sight of Elsa standing near him, and suddenly, it all came to her. "Oh, honey! You must be Elsa. The children can't stop talking about you."

"Hi." With a tight smile on her face, Elsa stuck out her hand.

Ronan managed to keep the laugh inside, but he put his arm around her because he sensed her anxiety level rise.

Sure enough, Aunt Lorna pulled her into a hug. "I'm a hugger! Welcome! I'm so very glad you came."

It wasn't long before everyone descended on them. Uncle Dan, Finn, and Declan with fist bumps, Michelle, and Amy with hugs.

Once again Ronan felt the rogue wave of unconditional love wash over him. And he hoped Elsa felt it, too.

He'd *held her hand*. Ronan had reached out for Elsa's hand, and when his big hand covered hers with a deep warmth, something inside of her ripped wide open. Speaking of rogue waves of love, she'd been pulled under by one even before Ronan opened the front door.

The rooms were filled with beautiful skylights, and large bay windows. The wood floors gleamed, and the kitchen was large enough for an island and housed modern cabinets in a dark cherry wood. The holiday decorations were a bit more generous inside, a large artificial white tree in a corner of the family room shining brightly with red blinking lights, wrapped presents already under it. Green garlands decorated the banister of the staircase leading upstairs, and on the fireplace mantel, Christmas stockings hung from hooks. There were candles in the windows. The lovely smell of cinnamon and apple cider laced the air. Elsa took it all in like a kid at Christmastime.

The house was incredible, but the people inside it even more so.

Ronan might technically be an orphan, but she envied him most of all for his family. They were all so delightful and interesting, too. Dan had worked for the post office in addition to coaching. Lorna sold real estate. Elsa already knew that Michelle was a family-law attorney, but she learned Finn was a former Olympian with an actual gold medal. And you could have knocked her over with a feather when she discovered that Declan was an amazing baseball player who'd had a short career with the MLB.

A family of overachievers, but with an actual *coach* as their patriarch, it wasn't surprising. He was already starting with the kids, too, praising them at every turn even for doing the simplest of things. The kids were incredibly well-behaved, too.

"Good job cleaning your plate, young man!" Dan Sheridan said to David.

"Dad, he's going to eat us out of house and home." Declan laughed.

"He's a growing boy." Lorna passed more potatoes to David. "And it's a compliment to my cooking."

"The roast was delicious, Mrs. Sheridan," Elsa said. "Everything is perfect."

"Yeah, Ma, you didn't even overcook the potatoes this time." Finn gave her a sly smile.

Michelle elbowed him. "Be nice."

"I'm always nice."

Lorna ignored her oldest and patted Elsa's arm. "Call me Lorna, honey. You are always welcome in my home."

It was the second time Elsa wished she could stay in this town forever and forget she had any other past. The first time was when Ronan pulled that rake across the dirt and her stomach got tight with desire. The thought was ridiculous, of course, because at her age, she couldn't just start over. Everyone had a past, and she wanted to remember her mother most of all.

Mr. Sheridan stood, raising his glass of wine. "We have an announcement to make. Boys, you won't be able to reach us on Christmas Day."

"And why is that?" Declan said, eyes narrowed.

"Because we're going to visit the Motherland!" Lorna said, standing to join him.

"You're going to Ireland?" Ronan said.

"Why at Christmas?" Amy said.

"It just worked out that way," Lorna said. "You know

that house right on the beach, not far from the lighthouse? The one that belonged to the Silicon Valley multimillionaire? Well, get a load of this. He couldn't stand the Texas heat, so I got the listing and sold it in a week! To someone else from California! Ha!"

There were cheers. Spoons came out and hit the glasses. Elsa joined in, tapping at her glass.

"Here we are all together again at Christmastime, this time joined by the prodigal son." Dan glanced significantly at Ronan. "I don't have a fat calf to slay, but let's celebrate us all being together again. And I hope it's the first of many holidays as a family, welcoming new and old. It's been a long time since Lorna and I took some time for ourselves, and she's convinced me y'all will be dandy without me, so I'm going to take this trip with my bride. So, let's raise a glass to romantic love, and everything better still be standing when I return."

"It will be, honey," Lorna said as she touched her goblet to his.

"I'll drink to that!" Finn said, clinking glasses with Michelle. "Here's to romance."

"How's the wedding planning going, kids?" Dan asked Declan and Amy.

"Just fine," Amy said. "We'll probably do it this summer once we're both out on break from school."

"Let us know how we can contribute," Lorna said.

"It's going to be low-key. We just want to get started on the marriage." Declan draped his arm around Amy in a possessive way.

"That's the most important part!" Dan said. "You two have it right."

"Kids, you get to open your presents since we won't be

here on Christmas Day!" Lorna held her arms up triumphantly and led the way to the family room and the tree.

"Woo-hoo! Early presents!" David did a little jig.

She didn't have to ask the kids twice. Everyone followed suit, and as Elsa was walking behind Amy, Dan pulled her aside. "May I talk to you for a minute?"

She stopped in her tracks, glancing briefly at Ronan, who'd been right behind her. He nodded almost imperceptibly, and it was only then that Elsa realized she'd been taking all her cues from him.

It was likely nobody said no to Dan Sheridan or wanted to. "Thank you so much for having me in your lovely home."

"You're always welcome." Dan's dark blue eyes, so like his nephew's, were soft as he took her hand between his two. "I couldn't let you leave without acknowledging your situation. We can't pretend that you're not going through a difficult time."

"Thank you." She lowered her head.

"Listen, I see a winner in you. It shines through your every move. Whether or not you ever *remember* who you are, there's a fighter inside and I can see her. If you reach deep down, I bet you can recognize the spirit of a woman who likes to win."

"Maybe you're right."

She'd never thought of herself in that way but had to admit finding increasing similarities between her and Ronan. And God knew he liked to win at everything.

"I know I am. You fought for your life, and you're going to fight to get it back. I'm good at sensing winners, believe me. I saw it in Ronan at an early age. Did you know he was All-State in football? He could have gone all the way with it, but alas, my brother's influence was too great. Following his father's example in the military was all he ever wanted to do. He excelled there, too. But that boy has had a lot of loss in his life. I'm very protective over him. He'd hate me saying anything, but I see the way he looks at you. You've come to mean a lot to him."

"And he has to me, too. He saved my life and I'll never forget that."

Never mind that her growing feelings for him involved a whole lot more than feelings of friendship. She didn't even know if she had the right to be attracted to him, but that was her problem. Despite what his uncle said, Ronan's feelings didn't go deeper than wanting to protect the woman he'd saved. It was the kind of man he'd become, ironically, similar to his uncle in his protectiveness.

"He's had his heart broken before by a high school sweetheart who couldn't wait for him to get back. Imagine, he's off fighting for his country, and his best friend moves in on him and his girl. I'm only asking that you consider his feelings *when*, not if, your memory returns. Your lifestyle and goals might be very different from his. You might come from two entirely separate kind of worlds. Let him down easy, in other words." He patted her hand gently.

She didn't understand why he worried she'd walk away from Ronan. The only way she would is if she already had a commitment to someone else. If only she could remember…

"Hey." Ronan walked back, interrupting them. "You're not going to want to miss this. They gave David his first drum set and Declan is acting happy about it just to annoy Finn. It's classic Sheridan."

"Oh boy." Dan hurried back into the family room.

"You okay?" Ronan took her hand. "Don't listen to anything he says. He worries about me too much sometimes, but I'm a big boy and fight my own battles."

She squeezed his hand. "He said your high school girlfriend abandoned you when you were overseas. Is that true?"

Ronan shut his eyes. "Now he's got you feeling sorry for me. Don't do that."

"I don't feel sorry for you, I'm angry on your behalf."

"It's not worth being angry over anymore. Even if this is the first time I've been back since then, it all happened a couple of years ago. I'm over it and I wish people would understand that."

"I do. I might be stuck right now, but I'd want to be move on, too. There's no point to wasting time on people who can't be faithful and loyal."

"Exactly." He tweaked her chin. "You get it."

On a deeply fundamental level, she understood. It was the reason she had to stop these growing feelings for Ronan.

He was free but she might not be.

Chapter Eleven

After the plethora of heartfelt gifts, which included a colorful scarf and perfume for her from the Sheridans, Elsa and Ronan headed back. They were quiet on the ride back, listening to Christmas music, filling her with nostalgia for sweeter times. At times like these, her memories seemed close enough to touch.

"Do you want something to drink, or are you going to bed?" Ronan asked once they were inside.

"I'm good."

"Yeah, that was a lot of food." He patted his flat stomach. "I joined the gym but I might have to start running, too."

She almost laughed, but instead took a seat on the couch, kicking off her shoes. "Oh please. You're perfect."

He quirked a brow. "Um, okay. *Nobody's* perfect."

"You're pretty close." An ache pulsed through her chest. "You're also *lucky*, no matter what you believe. I don't think I have this in my life, not a family like this."

His head whipped around to face her. "Why? Do you remember?"

"No, I don't." She folded her hands on her lap. "But I believe I'd know if I had something this special. I'd feel it in my heart."

He joined her on the couch. "Everyone has family, Elsa."

"Not like yours."

"I'll bet you do." He reached for her hand and squeezed it. "They're out there looking for you but maybe they don't have the resources or ability to put boots on the ground. It's going to take a while. Either they find you first, or you remember where you belong."

"No." Tears filled her eyes, and she pushed them back with the pads of her fingers. "I don't have anyone. I just know it."

Despite her best efforts to keep it together, she broke down, and heaving sobs wracked her body. With everything she'd been through, it was a wonder she hadn't reached this place before this moment. She thought of herself as a strong person, but she may have finally reached her limit. Maybe it was because of the wine she'd enjoyed tonight. Yes, that had to be it. Her inhibitions were lowered, and she couldn't keep the despair inside a minute longer. She wanted to be loved. To be wanted. That wasn't such a crazy desire.

Or maybe, instead of the alcohol, it had been watching Finn and Declan, so in love with their partners. Those women didn't know how lucky they were.

She felt her body being tugged into a pair of strong arms and then Ronan was speaking softly near the shell of her ear.

"C'mon, Elsa, honey. Hush. Don't cry. You know that's true. You're a great person, why would you be alone? Maybe you have found family, or biological, but you have *someone*. Believe me."

"It's been almost a *week*! If you had someone special in your life, I'll bet you wouldn't stop looking for her the moment you realized she was missing. And it wouldn't take you a *week* to realize it, either!"

He reached over and handed her a tissue. "That's true but maybe an unfair comparison. I have resources."

"And you *care*. You don't just care about your family, but you care about a complete stranger who needs you. You opened up your house to me. I don't know where I'd be without you." She clung to him, her safety, her rock.

"Don't make me sound like a saint." He continued to rub her arms in soothing strokes and made a sound that sounded like a groan. "That's not me. Living with you is not a *hardship*."

It was to her, knowing she wanted him but couldn't pursue anything until she knew something about herself. Anything at all would do. She didn't honestly believe this, but if she was a terrible person who'd done such harm that someone had tried to get rid of her, she didn't want Ronan involved. She didn't want to take him down a dark road he didn't need to visit. He deserved better.

"But y-you haven't been able t-to r-relax around me."

Now that her sobs were ebbing, her words were hiccupping sounds, and she dabbed at the mascara rolling down her cheeks. This wouldn't happen if she had falsies.

He chuckled. "If I can't relax, it's because of the way you look in this dress."

That shocked her enough to be distracted and she stilled. Then she straightened in his arms, which brought her awfully close to his face. That wonderful, gorgeous face with deep blue eyes the color of twilight.

He met her gaze, his eyes hooded. "You're not the only one who wishes you would remember. Who wishes someone would find you, so I could finally know if...if I can kiss you, or if you belong to someone else."

She didn't hesitate. "I feel the same way."

"Yeah?" He tugged on a lock of her hair and a lazy smile

quirked one corner of his mouth. "But my ex cheated on me, and I'm not the kind of man to come between two people. So, I can't touch you the way I want to until you know whether there's someone else."

"I want to think there's no one else or I couldn't possibly feel like this. I want to know if I can kiss you." She framed his face. "But I want to do a lot more than *kiss* you."

"Don't tease me." He literally pulled away from her, and now that she'd stopped weeping, he could.

But she didn't feel the slightest bit rejected. "Okay, I won't. I just hope I'm free for *your* sake as well as mine. Because I feel like I'd be good at sex."

"I have no doubt." Then he groaned again.

He made her laugh, something a few minutes ago, she couldn't have imagined. "If I go get out of this dress..."

He lifted his head and widened his eyes.

She bit back a smile. "And put on some *sweats*, can we cuddle?"

"You want to *cuddle*?"

"And binge Netflix. Amy told me she and Declan do that sometimes. It sounds low-key. And you need to watch *Outlander*, so you can get some pointers on how to be a great Jamie."

He scowled. "What's the point? I'll always be Irish."

"I wouldn't want you to change that even if you could, but you want to win, don't you?"

"The winning will be in simply *cuddling* and not doing anything else." He leaned back. "And I'm up to the challenge."

Ronan's emotions were all over the place.

Last night, he'd gone from zero to sixty when he'd come to the realization that Elsa felt the way he did. But where did that leave them? In an impossible situation. They were living together, having deep feelings for each other, but couldn't do anything about it. Not even a kiss. He'd never want to be the reason she would betray someone. With his history, he'd have to hate himself for that.

So, they'd cuddled in front of the TV, watching her show. He'd probably do anything at this point to please her so *Outlander* was not difficult. He discovered there were other things going on in the show besides romance, like wars and political conflict. It turned out to be a time travel series, something which had always interested him. Still not enough action, but he appreciated the effort. He insisted, and she agreed, to skip the graphic sex scenes, as that was pure torture and deeply awkward. The entire time he'd done nothing more than keep his arm around her while she leaned on his shoulder, her arm curled around his stomach. After, he'd led Elsa to her bedroom, and they'd said goodnight without so much as a chaste kiss at the door.

Next morning, Elsa was still sleeping when he left for the docks early, where he'd agreed to help Finn. A little over a year now, Finn's good friend Noah had bought a business, Nacho Boat Adventures, and Finn went in as a partner. They were a bit shorthanded today, and since Ronan had all this free time on his hands for the first time in years, he might as well help where and when he could. The situation with Elsa felt more settled and she had things to do around the house to keep busy.

He should probably look into buying her a new phone, even if he sensed her shame every time he paid for something. But he felt confident she'd be all right alone for a few hours. Besides, he would have to stay out of her way if he wanted to behave himself around her. There was still the night of the bookstore contest to get through, and God only knew how much more time before she remembered, or someone came for her. He both dreaded and looked forward to the day. It had only been a week, he reminded himself. One week. Not long enough. Even he, trained in reconnaissance, might need a week to find someone with few clues.

It was a cool morning, typical for December, and Ronan wore his windbreaker when he climbed the gangplank. Finn stood waving to him from the catamaran.

"Morning." Ronan boarded. "Can you believe they're actually going to Ireland?"

"It's about time he took some days off." Finn handed Ronan a cup of coffee from The Green Bean. "He never slowed down after he retired from the post office. Now he's coaching Little League when he isn't renovating the house. Honestly, there's no off switch with him."

Ronan chuckled because it was the truth. "I can't believe I listened to his advice to start fishing."

"He needs to take his own advice. I can't remember the last time *he* went fishing."

Ronan groaned. "Foiled again by the master."

"Face it, he'd do anything to get you to stay. We all would." Finn drank from his cup, then lowered it, and met Ronan's gaze. "And how's that going? Any decisions?"

"None so far."

"I imagine it's far more complicated now."

Finn had him dialed. He always had.

"Yeah," Ronan said, running a hand through his hair. "Much more. I can't seem to help the way I feel and I've tried. Last night, we discovered we're both attracted. But we can't do a damn thing about it until we know if she's free. I want her to remember her life, but it kills me to think there's a man out there looking for her."

"I can't say that I blame you. She's beautiful and intelligent. As if that isn't enough, she really slides into our family like she's been there all along."

Ronan thought the same, watching the way she interacted with his aunt and uncle, with the children. It was enough to get him to fall in love with her. He couldn't do that to himself, or her.

"Not that it matters. For all I know, she'll be gone tomorrow."

Finn above all people understood how painful that might be for Ronan. Losing Belinda was only one loss. Finn had seen firsthand how difficult losing Ronan's mother had been, the last tie to his nuclear family. He was alone in the world. But loss was a part of Ronan's life, whether his father, mother, girlfriend, or too many of his friends.

"Whatever happens, we're here for you." Finn clapped Ronan's shoulder.

"I know you are."

Before it got mushy, they got busy getting ready for the passengers they'd have today. Apparently they'd be hosting the law firm of Pierce & Pierce, a father-son company, which had fired Michelle last year. They were doing a team-building event.

"Seriously? They *fired* her? And you're letting them board?"

"Long story, and it worked out to be the best thing to happen to us. She and Arthur get along now and work together. Michelle doesn't do divorce cases anymore, and that's all Arthur does."

"All right, but what the hell's an office team-building event?"

Finn explained, and Ronan bit back a laugh. In his world, every day was a team-building event. You didn't spend time in a war zone with someone you couldn't trust. If ever there was a wild card, and it had only happened once, he stayed firmly in front of Ronan. He only gave his six to a handful of people. Fortunately, Finn was one of them.

They'd just finished prep when the first of the passengers showed up. An older white-haired gentleman and a younger man bringing up the rear.

The older man shook Finn's hand. "Thank you for doing this again. Last time didn't work so well but we're giving this another try."

Finn pointed to Ronan. "Arthur, I want you to meet my cousin, Ronan Sheridan. He's moved here to Charming and is helping me out today."

Ronan winced. It wasn't exactly true that he'd *moved* here. This was all temporary until he decided.

Still, he shook Arthur's hand. "Nice to meet you, sir."

"Rest assured, you're in good hands with Ronan. He's a strong swimmer, former Navy SEAL, and I'd want him with me in any emergency," Finn said. "Best to be prepared, but we won't have any trouble today. The bay is calm."

"I'm sure we won't," the younger man said. "I made sure everyone took motion sickness pills just to be on the safe side. We sure don't want what happened last time."

Ronan glanced at Finn, but he shook his head softly to indicate "no big deal."

The younger man was Arthur Jr., son and also a partner, hence the name Pierce & Pierce. After the group boarded, he met an associate attorney named Bill, and Sasha, the receptionist. She got chatty with Ronan and explained that she'd taken the place of Rachel, who'd gone with Michelle when she started her own firm.

They shoved off, Finn at the wheel, taking them farther out into the bay. It was a calm December day, never guaranteed along the coast, but they were decidedly past hurricane season. While he monitored the sails and ties, working in tandem with Finn, the group of coworkers chatted amiably. He heard Sasha say, "Trust exercise."

It was hard not to laugh when they lined up, and one by one each tried to fall into the arms of another, who would catch them. It worked best with Sasha, of course, and was a bit more disconcerting when she stood behind Bill as if to catch him. He had to weigh 180 pounds, at least.

"Okay, let's try this again," the senior Arthur said, who'd gone red-faced, with a trickle of sweat gliding down his cheek.

Odd, given the nice cool breeze coming off the bay, but he seemed fine otherwise.

Ronan was enjoying the sail, thinking about how much he loved the sea, particularly when he wasn't dropping down into the black night of an ocean on the other side of the world for a covert rescue.

Maybe Uncle Dan was right and he could do some good here.

"Help!" someone said, and Ronan whipped around. "I think my father is having a heart attack!"

Chapter Twelve

Ronan reached Arthur Sr. to find the man had collapsed in the few seconds since he'd last seen him.

"What happened?" Ronan immediately noted the man's pallor.

He'd gone from the red face to a pasty white. Not good.

"We were just talking, and…and he fell down. He was supposed to wait for me to be ready!" Arthur Jr. yelled.

"I don't think he meant to fall down," Sasha said. "This wasn't part of the trust exercise, dummy."

"Is he all right?" Bill said. "Should we call the coast guard?"

Ronan barely heard them in the background as the sounds of his heart pounded in his ears and adrenaline coursed through his veins. He ripped open Arthur's shirt and began CPR.

"Does he have any heart problems?" Ronan called out.

"Yes," Arthur Jr. said. "A bunch of them. Um, he's on blood thinners."

"He's had a heart attack before," Sasha said.

"A couple of them," Arthur Jr. said.

"Does he have a pacemaker?" Ronan called out. The more he knew about his patient, the better.

"No," his son said.

Finn, who'd rushed to anchor sooner than planned, came to assist. "How's he doing?"

"Not good," Ronan said softly between his compressions. "Do you have a defibrillator on board?"

"Yeah." Finn took off at a run and returned with the pad. "Is it that bad?"

"Think so," Ronan said, setting it up. He was gratified to know his cousin had prepared for a possibility like this.

"C'mon, Arthur." Finn squatted beside them. "Don't do this."

"Get us back to shore," Ronan said, and Finn jumped up and returned to the wheel.

Ronan continued to do chest compressions and breaths after he'd shocked Arthur's heart into a normal sinus rhythm. Behind him, Arthur Jr. and Sasha were openly crying, holding on to each other. Bill kept repeating, "Let's call the coast guard. Why isn't anyone calling the coast guard?"

"Shut up, you idiot," Arthur Jr. said.

Ronan wondered why this always happened to him. He must be the unluckiest man on the planet. In the space of one week, he'd performed CPR on two different people. One near drowning, one heart attack. He'd heard of a black cloud before, often referred to in emergency responder circles as being someone always in the middle of the action, but he'd never thought of himself that way. Then again, he'd mostly been in a war zone, where every damn day was a black cloud over them all. It was like his past had followed him here. He did not want to keep rescuing people!

Finally, thank You, God, for all his efforts, Ronan had a weak pulse from Arthur. Weak, but there.

His eyes fluttered open and he weakly said, "My wife is going to kill me for this. No more team-building exercises. *Ever.*"

"Dad, you're okay." Arthur Jr. squatted next to his father.

"But sir, you might want to think about retiring," Ronan said.

I know I am.

"Yeah, Dad, you've worked hard enough. Enjoy the easy life for a while."

The ambulance was there to meet them when they docked, and father and son boarded the bus together. Ronan briefly conferred for the second time that week with the first responders and off they all were to the hospital. Arthur wasn't out of the woods yet, but at least he was alive and breathing. The rest would have to be checked out at the hospital.

"Wow," Finn said, clapping an arm around Ronan. "Do you realize if you hadn't come with me, Arthur might have actually died here today?"

"He might still die," Ronan said, being realistic. "But I did what I could. The rest will be up to the team of doctors at the hospital."

"You saved him," Sasha said, coming up to Ronan to thank him, shaking his hand and holding it a little too long.

Bill shook Ronan's hand, too. "I'm new here. Sorry if I wasn't much help."

"You all did good, staying out of my way." Ronan pulled a hand through his hair.

God, he needed a beer and it wasn't even lunchtime.

"Hey," Finn said. "You know what I was thinking? We don't have a security point person on our team. It would be a perfect job for you."

Ronan stared at him. Another blatant attempt to get him to stay. "Don't create a job for me. That would be stupid."

"After today? I don't think so. We might not always

need a medic on board, but we need a detailed security plan in place."

"It would only take me a few hours to write one up for you."

"Did you know that Arthur is on his third wife? He's always preaching about work-life balance. He actually dialed it back for a bit, only working part-time. But I think since Michelle has been gone, he's working too hard, and the associate just recently came on board. Michelle is going to hate hearing about this."

Ronan pictured a man working hard all his life, dreaming of retirement, then finally retiring, and dropping dead of a heart attack a month later. It happened far too often. He did not want it to happen to him. Life was unpredictable. There might only be a few years good years left in him and he wanted to enjoy them with a wife, a couple of kids. He certainly did not want to retire with full military benefits, only to come home and be hit by a car.

"I think I'm going to call it a day," Finn said, after their passengers deboarded. "How about you meet me tonight at the Salty Dog? My treat."

"Sure." It sounded good, and after this, he needed to decompress with a glass of Guinness or two. "Don't give me a hard time, but I'll have to bring Elsa along. I don't like to leave her alone for too long."

Finn slid him a knowing grin. "It's not like I hadn't planned on bringing my wife."

When Elsa woke the next morning, the house was too quiet. She always heard Ronan bustling about the place, an early riser. After dressing in some of her newly donated jeans and a sweater, she padded into the empty kitchen to find him. No Ronan. He wasn't outside, either.

For a moment she wondered if she'd pushed things too far with him the night before, asking to cuddle and nothing else. It was a lot to ask from any red-blooded male who'd expressed his attraction. It wasn't easy for her, either, but without knowing she wasn't part of a committed relationship, she couldn't act on her impulses. She couldn't run her fingers through Ronan's golden hair, and plant kisses along that strong jawline all the way up to his lips.

Okay, she had to stop thinking about kissing Ronan! Now.

Last night was a watershed moment when she broke down, realizing the cozy family dinner around the Sheridan table did not feel at all familiar. She'd concluded she probably didn't have a family, at least not like his. She hoped Ronan was right and she'd simply forgotten like everything else. She had someone out there, or several someones who loved her, whether it be a husband and children, or parents and siblings.

She reached the coffee pot to find it full and a sticky note from Ronan.

> I've gone down to the marina to help Finn. Should be back later this afternoon. Call if you need me. ~ R

She poured herself a cup of coffee and added more fat milk, because forget skim milk when she had this golden stuff. Now she felt guilty Ronan had been so accommodating that he'd bought what she thought she wanted. How funny to remember such insignificant things and then later change her mind about them.

Now she had the rest of the day to herself and no idea how to keep busy. Eating breakfast, showering, and watering the garden wouldn't take long. It struck her how much she'd come to rely on Ronan's presence as her rock. Her safety. Maybe in her real life she depended on someone else the way she now did with Ronan. It killed her to think someone was waiting for her to show up, maybe looking for her and not having any idea where to find her.

The thought made her pick up the phone and call the police station to ask for any updates.

"Any news?"

"Nothing yet, ma'am," the officer said. "But we're trying surrounding cities, so it won't be long."

Disillusioned, she hung up. They police were doing everything they could.

After showering, changing, and watering and weeding the garden Elsa didn't want to watch another episode of *Outlander*. That show was messing with her head. She kept picturing herself as Claire and Ronan as Jamie. In a way, she and Claire had some similarities, both with dark hair, both being thrust into a world they didn't know. Thankfully, Elsa's was a modern one. Bored out of her mind within the hour, she thought of Amy right next door. What were the odds a mom of two would need help with something around the house during the holidays? She'd guess they were astronomical. Elsa could offer to wrap presents, vacuum, or clean the kitchen.

When Amy opened the front door, she smiled weakly. "Come in, I'm not feeling well but I'm pretty sure it was something I ate last night. I shouldn't be contagious."

"The food was rich, that's for sure." Even Elsa's stomach felt a little queasy after all that fat and sugar. "Do the Irish always eat like that?"

Amy laughed. "Only during the holidays. Mr. Sheridan is pretty much a health nut."

One look at Amy's pallor and Elsa wanted to order her to bed. "Is Declan around?"

"No, he took the kids shopping. They want to surprise me with their Christmas gifts. When he saw I was sick he wanted to cancel but I wouldn't let him. The kids are counting on it. I'm sure they'll be back by lunch, unless they talk him into fast food again." She shook her head, smiling.

Elsa hooked a thumb in the direction of Ronan's house. "Ronan went to help Finn at the marina. I've already done everything I can do today, and it's either offer my services to you or watch another episode of *Outlander*. And I like to watch that show with Ronan, anyway."

"Are you serious? You've been through so much. I hate to bother you with my load."

"Please, bother away! There's not much I can do until I find out who I am, and I like to keep busy."

For the next two hours, Elsa washed, dried, folded, and sorted laundry. With a family of four, it was like washing towels for a small nation or a B and B. Good grief. Elsa wanted to suggest they give each family member a color, and each member uses that color of towels and washrags. Seriously, a towel wasn't dirty after drying your clean body with it. They could be used more than once. She understood brothers and sister might not want to share towels, which is where the color scheme came in. Hmm. Wonder if this was a problem she had in her own home and had found a way to solve it. She seemed to be a bit of a problem solver. The glare on the TV in Ronan's living room, the towel issue here.

On the way back from the laundry room, Elsa overheard Amy throwing up in the bathroom and waited for her to come out.

"Please, Amy, just rest. You want to be better by the night of the costume party."

"But I still have so much to do. Presents to wrap, and the dishwasher needs to be unloaded," Amy protested. "I'm actually feeling better now that I threw up."

"I've got you!" With hands on Amy's back, Elsa gently pushed her to her bedroom. "Leave it to me."

While Amy slept Elsa unloaded the dishwasher, swept and mopped the kitchen floor, vacuumed the carpet, and cleaned the forward-facing windows. She hadn't realized how much time must have gone by because suddenly Declan and the kids were back.

"Hey, y'all," she greeted them. "Did you buy something fun for your mommy?"

Naomi nodded, her pigtails bouncing. "She's going to love it!"

"Sh, don't tell her," David said.

"I wasn't going to *tell her*," Naomi said. "But anyway, I betcha she can keep a secret."

"Where's Amy?" Declan asked, coming in behind the kids.

"I made her lie down and rest," Elsa said. "She wasn't feeling well."

"Still?" Declan brushed by her on the way to the bedroom.

"Actually, she feels better, but—"

But Declan had already opened and shut the door behind him.

Elsa finished anyway, for the sake of the kids. "I made her rest, but she's much better."

They were both staring up at her expectantly, almost a little hopefully, like they thought she might spontaneously burst into song. Unfortunately, this Elsa couldn't sing.

"You still don't know who you are?" David said, voice filled with awe.

She wanted to tell him it had only been about a week, but it wasn't as if she'd lost her car keys. "No, I don't."

"Weird," David whispered, shaking his head.

They were both still staring at her, and if they weren't children, she'd have to call them rude. She wasn't a sideshow attraction at the circus, even if she currently felt like one.

"Wait right here," Naomi said, then took off at a run down the hall.

David was still staring. He scratched his head. "Does this *happen* to people? Forgetting who they are?"

"I don't think it happens often," Elsa said. "But I hit my head pretty hard, and that's one of the reasons."

Naomi came back holding a book in her hands. "You can borrow this book. Maybe it will help."

It was a Nancy Drew mystery, *The Girl Who Couldn't Remember*.

"I used to love reading Nancy Drew mysteries," Elsa said, turning the book over in her hands.

"You *remember*?" David said, as if they'd solved the entire problem with a book.

"Not everything," Elsa said. "I do know certain things but not the big things yet."

Like who I am.

"I betcha reading the book will help!" Naomi said.

"Maybe you're right."

If nothing else, Elsa now had reading material.

She excused herself to go next door and wait for Ronan, who arrived when she was halfway done with the book.

"Hey, I brought us some lunch."

"You're home early!" It was hard not to rush to him, throw her arms around him and thank him for coming back.

"Finn didn't need me after all," he said, setting his keys and wrapped sandwiches down on the counter. "Hope you weren't too bored."

"I made myself useful." She set her book down.

"Nancy Drew?" He gave her a slow grin.

She turned the book over, revealing its title. "Naomi thought it might help."

"Ah," Ronan said. "Has it?"

Elsa shook her head. "Just making me feel old."

"Listen, Finn invited me to dinner tonight with him and Michelle. Want to come along?"

She couldn't say yes fast enough.

"This is it." Ronan parked, finding a space near the Salty Dog Bar & Grill. "Finn and Michelle hang out here a lot, and Declan worked as a bartender. I'd say it has the Sheridan stamp of approval."

Elsa was once more near the boardwalk where they'd been the night of the tree-lighting ceremony. "And it's not even an Irish pub. High praise indeed."

When he'd asked Elsa to come along tonight, she'd probably spent too much time getting ready again. But she had so little to work with that it took her time to pull together an outfit. After all, she was on a date, because *friends* could date. Hot guy, restaurant, nice outfit, Saturday night. A feeling of utter normalcy fell over her. In her real life, she probably went out a lot and socialized.

As they drove to the restaurant, Ronan's delicious scent tugged at a memory. "Are you wearing *Dior*?"

She had no idea why she would even know the name of a cologne's brand, but it just came out of her. So did the advertising line for some odd reason. She'd probably seen the commercial one too many times.

"I don't know," he chuckled. "It's whatever Aunt Lorna gave me for Christmas. If that's your way of telling me I smell good, thank you."

"Lorna has expensive taste. I'm wearing the perfume she gave me. Yves Saint Laurent."

His hand low on her back felt like a warm brand when he slowly guided her into the establishment, opening doors for her as he went. She didn't know for sure, but she didn't believe they made men like Ronan Sheridan anymore, a mix of both modern and somewhat old-school. At least tonight, she wouldn't feel uneasy about him paying for dinner. She would bet that Ronan never let his dates pay.

Inside, the mood epitomized jovial holiday festivities, and there didn't seem to be an empty seat. The hostess approached them, but Elsa recognized Michelle waving to them from a booth on the far side of the restaurant. Ronan took her hand and proceeded to lead Elsa past the hostess.

Elsa didn't miss the appreciative gaze she gave Ronan as he passed by. *Back off, he's mine!* Hold up, where had *that* thought come from? He wasn't *hers*. But the sense of competition was…vaguely familiar.

"We already ordered appetizers," Michelle said. "Have a seat and take a load off."

"Thanks, I will. It's been a day," Ronan said, waiting until Elsa took her place and sliding in next to her.

"I heard," Michelle said. "And don't worry, I called Arthur's wife and he's doing fine. He'll be in the hospital a few days, obviously."

"Ah, that's a relief." Ronan rolled a hand down his face. "I wasn't sure he would make it."

"Well, he is probably going to need another bypass and

I do think practicing law is firmly in his rear view, but he's going to live. That means a lot to his family," Michelle said.

"What are y'all talking about?" Elsa interrupted, feeling lost.

"This guy didn't tell you?" Finn pointed to Ronan. "He saved one of our passengers this morning, Michelle's old boss. The guy had a heart attack while we were out on the bay. Honestly, if Ronan hadn't been there…"

"Why didn't you tell me?" Elsa placed her hand on his thigh. "You acted as if you'd had a regular morning."

He'd brought back lunch, sandwiches from the deli, and they'd eaten together before they went out to tend to the garden. Not a word about saving anyone's life. Again.

Ronan shifted in his seat. "I didn't want to upset you with any bad memories."

The waitress interrupted, bringing a platter of loaded nachos and taking their drink orders before she was off again.

"I'm not upset," Elsa said, but she felt awful for Ronan. "You always seem to be in the right place at the right time."

His saving two people in the space of a week would be impressive work to most people, but Ronan behaved as if it was business as usual. Still, it couldn't be. Just the adrenaline rushes were stressful. If he had intended to relax, he was getting the opposite.

Finn nodded. "Which is the reason I'm trying to talk him into joining my company. I've been thinking we need security detail, especially since lately we've been getting requests from celebrities. You know, like those party boats they enjoy. And having a medic around couldn't hurt, either."

"Stop trying to create a position for me so I'll stay in town."

"What's wrong with that?" Michelle batted her eyelashes. "He knows talent when he sees it."

Elsa had been so wrapped up in her own problems that she hadn't even asked lately whether Ronan was close to deciding. Now, more than ever, the outcome mattered to her. Like his Uncle Dan, she didn't want him to risk his life, even if their country needed him. They could find someone else. Maybe she could ask him to resign, as a favor. He had feelings for her, and she wasn't above begging.

"All right, all right." Ronan put up his palms. "I'll seriously *think* about it."

"I'll drink to that," said Finn, just as the waitress arrived with their cocktails.

"You're Irish, baby. You'll drink to anything." Michelle kissed him.

Elsa watched those two with no small pinch of envy. That's exactly how she wanted to kiss Ronan, putting her whole body into it. God, she wished she remembered something *useful* for a change.

Ronan cleared his throat like maybe this display bothered him, too. "What are you two doing for this costume contest tomorrow night? I have to dress as a Scottish highlander, and Declan is Romeo, which is fitting. What about you?"

Finn's grin went ear to ear. "Well, you see, Michelle's favorite movie is *Rebecca*, based on the book by Daphne du Maurier."

"So, you're going as a rich white guy dressed in a three-piece suit from the 1930s?" Ronan said.

"Yep," Michelle said. "But for a man who lives his life in a T-shirt and board shorts, this was a win. The last time he wore a suit was on our wedding day."

Finn grinned and once again kissed Michelle. "Thank you for not putting me in a kilt."

"Some guys have all the luck." But Ronan winked at Elsa and squeezed her hand.

In that touch she imagined him saying: *I would do anything for you.*

And suddenly, despite all her troubles, Elsa felt like the lucky one.

Chapter Thirteen

"I look ridiculous," Ronan grumbled before he opened the doors of Once Upon a Book for Elsa.

"You look amazing. The green tartan complements your coloring."

Ronan didn't know about that, but Elsa certainly seemed fascinated by his legs. He caught her appreciating them, which was gratifying, even if he was wearing a *skirt*. He'd gained a new perspective and newfound sympathy for women. Even if he loved a woman in a short dress or skirt, they were awfully...exposed. It was entirely different from wearing shorts and he didn't care what anyone said. A nice gust of wind, and he was going to be cold in...places.

He felt better that the Irish wore kilts, too. Now he could wear one and not completely betray his heritage by portraying a Scottish Highlander. At least he wasn't Romeo. He smirked at Declan's costume. Decked out in puffy pants, a jacket, tights, and buckle shoes, Declan was the only reason Ronan didn't feel humiliated.

"Welcome, guys," Twyla, the owner, greeted them. She was dressed in a gown with a big poofy skirt. "Here's your prize ticket since you're in full costume. Oh, and Ronan, don't you look great? A *kilt*!"

"He's Jamie from *Outlander* minus the red hair," Elsa said. "We love the series."

"One of my all-time favorites by Diana Gabaldon. She's amazing. We have a lot of her *Outlander* series in stock and I'm always selling out." She handed them each a ticket with a series of numbers. "The best costume wins gift cards donated by all our local vendors. You probably heard this is a fundraiser, too, and we selected a literacy charity. Check out our giving tree, too, where you can buy a book for a child in need."

For a bookstore, the shop was packed wall-to-wall with people, but then again, it was the season for shopping. Ronan wasn't much of a fiction reader, though with books like *Outlander* he might have to start. Then he could privately read those salacious scenes he had to keep fast forwarding through while in Elsa's presence. He'd recently discovered he loved to torture himself, otherwise he wouldn't continually "cuddle" on the couch with Elsa but excuse himself and find some reason he couldn't. Newsflash: It also wasn't relaxing to have a beautiful woman practically crawl into his lap but have to keep his hands from exploring. He was trying to be a gentleman, but he wasn't exactly a saint.

"Oh my God, look!" Elsa pointed. "It's Rhett Butler from *Gone with the Wind*!"

It was none other than Noah Cavell, Twyla's husband. Obviously, Twyla was supposed to be Scarlett O'Hara.

"That's Noah. You should meet him. He's Finn's business partner." He tugged on her hand and led her through the crowd of people.

"Hey! Ronan!" Noah approached as soon as he caught sight of them and fist-bumped with Ronan. "And you must be Elsa. I've heard so much about you from Finn."

"Nice to meet you," Elsa said. "Was that your wife, Twyla, as Scarlett?"

"That's my bride. Last year, I came as Mr. Darcy, but this is much better. Man, I feel so dashing." He twirled his fake mustache.

The bubble of laughter that came out of Elsa stirred something in him. He hadn't heard her laugh with an unbridled, can't-hold-it-back tummy laugh. She was…delightful.

Noah stopped twirling and pulled on the lapels of his jacket. "Finn told me what happened with Arthur."

"It was nothing," Ronan grunted.

"He said the same thing about fishing me out of the bay," Elsa said. "I wouldn't listen to him."

"No, I get it," Noah said. "But Finn made some good points about bringing you on for security. We could use you."

"You're a first responder yourself. Don't let my cousin talk you into creating a job for me," Ronan protested. "I'm not sure you could afford me."

"What about doing a little bit of consulting for us on the side?" Noah said. "I'm serious, we could use a better plan. We're all good swimmers, but sometimes that's not enough."

"I definitely think a reputable company needs a plan that considers every possible outcome," Elsa said, then with wide eyes, she seemed surprised she'd said it.

"*Listen* to her." Noah nudged his chin to Elsa.

"I told Finn I'd *think* about it."

"Did someone mention my name?" Finn appeared, dressed in a dapper suit, Michelle at his side in a slinky dress.

"I don't see how that counts as a costume," Ronan muttered.

"Well, it does," Finn said, pulling a fake pipe out of his smoking jacket. "It's called winning."

David and Naomi rushed up to them.

"I'm *Anne of Green Gables*!" Naomi said, twirling in her dress. "And guess who David is? Guess!"

It was clear David, with his round spectacles, was dressed as the most famous of all young wizards.

"Batman?" Ronan teased.

"I wanted to go as Batman," David muttered. "But he's not in a *real* book. Just a comic."

"We have to do real books. On Halloween you can go as anyone you want, *David*." Naomi went hands on hips, schooling her twin brother.

"Whatever," he sighed and twirled his wand in the air. "At least I have this."

"Do you know who I am?" Elsa said.

"You're a lady from the olden days," Naomi said. "But I'm not sure of the book."

"It's above your reading level," Elsa said.

"Naomi has a really *high* reading level," David said.

"Well, your mommy wouldn't want her reading this book just yet," Elsa said, continuing to dig herself a grave.

"Why not?" Naomi said. "She lets me read anything I want."

"Well…this book is for grown-ups." Elsa's cheeks pinked.

"Oh!" Naomi said. "Eighteen plus? Yeah, I can't read those yet."

The kids were distracted by some friends who'd come in, and ran off.

"We're going to go buy a book." Ronan took Elsa's hand and led her to the giving tree, an interesting stack of books in the shape of a tree, lights strung through the books. There were tags on each book, with requests. "Which one?"

Elsa flipped through them. "I wish I had some money of my own. I'd buy each one. A kid should have their own book."

"Let's get a couple, then." Ronan picked out a card that asked for a Harry Potter book. "One from you and one from me."

"This one," Elsa said after a few minutes of studying each one intently. "She wants *Goodnight, Moon*."

"I remember that book."

His mother used to read it to him every night before bed. He paid for the books which would be filled and delivered to each child before Christmas. Making the rounds, they chatted with everyone there, many of them just now hearing about Elsa's situation, and fascinated. A few senior citizens who were huddled together said they'd put their investigative skills to use and try to find out more about Elsa.

"We have a book club and used to be accidental matchmakers," Mrs. Villanueva said. "But we've switched to solving mysteries. You know, the cozy kind."

When it was time to announce the winner, Ronan squared off with Declan. They both stood across from each other, stretched, as if their height and posture would ensure a win.

But the winner was neither one of them. The costume voted best by the owners of the bookstore was Naomi, as *Anne of Green Gables*. Rivalry forgotten, Ronan helped Declan and hoisted Naomi between their shoulders and carried her in a victory lap.

"I won! I won!" Naomi squealed, pumping her little arms.

She was so adorable.

A few minutes later, he rejoined Elsa. "Want to go home?"

Just as Ronan began to make the rounds to say goodbye, Ava came up to them, her husband, Max, behind her. She was dressed as a peasant woman, next to a dark haired man dressed as... Don Quixote?

"Hi, Ronan. Elsa, this is my husband, Max," Ava said.

"Nice to meet you." He bowed, brandishing a toy sword.

"You two look so cute." Elsa pointed to them. "Don Quixote, and you must be Dulcinea."

"Yes. I'm sure you remember I told you I'd do what I could to help." Ava's eyes were wide. "See, I have family in Dallas?"

"O-kay," Elsa said slowly. "Did you learn anything?"

When Ava hesitated, Ronan's stomach clenched. Who did Ava think Elsa might be? Was she married?

Ava touched Elsa's hand in a comforting gesture. "Dallas is a huge city, as you know, but my mother mentioned the wife of a CEO, who's on a committee with her, said that one of his ad executives is missing. She's going to send me a photo tomorrow so we can know for sure."

"Oh."

Advertising. It made some sense she'd be an executive, because of the dress she'd been wearing. He'd heard a nurse at the hospital refer to it as designer and "not off-the-rack."

"You might be just a day away from knowing who you are," Ava said. "I hope that's good news."

"Yes, thank you, it is. I'm thrilled." Elsa turned to Ronan and smiled.

It looked a bit forced. She was worried, he could tell. So was he.

By tomorrow, they'd know whether or not she was free, and he might be saying goodbye to Elsa forever.

***

"Everyone was so kind to me tonight," Elsa said, leaning her head against his shoulder. "As if I belong here."

"Maybe you do."

He let that remark settle between them, like a live grenade.

When Ronan pulled into the driveway, he almost didn't notice the luxury sedan parked on the curb in front of his home. He was too busy admiring his lights display, which, if he said so himself, was far superior to Declan's. His attention was pulled back when a silver-haired, smartly dressed gentleman climbed out of the driver's side. In a flash, Ronan wondered if this was the end of his story with Elsa, far sooner than tomorrow. Her father, perhaps, had found her. But unless she suddenly remembered, he wouldn't take anyone's word for it. Proof would be required.

"Lauren!" the man said, stalking toward them.

"I'm Ronan Sheridan." Ronan stepped in front of her, blocking the man from coming too close. "Can I help you?"

"I'm sorry to barge in on you like this. You see, it took me a while to find Lauren. I didn't even know she was missing." He put a hand to his chest. "My name is Harry Poindexter."

"Are you...my *father*?" Elsa's voice was a small squeak in the quiet of the evening.

"No." He shook his head. "You work for me. You're Lauren Montez, and you went missing last week after our company yacht party here on the bay, and we've all been looking for you since we realized what must have happened."

I'm pretty sure my name starts with an l, she'd told him. But hell, a lot of names started with an *l*. Linda, Liz, Lynn, to name three. Ronan wasn't going to let this man, whoever he claimed to be, just waltz into their lives without some kind of proof.

"I don't remember." Elsa clutched his arm, her nails nearly piercing his skin. "I—I don't recognize him."

"What *happened* to you?" Harry addressed Lauren.

"She has amnesia," Ronan said, answering for her when she didn't, "and doesn't remember anything about her life."

"My God." Harry went ashen gray. "So, it's true. *Unbelievable*."

"I'm sorry," Ronan said. "But before we can talk, we're going to need some kind of proof that you know her."

"Of course." Harry dug into the breast pockets of his tailored suit. "I've got photos on my phone of our holiday Christmas party. And this is your clutch, with your wallet and your ID. Someone on the yacht found it after we'd all left and simply put it in the mail to you without *telling* anyone. I hired a private investigator and he's the one who located you and said the police here were calling you a Jane Doe."

"She fell overboard," Ronan said.

"I was afraid of that." Harry closed his eyes and pinched the bridge of his nose. "We didn't know."

"*How* could you not know?" Ronan fought to keep his anger tamped down.

"It's quite embarrassing, actually. First, we had to dock ahead of time when a fight ensued between my son and the woman he'd brought to the party. It got...physical. She was hostile and went at him hard. Punched him the stomach. He was a mess. We docked, the police were called, and in the melee, everyone dispersed. I honestly thought you'd left early because...turns out the fight was about you."

"*Me?* Why? Was he cheating on me? Is your son my boyfriend?"

She squeezed Ronan's arm so hard she would have drawn blood had he not been wearing long sleeves. He too held his breath, waiting to hear that Elsa or Lauren or whoever would be back with her boyfriend tonight. But no, if that were true, wouldn't *he* be here? Ronan would be.

"I wish." Harry shook his head. "No, you two have never dated, but the woman must have believed you were flirting. My son denies this. Who knows what's true? It doesn't matter now. The important thing is that you were scheduled to go on vacation the following week, so I didn't even realize you were missing. It wasn't until you didn't come to work that we began asking questions. None of your neighbors had seen you and we discovered you'd failed to show up for an interview at one of our competitors. Then no one could recall actually seeing you on the boat *during* the big fight. That's when I had to bring in a private investigator to track you down. It didn't take him long."

It was an awful lot of effort for an employee, and Ronan was beginning to wonder why he hadn't just reported her missing to the authorities. Obviously, he wanted to find her and fast.

Then Elsa spoke up with thoughts similar to his. "You did all that for *me*?"

"I wanted results and I wanted them fast. You don't just work for me, Lauren, you're vital to my organization. I'm the CEO of Raven Advertising, and I rely on and pay you *extremely* well because I simply can't run my company without you."

Ronan heard Elsa gasp just as a punch went straight to his heart.

Chapter Fourteen

Lauren flipped through her Kate Spade wallet and found no fewer than ten credit cards, one debit card, and over two hundred dollars of cash. She scrolled through photos on Mr. Poindexter's phone. He'd asked her to call him *Harry* but she couldn't. He was a stranger to her. She still didn't recognize this other life, in which she was apparently a powerhouse ad executive. Mr. Poindexter couldn't run his company without her, or so he claimed. It sounded like someone else's life. This didn't feel familiar or natural.

The photos on his phone were from the night she'd fallen overboard. A company party on a luxury yacht, complete with a dance floor and a hot tub. She was in many of the photos, dancing with several men, including a dark-haired younger man in a double-breasted suit, Drew Poindexter. All she could remember from the night was the dress she'd been wearing, the one that had been ruined, a beautiful red-and-white, slinky short dress. According to photos, she'd worn matching red strap-on heels. Her makeup was flawless, and clearly, she'd been wearing hair extensions. Those must have been lost in the accident, along with her shoes and phone.

She sat on the couch next to Mr. Poindexter for a couple of hours, rediscovering a part of her life. She'd learned nothing so far about her personal life. Lauren glanced up when Ronan reentered carrying cups of coffee. He'd changed into jeans and a long-sleeved cotton shirt but she was still dressed in her gown. Ironic, since this felt a bit like a time travel show, less the war, famine, and beautiful Scottish Highlands.

Now she was comfortable, at peace, and this man had come to turn everything in her new world upside down. Yes, she wanted to know *who* she was, but she didn't want everything to change.

"I had an interview with one of your competitors?" Elsa was a loyal person, she felt that in her heart. "Wasn't I happy at your company?"

"I thought you were. You never said anything to me. Believe me, I would have fixed it if you had."

Ronan sat beside her on the couch and she automatically reached for him when she asked Mr. Poindexter the question that had been heavy on her mind. She now assumed she wasn't married or her husband would have come.

"Do I have someone special in my life? A boyfriend or fiancé? A significant other?"

"No, you're very much a loner and workaholic like me. To us, it's not work, it's fun. You've always excelled at everything you tackled. To my knowledge, you never had any serious relationships, and I believe I'd know if you did. We're close and socialize outside of work."

She sighed in relief, because she wanted to believe she wouldn't have the feelings she had for Ronan if she'd ever been in love with someone else. Her instincts were correct and her desires normal. Good to know.

"What about my family? My parents? Do I have brothers and sisters? Have they been looking for me?"

Mr. Poindexter's eyes widened. "You really don't remember."

"Her type of amnesia is rare, but it's likely everything will come back to her eventually," Ronan said, his hand protectively on her knee.

"And if it doesn't?" Mr. Poindexter said. "What happens if—"

"What about *my family*?" Lauren interrupted.

She couldn't shake the feeling he was concerned about all the time she'd missed from work. That was *his* problem. Who were her friends and family? Surely she had them.

He shook his head. "I'm sorry. You told me your father left when you were quite young and there's no relationship with him. Your mother died when you were ten. You went to live with your grandparents in San Antonio. They're no longer alive. Apparently your family never had much money, so you got an academic scholarship and attended university, then started to work your way up in the advertising world. Because of your unique background, you have a talent for coming up with the right angle to approach marketing so it seems personal and approachable to Middle America."

Seems but isn't? Either way, he'd gone back to talking business when all she wanted was information about her life.

Mr. Poindexter leaned forward. "Lauren, dear, I was thinking you could go back to Dallas with me tonight. I'll take you to see your condo, neighbors, and maybe something might come back to you."

A week ago, she might have agreed, and he had a point. Familiar surroundings would trigger memories. She didn't want to leave, but there was the issue that she'd been a charity case for everyone. Maybe Ronan wanted her to go so he could get on with his life. She glanced at him, hoping to get some confirmation that he might be okay with her staying a little while longer. Just until she remembered or gathered the courage to go *be* this other woman.

"That's...probably a good idea. You can go if you want to." Ronan didn't meet her eyes and his voice sounded almost foreign to her. Detached.

"What if I don't want to?" She reached for his hand. "I'm still scared."

"Then, *don't* go." He squeezed her hand, turning to Mr. Poindexter. "She's not leaving with you. Not now."

"All right, fine. I can arrange for a car to pick you up tomorrow if you'd prefer," Mr. Poindexter said.

Dallas was a long way from Charming, but yes, she'd been right all along. She was a Texan through and through.

"Thank you, but I'm sorry. I'll need a few days. You have to understand, I've been here over a week and I'm..."

Not ready to go. This feels like my home.

It's almost Christmas. Please don't make me go.

"I think I understand." Mr. Poindexter scowled. "But just know, when you're ready, we're here for you. Me, and everyone at the agency. You will always have a position there."

"Thank you." Lauren walked him to the front door. "You can't know what it means to me that you cared enough to hire someone to find me. If not for you, maybe I'd be lost forever. But the thing is, Ronan saved my life. He fished me out of that bay when I was drowning."

Mr. Poindexter shut his eyes briefly and cursed under his breath. "I didn't know that."

"I was at the hospital for a day getting checked out and when they released me, he took me in. He and his family have paid for everything. My clothes, my food, everything. I had nothing. Not even a name."

"I don't know quite how to say this, but you have a lot to

give them back financially. You'll be absolutely fine from this point forward and never dependent on anyone again."

Funny how those instincts of hers had been so accurate. She'd never depended on anyone, but the experience of having to had humbled her.

"Um, Harry." The name felt odd on her lips when she tried it out. "Did I ever work on a commercial for a winery in California?"

He smiled for the first time since she'd met him. "That was your account, yes. You came up with such a great campaign that they switched from the agency they'd worked with for years."

No wonder everything in California had seemed so familiar. Yet even now, she couldn't remember what she'd done for that company.

"I wish I could remember."

"Have patience. I won't lie. I had hoped seeing me would be the catalyst you needed. But maybe you need to visit your condo, and the setting where you lived and worked. Take your time, of course. Oh, and I can arrange for your car to be delivered to you if you'd like. That way you can drive home when you're ready."

Home. It was odd to think of Dallas as home.

"I appreciate that. It's been tough to be dependent on everyone, especially Ronan. He's been stuck with me."

"I wouldn't say he feels 'stuck', but I admit you almost seem like a different person. Maybe the time away from the city has been good for you. You always had a tough time unwinding. Kind of like me." He patted her arm. "Please connect with me soon."

Lauren stood in the doorway and watched him drive off in his dark luxury sedan. She quietly shut the door. Ronan was only a few feet behind her, as if ready to catch her when she fell from the shock.

"Are you okay?"

His deep blue gaze said it all. He would continue to give her everything she needed because that's the kind of man he was.

"I'm not Elsa anymore. Is it going to be tough to call me Lauren?"

He shoved hands in the pockets of his jeans and cocked his head. "Lauren is a much better name anyway. It suits you."

"Does it?" She nibbled on a fingernail. "You heard him. I sound like a *terrible* person."

"No, you don't. I'm not surprised you're an overachiever. Since you've been here, you have to keep busy. But keep in mind the professional side is the only side of you Poindexter truly knows."

Lauren had to consider a secret boyfriend, someone else she worked with, information she hadn't shared with her boss. It was possible, but unlikely. And if that person hadn't thought enough to come after her, the relationship was over anyway. She was calling it quits on the imaginary, possible-secret boyfriend she didn't remember.

"There might be more of your life outside of work you didn't tell him about, so he wouldn't know," Ronan continued.

"Like friends who can't be bothered to report me *missing*? What kind of person am I? Someone who works so hard at her job I didn't make time to date, nurture friendships, or fall in love!"

Ronan threw his arms wide open. "You're looking at one."

"Not you! You have your family and you're always helping people. How can you even *say* that?"

"Why do you think my uncle wanted me to find a way to unwind while I'm here? Because my whole life has always been wrapped up in what I do. I felt in many ways that my career defined me. It's who I am."

"Is that why your ex left you?"

He shook his head. "She left because she didn't understand the meaning of loyalty. We were high school sweethearts, but she couldn't hang in there and wait for the good part. And of course, it didn't help that my former best friend decided to ease her loneliness on those long months when I was away. I'm not blaming her."

"Oh, Ronan. I'm sorry."

So much loss in his life. They were two of a kind in a way.

"It happened and I'm over it. Maybe it's true I worked too hard. My uncle isn't exactly the type of person to discourage anyone from being the best at what they do. In my case, unfortunately, the process of reaching the top might mean the end for me. Literally. But since my entire life has been the military, all I had after Belinda was short-lived relationships. Nothing serious. I sound like the male version of you, but GI Joe–style." He shrugged.

"Well, GI Joe, tomorrow, I'm going to the bank with my debit card and get some money to pay you and everyone else back for all you've done for me."

Ronan closed the distance between them. "You don't need to do that."

"Why not? Apparently I have a ton of money. What good is it having money if I can't help my…my—" She got stuck on the next word, knowing what she felt for him was far deeper than friendship.

"Friends?" He took a step closer so that they were nearly hip to hip. "Because you should know you have them here."

She bit on her lower lip because him being so close heightened all her sensations. "Is that what you are? My friend?"

"Anything you want, *Lauren*. But more than friends, I hope." His eyelids were hooded, clear and powerful desire shimmering in them.

She smiled at his use of her real name, a little like meeting him for the first time. *Hello, Ronan, my name is Lauren.* Now she had something to give him.

Her real self.

She reached to thread her fingers through his hair. "I don't think you were my type. *Before*."

"We don't exactly travel in the same circles. You probably didn't have a chance to meet many military men."

"Clearly, I was an idiot. Had I known, I would have made time to hang out wherever it is naval ships dock."

He brought her hand to his lips and brushed a kiss across her knuckles. "You didn't know what you were missing."

A buzz of longing hit her, making her body pulse with energy. If he did this to her by kissing her fingers…then he bowed his head and kissed her lips. And though she'd probably been kissed before, this truly felt like the first time, a kiss so deep and intense she was lost to everything but this moment. No matter what happened when her memories came back, this kiss was going to be the headliner for the rest of her life.

After what seemed like hours, they finally broke apart with a gasp.

"Damn. I knew it would be good, but even I didn't know we would be like this." Ronan pulled her to him, belly to belly.

"If this is how we *kiss*, can you imagine?" She wound her arms around his neck, keeping him close.

"We don't have to imagine anymore."

"No, we don't." She met his intense gaze.

"Unless... I don't want to take advantage of the situation." But he said this at the same time as his hands lowered to her behind.

"You're not taking advantage. *You* are what *I* want."

"Why? Is it because you're vulnerable? Lost?"

"No, because I'm crazy about you and you're the hottest Irishman on the planet." To further demonstrate her desire, she settled her hands on his behind. "Also, you have the best legs on a man in recorded history."

The corner of his mouth quirked up in a smile. "Then, the kilt was totally worth it."

"Oh yes."

"C'mere," he said.

"I... I don't think I can get any closer."

"Try."

She did, pulling her entire body to his, wrapping herself around him like a tight scarf.

"You know what would make it easy to get closer? If we weren't wearing any clothes."

He quirked a brow. "That is true. Hard to argue the point."

She definitely wanted out of this gown and down to bare skin, but when Ronan's lips tugged her earlobe, then slid down the column of her neck, she stopped processing thoughts.

He led her to the couch and pulled her down. "I want to reenact that scene from *Outlander* we had to fast forward."

"Which one?"

There were so many. It seemed all Jamie and Claire ever did was have sex.

"Skirts can be sexy," Ronan said.

Then he proceeded to demonstrate, when his head dipped under her skirt, and oh yes, she remembered the scene.

Chapter Fifteen

Lauren woke up the next morning in Ronan's arms. Nothing in her world had ever come close or been as perfect as this moment. Last night, she'd been insatiable, reaching for him again and again. He was always ready for her, like he too couldn't get enough.

"Lauren?" His morning voice was deep and husky. "Babe."

"Hmm?" She didn't want to move or do anything to change this moment.

He shifted his weight, his hand slid up and down her bare arm. "Do you want some coffee?"

She should *probably* let him get up. "Yes, please."

"I'll be right back. Don't go anywhere." He pointed to her as he kicked off the covers and quickly pulled on pants.

Lauren sat up in bed, smoothed her tousled hair, and pulled the sheet up to her naked breasts. She felt a little body conscious after getting a full view of Ronan's Greek god physique. She shouldn't be, at least not according to his comments when he undressed her, calling her *beautiful* and *perfect*, kissing every inch of exposed skin.

She hadn't even stepped foot inside Ronan's bedroom before this, wanting to give him his privacy. Now she took it all in, the low-key space with simple decorations. The king-size bed with a dark wood headboard dominated the small room. Natural light filtered in through the gray curtains. The focal point on his functional dresser was an oval-framed photo of an older woman with a sweet smile and Ronan's eyes. It *had* to be his mother.

Lauren was slowly getting more memories back, so maybe seeing Mr. Poindexter had done something. Last night, she'd dreamed of a dark-haired woman who looked like her. But all the memories were decades before, sweet memories of life with her grandparents, who'd lived and worked on a small farm outside San Antonio and kept the memory of her mother alive. She could remember all the way to her high school graduation, where she'd been summa cum laude, her grandparents so proud they could bust.

Slowly, she'd get everything back, even the last ten years. Good thing, because she'd like to know where everything had veered off course. The woman Mr. Poindexter described seemed closed off to people, far too materialistic, and Lauren hadn't been raised that way.

Ronan reentered the bedroom with two mugs of coffee and handed her one. "How did you sleep?"

"Better than I have in years." She glanced at him shyly because he still didn't have a shirt on and she'd lost another brain cell. "If I remember correctly."

"Same." He took a sip of his coffee, giving her a wink. "Last night was—"

"Intense. And glorious."

"And you were right. You are *very* good at this."

"So are you."

He set his mug down and hers, then drew her into his arms. "What do you think you're going to do now that you know where you belong?"

"I... I don't know yet."

He settled his chin on her head. "You'll let me know if I can help."

It was as if now that they'd had sex, he couldn't wait to get rid of her.

"Why?" She pulled away. "Are you in a rush? Do you want me to go? Just *tell* me."

"Hey, no. Babe, listen, I don't *want* you to go."

"You sound awfully eager for me to get on with it. I just learned *last night*."

"I'm making a mess of this." He palmed his face. "No, I'm not eager. Not even close. I'm asking because I'm worried."

"Worried?"

"You have an entire life anyone would be eager to get back to and not a single person could blame you. It's going to be tough to see you go, but if that's what you want, I can't hold you back."

"But is it what *you* want?" she pressed.

"Hell, no. Listen. If I had my way, if I could for once have it all the way I want it, you'd never go. You'd stay with me."

Delight pulsed through her, wrapping around her heart. *"Really?"*

He nodded. "I'll be honest. I'm falling in love with you."

Her breath caught because this couldn't be true. This was too much. She didn't feel deserving of this man's love. Not yet.

"Ronan," she whispered.

"Don't say anything." He pressed his lips to hers. "You don't have to. Just know this is the first time in a while where I can say that wholeheartedly."

It was huge. She wanted to tell him she loved him, too,

because her heart said she did. But it wasn't fair to tell him before she truly knew and understood every part of herself.

"You should know, I'm remembering more, just not *everything*. Not the past ten years. So far. I don't know why, but maybe when he mentioned my mother last night, he confirmed what I suspected and feared. Knowing I lost her a long time ago…it may have triggered something."

"Please tell me it wasn't like grieving her all over again."

"No," She reached for him, thinking of his more recent loss. "But I don't think the grief ever really ends. It becomes a part of the fabric of who we are and the pain isn't as fresh. I'm sure we were close. Were you close with your mother?"

"Yes, very." Ronan kissed her temple. "My father was deployed so often, many times it was just the two of us. She was a young mom, only twenty when she had me, and in a way we grew up together. Things changed a little when we moved to Charming to be closer to Uncle Dan, and my world broadened. But we were definitely a little unit."

"I remember that's how it was with my mother. Just the two of us and it was everything. It was enough. I adored her. She was funny and smart and she could sing a ballad just like Celine Dion, I swear. I was lost without her. My grandparents were great. Don't get me wrong."

"Yeah, but they weren't her."

"Exactly."

Funny, they had so much in common. Similar beginnings, though, somewhere along the line, they took entirely different turns. His, a lifetime of service in memory of his father. Her, a choice to use her talents to pursue wealth. She felt lucky to have met this man at the right time, and if not for falling overboard, they would never met. Well, there was no "maybe" about it. They lived in entirely different worlds. He was from the military complex, she lived in the corporate world.

And sooner or later, she would have to go back.

Later that morning, Ronan left Lauren alone in his room so she could go spend some time researching her life on his laptop. Now that she knew her name, she wanted to look up social media accounts, sign into her cloud, call her bank. Because, damn, everything had changed, even if she still didn't remember it all. She had a life to get back. The woman entirely dependent on Ronan and the kindness of strangers didn't need him anymore. She didn't need anyone and it seemed that's the way she'd chosen to live her life.

She didn't seem all that different from him, honestly.

Yet she was still here, with him, lying on his bed. Choosing to stay. He was going to be satisfied with that for the moment. One day at a time. He'd just finished working outside in the garden, noting how tiny shoots of green were already beginning to emerge from the dirt, when there was a knock on his door.

Not surprisingly, Declan.

He hooked a thumb to the curb. "So, who drove that fancy luxury sedan parked in front of your house last night?"

"Everything has changed." Ronan waved him inside. "Come in."

"She remembers?"

"No, but someone finally found her." Ronan walked into the kitchen, Declan following. "It was about time someone cared enough."

"Don't tell me. The owner of the sedan? Her man?"

"Not a husband or boyfriend. It was her boss."

Declan blinked. "*What?* Did he think she was playing

hooky and had to track her down? Gives new meaning to overtime."

"She's a high-powered ad executive and went missing from one of those yacht luxury parties. No one reported her missing because they didn't even realize it."

Ronan told his cousin everything, and watched as Declan's eyes widened, and he shook his head in disbelief.

"Now what happens?"

"Her boss wanted to take her back to Dallas, but…she's not ready. She wants to stay a while longer, asked me if it was okay with me."

"And you said yes?" Declan grinned. "Because you're not a crazy man."

"She can stay however long she likes."

"Of course she can." Declan tipped back on his heels, then narrowed his eyes. "Know what? You literally fished a beautiful woman out of the bay. I'm beginning to suspect *you're* the one who inherited all the Irish luck in our family."

"Ha! Not you, the man who gets a second chance with literally *the girl next door*?"

"Okay, you got me there." Declan shrugged with a goofy smile.

"Besides, I'm not *lucky* that the first woman I've been interested in in years lives in Dallas and is probably going to leave, sooner rather than later."

"True, but you could change that. There are some women, few that they are, who claim you're quite the catch."

Ronan snorted. "You're a regular comedian."

Just then, Lauren emerged from his bedroom. "Babe! Wait till you hear this!"

Declan quirked a single brow to Ronan, grinned, and

crossed his arms. "Well, well. Good morning. I think I'll go see what Amy's doing."

Lauren stopped in her tracks and set the laptop on the counter. "Oh, hi, Declan. Did you hear the news?"

"I heard." Declan smiled. "And I'm happy for you."

"As soon as I get a few things figured out, I'll come over and tell Amy everything. I'm sure she wants an update."

"No rush, but you're definitely going to need to come by before you leave and say goodbye."

"I have so much to be grateful for and I want to repay everyone. You don't know what it means to me that you all took in a stranger and made me feel like I belonged."

"No one more than this guy over there did." Declan jutted his chin toward Ronan. "Pretty sure he'd do anything for you."

Ronan turned to Lauren. "He's not wrong."

"Thank you," she said, her dark eyes shimmering.

Declan left, and Lauren pulled him by the hand to the open laptop. She pointed to the screen; he leaned over her shoulder and couldn't believe what he saw.

Chapter Sixteen

One thing became abundantly clear. Lauren was flush. It had taken her an hour on the phone to get logged back into her account after being forced to change the password, but once she did, her eyes bugged out. All those zeroes. She wondered if it could be a mistake. When Mr. Poindexter said he paid her extremely well, he'd meant it. The automatic payroll deposits plus bonuses from the advertising agency were like funny money. And as much as she clearly blew through cash, she had plenty to spare. Then again, she hadn't spent anything in over a week.

She could tell Ronan was equally amazed, given his utter and complete silence.

"Most of the charges are for incidentals like gasoline and eating out. I spend way too much money at an Italian restaurant. And on my rent, for God's sake. That's a ridiculous amount to pay for a condo!" She turned to him. "Isn't it?"

"Maybe it's a gated and exclusive community."

"Whatever it is, it's not worth it. I probably don't even spend much time there according to Mr. Poindexter."

When Lauren thought of the way she'd grown up, and how her grandparents sacrificed, it seemed a sinful waste of resources. There were also plenty of trips to a local day spa and daily charges at a coffee shop. She'd spent an alarming amount of money at a local art gallery.

Distracted by Ronan starting to nibble on her neck, she turned, shutting the laptop. "I'm sorry I walked in on that conversation. I didn't know Declan was here."

"It's fine."

"But I... He probably thinks..."

"That you're taking advantage of me now that you know you're free to?" He gave her a slow, easy smile.

"Maybe he's worried about you. He might think I'm an opportunist, staying with you even though I have a place to go now. He's wondering what my angle could be."

"No, Declan won't judge."

"Your uncle was worried." She bit on her lower lip, not wondering how much she should say. But Dan hadn't asked her to keep his confidence.

"I knew something was going on when I interrupted you two."

"He just... He said the way you looked at me, he could tell you were interested. And he was thinking I should let you down easy because you've already had so much loss in your life."

Ronan groaned. "I'm a big boy and I wish he'd stop worrying about me."

"He loves you so much. And I completely see why."

He took one of her hands up to his lips and brushed a kiss against her palm. She was beginning to discover, to her delight, that Ronan was one of those men who liked to touch...often. Foreplay was his jam. No doubt about it, she could get used to this kind of treatment. No wonder she didn't want to rush off to Dallas and her apparently lonely spinster life when Ronan was here to keep her warm.

"I have an idea," Lauren said, pressing her forehead to

his. "Would you take me shopping after I cook you breakfast?"

Interestingly enough, Ronan agreed without asking any questions. He ate the scrambled eggs and toast she made without complaint, even though she'd burned the toast. It may have gone down easier when she crawled into his lap to feed him the last few bites. Her lack of ability in the kitchen now explained all those restaurants and coffee shop charges.

Only once they were in his truck, rolling out the driveway, he asked, "Where to?"

"Once Upon a Book!" she announced.

"We were just there last night."

"But I didn't have any *money*." She pulled out her debit card and waved it. "Time for some retail therapy."

"At a bookstore?" He sounded incredulous.

Lauren found Twyla behind the counter, no longer dressed in costume as Scarlett O'Hara, but in a cute red-and-green polka-dot dress. She wore a reindeer headband.

"Welcome in!" she called out. "Oh, it's you, Elsa. And Ronan. How are y'all doing? Recovered from last night?"

Lauren waltzed in. "My name is Lauren, for starters."

"You remember?" Her eyes went wide.

"Not exactly, but one piece of the puzzle is solved. I've got my identity back and I assume the rest of my memories will surface soon. I recall everything but the last ten years."

"That's certainly progress!" She came around the counter. "Can I help you find a certain book? I have an entire self-help section. Maybe it will help with your memory."

While that might make more sense in her situation, Lauren went straight to the giving tree and began stripping off tags. "I want to buy every book left on the wish tree."

Ronan assisted, tearing them off and handing them to Twyla.

"You mean it?" Twyla gaped. "Some of these books are expensive."

"Not a problem," Lauren said. "Oh, and also, I want to get Naomi a book she *doesn't* have. Can you help?"

"Absolutely," Twyla said, making her way to the children's section. "Amy and the kids are regulars and they all have wish lists."

When Twyla finished ringing them up, including books for the entire family, Lauren had to blink twice at the total. But she'd just seen her bank account and knew she had the money. Bonus, she was helping the small business of a sweet woman whose family, she'd been told, had been running it for generations.

"You want to slow down, big spender?" Ronan said, opening the door to the shop.

"Nope, I'm just getting started with my Christmas shopping."

This was a little like being Santa Claus, the female ad executive version. She wondered if in the past she'd been this generous with others. Then again, there hadn't been "others." Hopefully, she rewarded her assistant or assistants on a regular basis. She'd like to believe so, and that they'd all be anxious to have her back at the agency. Even if they didn't have more than a professional relationship, that was at least a *type* of relationship.

"Next stop, the hospital! I told the nurses who took care of me that I'd come by once I remembered. They had such faith that I would."

They'd been so kind, giving her scrubs and shoes and cookies. It wasn't much, but it was everything they had. Most of all, they'd been compassionate and caring.

She stopped by the gift shop and loaded up on flowers, stuffed animals, and candy. Most everything was Christmas themed and that was fine with Lauren.

"Hey, aren't you the amnesiac girl? Our Jane Doe?" the salesclerk said.

"That's me," Lauren said. "But I preferred Elsa. It turns out my real name is Lauren."

She rang Lauren up, then looked up shyly. "Can I have a photo with you?"

"Sure!" Lauren and the clerk smiled into the camera as she took a selfie with her phone.

Ronan helped her carry all the various items and they went up to the second floor where she'd been admitted. Lauren immediately recognized the nurse who'd given her the cookies.

"I'm back!" she announced.

"Jane," the nurse said. "So good to see you again, hon."

"Actually, my name is Lauren. Someone finally realized I was missing, so now at least I know who I am. Not all the memories are back—"

"But they'll come," Ronan said with such assurance that Lauren wanted to kiss him.

"This is for you all, because you took such good care of me, and I can't thank you enough." Lauren set two bouquets of flowers on the nurse's desk and handed her the candy boxes.

Ronan set the rest of the flowers and stuffed animals down, and they covered every inch of counter space available.

"Oh goodness! This is a lot," she said. "I'll spread them around. We have some very sick patients who won't be home by Christmas, and it's tough to be hospitalized at this time of the year as you know."

Lauren nodded, remembering that part all too well. "Please give these to whoever needs cheering up."

His hands empty, Ronan draped an arm around Lauren, the obvious affection endearing, and she sunk into him, wrapping her arms around his waist.

"Look at this," the nurse said. "Reunited! Are you her husband?"

Lauren shook her head. "Ronan fished me out of the bay, and then took care of me until I could find out where I belong."

"It seems to me you already know where you belong." The nurse winked.

The visit wasn't over until all of the staff gathered around Lauren, and Ronan snapped a photo of them.

Next, Ronan drove her to Glamtique, where Zoey had a crowd today. While she was busy with other customers, Lauren picked out the green dress she'd caught Amy admiring. As a mother of two and a teacher planning a wedding, it's no wonder she wouldn't buy it for herself. But she'd have it anyway, just because. Lauren paired it with the red heels she'd drooled over. Amy would love these, too. Nothing for Lauren today. She couldn't imagine what she had waiting for her in the closet at the condo. Enough clothes and shoes for a lifetime, she'd guess.

She spied a gorgeous man's leather jacket on her way out.

"Do you want this jacket?" She held it up to Ronan.

He took it and put it back on the hanger. "I don't need anything."

"But it would look sexy on you."

His response was to pull her out of the store. "Let's go before you tear a hole in the ozone layer with your spending."

"Too much?" she said.

"We don't love you because of what you can give us." He faced her, hands on her shoulders.

There was that word again. *Love.* He loved her, and she *wanted* to love him. But something unnamed stopped her, as if she couldn't let go of the past before she fully understood it. For now, maybe he was right in that she'd tried to substitute a gorgeous jacket for what she felt for him. Maybe that's where her trouble with materialism began.

"But... I'm just grateful for everything."

"Then, show me in other ways."

"Are we talking sexy times?" She cocked her head.

He smirked. "That's one way, but I'm sure you can find other creative ways. Listen, you don't owe me anything. I will accept your thanks and raise you with gratitude for the best week of my life so far."

"Well, let me see if I can top last week."

Later that day, after they'd returned from shopping, Ronan had an errand to run and asked if Lauren would be okay alone. It was a good time for her to make some calls she wasn't sure she wanted to make in his presence. She dialed the agency because she wanted to check her work emails but had no idea how to go about it anymore. Poindexter had simply given her a work cell phone. The main operator connected her, and the voice that picked up the phone sounded young but smooth and professional.

"Good afternoon, you've reached the office of Lauren Montez. This is Katrina speaking. How may I help you?"

Katrina. It didn't sound familiar.

"Hi, Katrina. Um, it's me. Lauren Montez." The silence which followed made Lauren wondered if she'd been disconnected. *"Hello?"*

Lauren heard a sharp intake of breath on the other end of the phone. "Oh my God, Ms. Montez?"

"I'm sorry I disappeared," Lauren said. "Mr. Poindexter came by and told me everything. I apologize for having been away with no explanation."

"It's really *you*. Amnesia? I thought maybe this was all some kind of hoax and I wanted to warn Mr. Poindexter, but he insisted it had to be you, and he was right."

"It's true. And I'm so sorry to have worried you or... or left you with a bunch of questions you couldn't answer. That must have been so stressful."

"But it's not your fault. It's our fault for not realizing what happened to you! I'm *so* sorry, Ms. Montez. Had I known, I would have made them stop the yacht and go back for you. I was far too busy dancing and having a good time."

"You call me *Ms. Montez*?"

There was a slight pause. "What else would I call you?"

It sounded so official. "Aren't we friends?"

Another pause. "Friends?"

"We work together, but aren't we also friends? We were at the same party. Why don't you call me Lauren?"

"We're not *exactly* colleagues," Katrina said. "Early on, when you hired me, you made the point that because you're a woman in a man's world, you should be treated similarly. And I don't call Mr. Poindexter 'Harry,' none of the staff does, so... I mean, you're right about this."

"I see." Lauren hesitated a moment because while it sounded logical, it didn't feel right. "But I've changed my mind. Just call me Lauren."

"Um, o-kay."

"I'm trying to get back into my work emails so I can take a look at my life. I still don't remember the last ten years and I'm searching for things that might trigger my memories. There could be something in my emails."

"I can help with that. I'll call our IT department today and have them reinstate everything for you. They'll send you a link on your work phone and you can get set up again. Once we realized you were missing, we froze everything."

"Oh, and if you don't know anything about this, I understand but… Mr. Poindexter said something about a fight on the yacht that he thought might have been about me?" Lauren worried a fingernail between her teeth. This fell into the category of things she wanted to know but also feared.

"I don't want to gossip. I know how you feel about company rumors."

Old Lauren sounded so uptight!

"Whatever I said before, I'm giving you permission to tell me now." Lauren cleared her throat. "Please, and don't hold back. I need to remember, and you could help me put the pieces together."

"Well, it sort of looked like maybe you and Drew Poindexter might have had a little something going on that night."

Lauren sucked in a breath. "Doesn't he have a girlfriend?"

"I don't think it's serious. That night, he wanted to ditch his date for…you. You two were drinking and flirting a lot."

The unspoken words were that Drew probably had a good reason to believe Lauren would be okay with this. She must have given him some signal, if not just come right out and told him to get rid of his date.

"It isn't that you were trying to break them up!" Katrina corrected. "You always told me that you'd never settle down, that men were a fun diversion. Drew is very attractive, you have to admit. He's a serious flirt. Half of our female staff is in love with him."

"But... *I* wasn't in love with him, right?"

Katrina laughed. "No, I don't think so. You were determined to stay single and childless. At least, that's what you said that one time you took me out to lunch for my birthday."

One time? She'd taken her secretary out to lunch *one time*?

"How...how long have you worked for me?"

"You really don't remember?"

If Lauren had a nickel for every time someone said this! What did they expect her to say: No, I'm *kidding*! I'm just testing your knowledge.

"Sorry, it's so weird you don't know. I've been working for you five years now, since right after college. You hired me on the spot."

Five years and one lunch. Lauren wanted to ask so many things, like whether or not Katrina liked working for her. Whether she'd been a good and generous boss. It didn't sound like it.

And maybe there were some things she wasn't ready to know yet.

Chapter Seventeen

Ronan had postponed this meeting for too long. Yes, he'd been busy giving 100 percent of his attention to Lauren and his family, but he couldn't put this off much longer. It was time to decide and the appointment he had with his mentor was the catalyst. Even if Uncle Dan liked to think of himself as Ronan's advisor, he'd never been in the military. There were things he'd never understand, such as the closeness of the brotherhood in arms. At one low point in his career, Ronan was fortunate enough to find someone who understood the legacy Ronan wanted to follow. That someone was his former commander, John Mock, a first-generation Chinese-American who had served thirty years in the Navy and retired with full benefits. One guess what he thought Ronan should do.

Maybe that's why he'd been avoiding this meeting.

Separating from the Navy meant he'd leave only a few years shy of his twenty years of service and lose full benefits. He'd be on his own, a private citizen. A civilian. Sometimes he wondered if he could exist without a mission plan. Without a solid goal. On the other hand, his new plan would be survival of a *different* sort. An employee, looking for healthcare benefits and a livable wage. It was an entirely different kind of challenge, one regular people engaged in every day with admirable courage.

He drove to Houston to meet the commander in a small coffee shop downtown in a shopping strip mall. And yes, it was hard *not* to salute him.

The waitress poured coffee, and Ronan didn't want anything else.

"How are you?" Arthur asked when Ronan took a seat in the booth across from him.

"Stressed."

"Does that mean you've decided?"

Ronan studied his hands, clasped on the table in front of him. While he was giving up a lot, clearly there was still so much for him left in Texas. Two cousins who were more like brothers and would be growing their families soon. An aunt and uncle who wouldn't be around forever.

And a woman who'd come to mean everything to him in a short time.

Arthur grunted. "Just tell me it's love."

"What?" Ronan narrowed his eyes.

"You've giving up a lot, so it had better be a damn good reason. She had better be worth it."

Damn.

"She is," Ronan said without hesitation. "But she's not the reason. Besides, it might not work out with her anyway."

Arthur quirked a brow. "And you're still doing this?"

"I recently met with a man who had a heart attack and almost didn't make it. I had to conduct CPR on him. Turns out he was on the verge of retirement. He was on the brink of losing his entire life, so close to not seeing the reward of his service. I don't want that to be me."

"It will be tough becoming a civilian again. The military is structured and we color within the lines. Civilians are coloring outside the lines here. You're going to have to embrace that uncertainty or you won't catch up. There are rules, sure, but most don't fall in line. People break the rules all the time. It's chaos."

Lately, he was appreciating the mayhem more and more. Hence, his front yard filled with blinking lights and animated, singing ornaments. In his tightly controlled world, that would have been considered wasteful, and most of all, untidy. He now also had a newfound ability to function in the complete unknown, thanks to Lauren. He'd done some good there, too, and he didn't just mean the rescue. Because in some ways, she'd also rescued him. He'd learned it was possible to love someone unconditionally, because he'd loved her even before he knew who she was. The point was he knew her character. She, by far, was the most courageous person he'd ever met and he'd met many. She managed to inspire him even while going through a crisis.

"My goal was a legacy, in memory of my father. And I think I've accomplished that goal. Now there's a lot of good I can do right here. The one person I'd wanted to please and honor isn't among the living. And I believe his closest spokesperson is his younger brother so I'm taking his counsel and ending my service. Ultimately, the decision is mine and I feel good about it. I've done enough. I've given enough to my country."

Maybe he hadn't given as much as some of our friends, or his father, but he had to give his best efforts to the rest of his life. There was one other person who'd meant the world to him, and he knew that his mother would be happy with the choice he'd made.

"I've got plenty of contacts for you when you're ready. There are opportunities for someone like you. Executive protection agent, law enforcement, medical. The sky's the limit. And you can always count on me for a referral."

There were other ways to honor his father such as living an exemplary life, being someone's husband and someone's father.

He might as well start living now.

The first person he wanted to inform of his decision was his uncle, who was packing when Ronan called him from his truck.

"Do y'all need a ride to the airport?"

"No, we're trying one of those rideshare things. You kids are too busy. And hey, we actually had to buy winter gear. We're definitely having a white Christmas over there. I don't know how this Texan is going to handle the cold, but if you boys could do it, I can."

"Absolutely. By the way, when you get back, I'll still be here. Not going anywhere."

"Honey, Ronan isn't leaving!" Uncle Dan called out.

He could hear his aunt in the background. "Thank the good lord. My prayers have been answered!"

Ronan chuckled. "I'll have to start looking for a job, preferably one with health insurance. Let me know if you have any leads."

"Are you thinking the medical field? There are so many opportunities."

"Or security detail."

He's been thinking about what Finn said, and though he didn't think he'd be needed much at *Nacho Boat Adventures*, executive security detail was more in line with his expertise. He'd do some research into qualifications and experience.

"Between me and Lorna, we have a lot of contacts. And how is the lovely Elsa doing?"

"Well, first of all, her name is *Lauren Montez*."

"She remembers? That's wonderful!"

"Not exactly, but the man she works for tracked her down. So, she has her identity, but she still hasn't dredged up much of the past ten years."

"Tell me, who is she?"

Ronan told him everything, and if his uncle was worried, he didn't say it. But he wouldn't. Certainly not to Ronan. He'd only be encouraging and optimistic, helping him to see the world through the lens of opportunity.

"She's a winner! I could tell from the moment I met her. It's no wonder she gravitates toward you."

Ronan snorted. "She was kind of *stuck* with me."

"Even if that was true, now that she knows where she's from, some fancy job in Dallas, why is she still staying with you? I'll tell you why, because she knows you're the best thing to ever…"

Ronan allowed his uncle let loose with the pep talk, smiling and half listening as he drove home. Positive reinforcement never hurt anyone last he checked. After a decision like the one he'd made, he needed all the affirmation he could get. He didn't expect everything to be perfect from this point forward and there would be a lot of adjustments to make. But he could handle them.

Flush off the high of being assured he was one of the most wonderful beings on earth, Ronan opened the front door, and a flash of dark hair propelled herself into his arms.

Damn it, Lauren was covering her face and crying against his chest.

A rising sense of panic filled his chest. "What's wrong? What happened?"

He'd been gone two hours, tops, so not too much damage could have happened. Leading her to the couch, he sat and pulled her down next to him. "Tell me."

"I... I called my office and spoke to my secretary. And I'm such a bitch!"

"She *said* that?"

"No, of *course* not. I'm her boss so she was very nice, but... I can tell. I've taken her to lunch once in five years. Apparently I don't engage in gossip with her. I made her call me Ms. Montez."

"None of that sounds wrong to me."

Coming from the military complex, he appreciated and respected the chain of command. His superiors had taken him "to lunch" a total of zero times. Trust him, it didn't happen. The difference between the two worlds hit him.

One more area where he'd need to adjust expectations.

"I'm not generous even though I obviously have money. And I sound so *uptight*. I'm afraid of who I am. That's not the impression I want, or who I want to be in the world."

"You can be whoever you want to be. People change directions all the time. Not me, of course. Until now. I've been on one track for nearly twenty years."

She sighed against his neck, the move sending a jolt of awareness through him.

"You're a rock. So certain of everything."

"I was, but things have changed. I'm leaving the military."

Lauren didn't think she'd heard right. "You're not going back?"

He shook his head.

Until that moment, she hadn't been aware of how much she'd wanted him to walk away from that life. It was a life she admired, one of service and sacrifice such as she couldn't comprehend. But loving a military man had to be impossible. She didn't want to accept the idea of him taking life-threatening risks when she cared so much what happened to him. No matter where they wound up when all was said and done, she wanted him safe. She wanted to think of him living the happy life he deserved.

"I can't believe I've been so caught up in my stuff that I didn't stop to think what you must be going through. That's a huge decision." She framed his face. "I'm so sorry I haven't been more supportive."

"You've had your own issues and they were much bigger than mine. Besides, you've helped me understand that there's a lot of good I can do here."

"I wouldn't be here without you, and now I want to help you in any way I can."

"I'll be okay. Sure, it's going to be an adjustment, but I have a wide circle of support here. Pretty soon, I'm going to be on the job hunt." He took one of her hands and brushed a kiss across her knuckles.

She wanted to tell him the rest, about Drew and how she'd been flirting with him the night of the party, if you wanted to believe Katrina. How, even if she couldn't remember, she might have had plans to have sex with him that night. For the first time, she was grateful for falling overboard, if it had stopped her from making one of the worst decisions of her life. She didn't know, but the only explanation had to be she was lonely and desperate.

She couldn't tell Ronan about Drew. It mattered too much what he thought of her. She never wanted to believe she'd been the kind of woman for casual sex, for luring men away from their partners. If she'd ever been that kind of a woman, she wouldn't be any longer. Ronan was right. People could change, and she'd had the most significant emotional event to spur that change.

"I want you to relax today," Lauren said, pressing her hands to his chest. "I'm going to make you dinner."

He quirked a brow. "Are you sure?"

Boy, burn one piece of toast and get a bad reputation.

She elbowed him. "Mr. Poindexter gave me that cell phone, so I'll simply look it up on YouTube. What could go wrong?"

"I don't even want to think about it." He ran a hand through his hair.

"Ha ha." She stood. "Why don't you go do something fun while I figure this out?"

"O-kay," he said. "But you really don't have to do this. I'll take you out."

But according to her bank statement, eating out was what she did on a regular basis.

"It's so close to Christmas surely everyplace is going to be slammed. We should just stay in."

Look at her, all domesticated. Yeah, she could do this. Besides, she wanted to. She found a recipe for an easy pasta and had it on the table within an hour. What's more, Ronan enjoyed it, eating two helpings. Only a week ago, they'd been awkward with each other, bumping into one another in the kitchen, two strangers living together. Now they had an easy fluidity to their movements, and when Ronan bumped into her, it was clearly planned. He wrapped his arms around her, gave her shoulder a quick kiss, touched her behind. It all seemed so natural. Like two practiced lovers.

But later that night, after they'd washed and dried the

dishes, and watched some TV, it came time for bed. Lauren didn't know what to do. Did he want her to sleep with him every night or did he want his space? He wasn't ready for a live-in girlfriend, if that's what she could even be called. She was a guest. Guest with benefits? That sounded terrible. She couldn't just assume anything, so after he'd gone to his bedroom, she stood in the kitchen for several minutes, hesitating. Going in her own bedroom also sent a message. One she didn't want to send. And then it happened.

"Lauren?" Ronan called out. "Are you coming to bed?"

"Yes! Be right there." She nearly flew to his bedroom, where she stopped in the door frame, finding him already shirtless.

He winked. "What took you so long?"

"I... I didn't want to assume. Or intrude. You have your own bedroom, and I have mine."

"Well, that was before." He met her at the door and pulled her into his arms, his hands low on her back. "I don't know how I can make this clearer. You already know how I feel, so it's entirely up to you. No pressure. But I'm in love with you, so you have an open invitation into my bed."

She wanted to ask how he could say he loved her when he didn't even know who she was, but maybe he *did* know. Maybe he saw a side of her no one else had.

"Consider this my RSVP," she said, and pulled off her blouse. "I can't make it any clearer."

Chapter Eighteen

At first, Lauren couldn't locate the buzzing, which seemed to be in her head. She opened one eye, and realized the sound came from the work phone she'd been given.

Drew, the caller ID displayed, as if he'd been previously programmed into her phone. It was a work phone, and they worked together, so that made sense. He probably wanted to know when she'd be back. She let the call go to voicemail, because clearly, she was on vacation and not to be bothered. Settling back into Ronan's arms, she ignored Drew. From what she'd learned, he represented the worst parts of herself.

But instead of giving up, the phone began to ping. Ronan stirred and she didn't want to wake him, so she grabbed the phone and left the room.

Drew:
I want you to know how terrible I feel about what happened. If I hadn't been the victim of domestic violence that night, I might have noticed you were gone.

Lauren hesitated to respond, but after a moment, she texted back.

I'm sorry to hear what happened between you and your girlfriend. Please, if I had anything to do with that, I'm sorry. It wasn't my intention to come between you two.

Drew:
Are you kidding? We've been dancing around each other for weeks. It was finally going to happen that night but I blew it.

This was not what she wanted to hear. She was seriously going to sleep with Drew? What could she have been thinking?

You should know that after the trauma of what's happened to me, I've really changed. I'm probably not the woman you knew.

Drew:
You're still hot, aren't you?

Seriously?
She texted back.

That's hardly the point. I'm almost glad I fell overboard if it stopped me from doing something that stupid.

Drew:
Why stupid? I wouldn't have let it affect our professional relationship. You wouldn't have, either. It's all about the work. Relationships come and go. We're two of a kind, you and me.

No, no, no! She was *not* like Drew Poindexter. Refused to be.

I'm not like you. If I was before, I'm not anymore.

Drew:
Sorry, but people don't change who they are. Deep down, there's a lioness inside of you waiting to roar again. Everyone at our agency feared you. You had power and influence. Dad told me about the other night. You're not acting like yourself. I can't imagine what you've been through, but the truth is, if you don't get your act together soon, I'm afraid we'll have to replace you.

Lauren sucked in a breath. So, she had power and influence, but they were thinking of replacing her. It didn't sound right. Maybe Drew was pressuring her on behalf of his father, but it wouldn't work. She couldn't be rushed into going back to work when she barely had her life back.

But it's Christmastime!

Drew:
Christmas is a hallmark holiday. We're giving everyone the day off anyway.

One day? Gee, how generous of them!

Drew:
I assume by now you've seen your payroll deposits. Are you actually willing to give that up? All those years of hard work? There's a lot of good you can do when you have this kind of money. Think about it.

Exactly, but it didn't look like she'd been doing any good for others. She'd been spending her money on frivolous material things. Her grandparents and mother would be ashamed of her. Forget going back to work, she was going to continue to spread cheer around this town like a female Santa Claus.

Later that morning, Lauren wrapped her presents. Ronan had headed to Houston for an interview with an executive protection services agency and said he might not be back until much later. Lauren was filled with happiness that he'd decided to leave the military, and she didn't stop to consider until later, that being someone's bodyguard might be nearly as dangerous as what he'd been doing. Either way, she put it out of her mind. And at least, he was making strides toward his new life, having already made a decision, while she still seemed to be stalling.

Carrying her gifts, she headed next door.

"Hey!" A cheery Amy swung the door open. "Come on in, stranger."

"I hope I'm not intruding." Lauren stepped inside the cozy home. "But Ronan has an interview and I wanted to…to give you these just in case I'm not here on Christmas Day."

"Oh my! Thank you so much." Amy took the packages. "I'll put these under the tree. The kids are with their father and we're not opening anything until they get back. They'll be home on Christmas Day. He gets the week before and Christmas Eve. I get Christmas Day and the week after."

"They're only books from your wish list and a little something extra for you. I didn't know what to get Declan, so I got him a gift card."

"You didn't have to do that. How generous of you."

But far, the more generous person had been Amy, who'd shared what little she had when Lauren had nothing.

After placing the last present under the tree, Amy turned to face Lauren. "By the way, Declan told me everything."

"I was right about being a Texan, at least. Apparently I live in Dallas and I'm an ad executive."

"That explains so much about you."

"It does? How?"

"You're so sharp. We all noticed it right away. And there's your incredibly good taste and the way you drooled over fancy shoes. I bet you work hard to make all that money."

"Certainly not as hard as you do."

"Oh, but I love my job! It's really a calling, I'd say. I didn't get into teaching to become wealthy, that's for sure." Amy led her into the kitchen. "Let's have some iced tea."

Lauren followed Amy. "How's the wedding planning going?"

"It's going okay." Amy pulled out a pitcher from the fridge. "But this is my second wedding, so it makes sense for it to be low-key. My parents already paid for one wedding, and we don't want to ask Dan and Lorna for help. She's so excited about their trip to Ireland. I will say that Naomi was super excited about being a flower girl and scattering a trail of flowers down the church aisle. She'll just do that here in our own backyard."

"Why? No churches available nearby?"

"We're cutting costs where we can and venues are expensive. This way, we can spend more of the money on food and flowers."

"And what about your dress?"

"I can't very well wear white." Amy laughed and waved

her hand dismissively. "I'm just wearing one of my nicest dresses. Maybe I'll spring for a new one."

"That doesn't like much fun."

"Well, I'm interested in the marriage, not the wedding."

"But...didn't you say Declan was your first love? That's worth honoring with a big splash."

"Yes, but—"

"Please, please, please. Let me buy your dress!" Lauren clasped her hands together, prayer-like.

Finally, something she could give to Amy and Declan, who'd been so kind.

Amy blinked. "What? *No!* I can't let you do that."

"I just want to do good things with all I have. And you were so welcoming to me, you and your family. Ronan felt obligated, but y'all didn't have to do all you did. Bringing me clothes and hair product. Giving me a beautiful dress so I could dress up for the family dinner. Taking me shopping for a costume."

"That's not extraordinary. It's what we do and who we are. You needed help."

To her horror, Lauren started to cry. "I'm just... Please, I want to do this. Please let me. It's the least I can do. I don't remember everything about my life, but it seems like I've never helped or given much to anyone else."

Amy patted Lauren's shoulder. "I'm sure that's not true. You don't have all your memories back. When they come, you'll finally know all the meaningful things you've done for others. You're not the type of person to think only of herself."

But Amy didn't know everything, and Lauren hesitated to tell her what she'd learned wasn't encouraging. Then the compassion in Amy's eyes had Lauren spilling her guts.

"The thing is, now that I have a work phone, the CEO's

son has been in touch. He's leading me to believe all kinds of awful things about myself. Like, the fact that I was going to have sex with him the night I went missing, even though he had a date there."

If she'd judged Lauren in any way, Amy gave no hint of it. "And you believe him."

"I don't want to, but why would he lie?"

Amy quirked a brow. "I can think of a few reasons."

Maybe Amy was right and Lauren *was* being gullible. It could be he wanted to weaken her position at the agency in some way, perhaps even to subtly blackmail her. She hadn't even thought of that angle.

"I'm afraid of the person he thinks I am. Someone who's so driven that I have almost no friends outside of work."

"That's hard to accept, having met you."

"Does someone really change who they are at their core because of amnesia? I doubt it."

"No, but you might rediscover who you used to be. That's entirely possible. Maybe you lost yourself, your true self, somewhere along the way. It could have been for any number of reasons."

Lauren wanted to believe that. Something in her past may have led her to believe all that she meant to the people in her life was money. Status.

A loud clang and rattle sounded outside and Amy went to the window facing the street.

"What's this? It's some kind of tow truck service. Lauren, they're parking a car in Ronan's driveway. Did he buy a car?"

Lauren ran to the window. The sedan in question was a red Mercedes-Benz, and it looked more than a little out of place in front of Ronan's modest rental.

"That...that might be my car. My boss said he'd have it

delivered. This way, I don't have to depend on Ronan driving me around."

When the driver headed next door, Lauren met him.

"Signature, please." He handed her a clipboard and she signed her name. "Nice car. Enjoy."

He handed her the keys and left.

"Wow," Amy said from behind Lauren. "Granted, I don't know much about cars, but my ex used to drive a BMW for a while. This is a good car, right? I know how expensive they are."

"Funny, I have no memory of it. They could have brought me any car and I wouldn't have known the difference." She walked around the rear, dying a little inside when she saw vanity plates: #1ADGAL.

Dear God, she didn't even want to get inside this car. There was no better testament that her identity was wrapped up in her work than this.

"Go on, get inside, take it for a spin," Amy said. "Maybe it will trigger a memory or two."

Lauren clicked the key fob and opened the front passenger door. Amy stood on the sidewalk, arms crossed, watching as Lauren dug through the glove compartment. Either she didn't spend much time in her car, or she was meticulous about cleaning. No empty wrappers, no receipts, no papers. Only her registration and insurance card.

"You definitely don't have children." Amy shook her head. "This car is spotless."

"I'm not getting anything. But then again, either someone detailed this car or I am a clean freak."

"Seeing as you've been over to my house and not dropped dead, you can't be that OCD."

"Clearly, this car isn't very loved." Lauren hopped out. "How about you and I go for a ride and break it in?"

"To truly 'break it in' you'd need my kids." Amy held up air quotes. "But okay, I'm in."

With that, Lauren rushed inside to get her purse.

Chapter Nineteen

"Are you *sure* you know how to drive this car?" Amy said from the passenger front seat.

She sounded doubtful and Lauren didn't blame her lack of faith. They'd sat in the car for five minutes with Lauren trying to figure out how to start it. Everything in the car contained new technology, including a monitor and GPS system. The car even had seat warmers, as if she'd need them in Texas. Thank goodness it had a working air conditioner.

"I don't think I'd driven it for long, and it's obviously new. Okay, got it." The car started when she touched the key fob to the right spot.

Behind the wheel of the Mercedes, Lauren steered them onto the residential street. Actions like breathing, walking, eating, sex, and driving automatically came to her. She almost had everything she needed to be normal, but it was as if a part of her brain had a room that had been closed off. She was so close to knowing everything, that maybe it would help if she wanted to open that room. But with every piece of information she learned about the old Lauren, she wasn't sure whether or not that room should stay secured.

After a few minutes, she got a handle on the car, and the

responsive brakes. But not before she tapped on them and Amy jerked forward in her seat.

"Sorry." Lauren winced. "I'm obviously not used to this high-performance vehicle."

"Where are we going? Want to drive by the boardwalk and pick up some kettle corn? I'm craving it."

Amy had to give Lauren directions, but she drove down the coastal road, the Gulf on one side, sailboats in the distance, the December air clear and crisp. They turned into the boardwalk lot, parked, and walked down past all the storefronts. Lauren stopped frequently, exploring each one filled with touristy items. She bought candy, a waffle cone, saltwater taffy, and fudge. At the Lazy Mazy Kettle Corn Shop, she purchased a foot-long bag of the treat and brought it back to the car.

A jingle started to form in her head, ad copy, for the store. She should share it with the owners at some point. Apparently she was fairly good at this kind of thing. Or had been.

"Are you sure about this?" Amy said, once more inside the vehicle. "We don't have to eat in your *car*. Declan doesn't let the kids eat in his truck."

"It's a nice truck."

Amy nodded. "It's fairly new and he's incredibly fond of it."

"But we're not children. I think we can eat in my car." Lauren unwound the tie on the end of the bag and grabbed a handful, then handed it to Amy.

My God, it was *delicious*. Salty and sweet and crunchy. Her eyes almost rolled in the back in her head. She could eat this every day.

Amy took a handful. "Anything about the past coming back to you yet?"

"Not at all. I wonder how much time I spent in my car. Maybe I just drove to and from work." She turned back the way she'd come but then changed her mind. "Wait. Where's Glamtique? I want to go back, because I saw something there I want to get Ronan."

When they got there thirty minutes later, the shop was packed once again. Lauren rushed in because she wanted to get him the leather jacket, among other things.

"Hey, y'all!" Zoey greeted them. "Back so soon?"

"We're looking for a dress," Lauren said, grabbing the leather jacket off the rack. "A very special dress."

Amy met her eyes and she shook her head. "No. We talked about this."

"You bought *me* a dress. Turnabout is fair play."

"That dress wasn't expensive."

Zoey cleared her throat. "When you say special…what are we talking here? Evening gown? Tea length?"

"Well." Lauren cocked her head and smiled. "What do you have in *white*?"

Zoey's eyes widened along with her smile. "Oh!"

"No, no, not *white*!" Amy held up her palms, then lowered them. "Maybe…cream?"

"Come right this way." Zoey led them to a back area of the boutique where she had a full-length mirror and a small dressing room.

She turned and batted her lashes. "Is this perhaps, with any luck, a wedding?"

"Yes!" Lauren said. "And money is no object."

"You said the magic words, girl. It's my dream to get some wedding dresses in," Zoey said. "But they're difficult to store so I usually work on a case-by-case basis. If I had more time, I could order something from the catalog."

"By the way, I haven't agreed to any of this." Amy

pointed between them. "Right now, I'm just going to try on a dress."

"Yes, fine. Okay," Lauren said. "Got it."

Several minutes later, Amy was in the dressing room trying on the first dress. It was a tea-length, cream-color lace with satin, which to Lauren, looked way too matronly.

"She has a great pair of legs," Lauren said. "Anything shorter?"

"I agree on those legs, Mama!" Zoey got busy handing dresses over that might work to Lauren, who passed them on to Amy, after giving them the greenlight.

The second had way too much tulle, was a long gown, and actually white, so Amy rejected it outright. They had success on the fifth dress. Lauren knew it was the one when she saw the expression of longing in Amy's eyes as she saw herself in the mirror. The dress was a knee-length ivory sheath dress, in satin, which fit Amy like a glove. With a bateau neckline, the dress said both sexy and sweet.

"This is the one," Lauren declared. "Isn't it?"

It fit a big snug at the waistline, and Amy laughed, patting her little tummy. "I agree it's perfect, but check out my food baby. This is usually my size, but I just ate nearly my weight in kettle corn."

"Show me a bride who doesn't starve herself before her wedding day, and I'll show you a Texas without heat waves." Zoey fanned herself. "It can always be altered, if necessary."

"Lauren, are you sure?" Amy pressed, checking out the price tag. "You don't have to do this."

"I've already begged. Don't make me get down on my knees." Lauren clasped her hands together prayer-like.

"Okay, okay! Thank you." Amy chuckled. "Boy, you're a pain."

Lauren had already purchased Amy a pair of Jimmy Choos, which would work with the dress once she opened the box on Christmas Day. She grabbed the jacket Ronan pretended not to want and paid for everything with her credit card.

"Come again," Zoey said. "You're already my best customer."

Amy was scrolling on her phone as they left the store. "Wait until Declan sees this dress."

"Don't show him before the wedding. I heard it's bad luck."

"You're right. I'll play it safe, then. Hey, Declan texted that he wants to take me out to dinner tonight, so we need to get back soon."

"No problem." Lauren got back behind the wheel and started the car.

The past few hours had been so much fun. She couldn't recall having a girlfriend like this, but the only way to find out for sure would be to go back to Dallas. Maybe she had a close friend calling the condo obsessively and wondering where she'd been. Or perhaps a next-door neighbor who'd been instructed to water her plants. She assumed she didn't have a pet or Mr. Poindexter would have said something.

"Let me try this." Lauren punched the address into the GPS so the car could guide her back home.

Home. The house she'd lived in such a short time truly felt like her real home.

"Um, Lauren?" Amy broke the silence. "Just tell me if I'm being too nosy, but are you and Ronan officially a couple? Declan mentioned something."

Were they? She didn't know yet. They were sleeping together. He said he loved her and that meant everything. But the truth was, she wasn't going to be able to commit to anyone until she made some decisions. Until she remembered. And driving this stupid car hadn't helped. She was definitely going to need to go to Dallas soon.

"It was a bit embarrassing. Declan…sort of walked in on something."

"Oh no!" Amy gasped and covered her mouth.

"Not that kind of something." Lauren chuckled. "I came out of Ronan's bedroom, fully clothed by the way, and Declan sort of put it all together."

"Whew!" Amy rather comically wiped her brow. "Is this sort of a casual thing or is it going somewhere?"

Lauren would be an idiot not to want it to go somewhere, but though Ronan claimed to love her, how would he react to her past? He'd made excuses for her so far, but if she fell back into old patterns of caring more about material wealth than people… Ronan wouldn't be along for that ride.

"I… I don't know. I hope so."

"I'm sorry to put you on the spot. Forget I said anything."

"No, it's okay. I'm deeply attracted to Ronan and right now we seem to have so much in common. But is he going to love the person I really am?"

"And who is that?"

"A person who apparently chose my career over personal relationships."

"I think that might only matter if that's still who you want to be."

"Of course it *isn't*. But what if I change my mind when I remember everything? What if I can't help my nature and fall back into old patterns?"

Up ahead, traffic seemed to slow up as they reached the bend to take them from the coastal road toward the residential part of town. Some people were turning toward the boardwalk, others toward the main highway.

"Okay, listen. You know I was married before and it didn't work out. I desperately wanted to keep my family together, so in many ways, I tried too hard, changing who I was at my core. I joined the Junior League because he wanted me to. In other words, sometimes as women we change who we are, or cloak ourselves in who we need to be. You are a woman working in a male-dominated industry and at the top of your game. Maybe you felt you needed to change who you were to become that person and be accepted into the boy's club."

It was entirely possible, and hope rose because this version of her, a woman who bought Amy's dress simply because she wanted her to have it, was the woman she wanted to be. And if she'd changed once, she could do so again, back to being the woman she'd been ten years ago, when her grandparents were still around.

"Here's something I can tell you about Ronan—loyalty is extremely important to him. That's probably because of his military service. He excelled there and considers himself a man of honor. Yes, he might be a little bit uptight because in the world he came from, there's no gray areas. Honesty and living a life beyond reproach is most important to him. You want to know something funny? He discouraged Declan from dating me, even after I was already quite single."

"Why?"

"My ex-husband wanted to get back with me, after the divorce, simply because he had regrets. Mind you, the divorce was his idea and quite painful for me. But by then, I'd already fallen back in love with Declan and there was no turning back for me. I heard Ronan thought Declan should step aside and let me reunite with my ex. That's just the kind of guy he is. A little *too* honorable sometimes, but it's the military way."

Fear punched through her stomach. If Drew was right about her, she'd be just the kind of woman Ronan would not have anything to do with. She didn't want to remember the kind of person who'd been ready to take another woman's man away, if even for one night.

Especially for only one night.

"Loyalty is a good quality in a man if you ask me, even if maybe he could relax his views and understand we're all human. I figure that will happen more as he acclimates into civilian life. But, honestly, if you don't love Ronan—"

"Who said I don't love him?" Something snapped in Lauren, and the truth came pouring out. "I do love him. Who wouldn't? I'm crazy about him."

And as if the universe wanted to put a point on her statement, to make sure everyone would remember this moment, her car was suddenly pushed from behind with a force which caused the air bags to deploy.

Chapter Twenty

Lauren shoved the air bag out of her way. "Amy! Amy, are you okay?"

"I think so." Amy rubbed her head. "What happened?"

"I'm not sure but we got hit by the car behind us."

A moment later a dark-haired man rapped on her window. He made a motion for her to roll it down.

"Are you both okay in there?"

"Yes, I think so." Lauren reached for Amy's hand. "We're okay."

"I called 9-1-1. Just sit tight."

A few minutes later, the EMTs had arrived and were assessing Amy, Lauren, and the person who'd hit them with his economy car. His front end looked far more damaged than Lauren's luxury sedan, although that, too, looked like it would need some body work. She'd wanted to break the car in, but she hadn't meant it literally.

"I don't need to go to the hospital," Amy said. "I'll text my fiancé to pick me up. Really, I'm fine."

But the EMTs weren't having it. "You're both going to get checked out."

Lauren saw the man who'd come to her passenger side door speaking to a police officer. He gave his name as Adam Cruz and said he'd seen the accident happen. Apparently the man behind them was on his cell when traffic slowed, and he plowed into Lauren's sedan.

"She stopped suddenly!" the man protested when he overheard Adam talking to the police.

"Take it easy," the officer said. "We'll need a statement."

"Hey, aren't you the lady from last week?" the EMT said, while helping Lauren climb into the ambulance.

"Yes. I'm sorry about this. For some reason, I seem to attract trouble."

"Nah, that's not you. That's me." The second EMT thumped his chest. "I'm the black cloud in my unit."

But Lauren couldn't help feeling like some kind of magnet for bad energy. The car accident wasn't her fault, probably, even though she was still getting used to the brakes and may have stopped suddenly, as the other driver claimed. He also shouldn't have been texting. Thinking back to that night over a week ago, she still didn't know how or why she'd fallen off the yacht. No one else did, either, since she'd been alone. Assuming no one had pushed her off, could she have jumped in on purpose? She didn't think she'd ever do something like that, but on the other hand, her life sounded pretty empty.

When they arrived at the hospital, Amy and Lauren were taken into two separate bays, the curtains between them opened. Amy complained of a slight headache and they wanted to check her out for a concussion or whiplash. Guilt spliced through Lauren, sharp and blunt. This felt like her fault, even if it wasn't.

Everything in the emergency room moved quickly, as her vitals were checked along with Amy's. When Lauren didn't complain of a headache or neck pain, and didn't want another scan so soon after the first one, the doctor agreed. They said she'd be discharged, but they needed paperwork.

Then, for reasons Lauren didn't quite understand, a nurse closed the drapes between her and Amy. There were hushed tones and Lauren strained to hear. If anything happened to Amy, she'd never forgive herself.

They wheeled Amy away for a scan and she came back shortly afterward. They'd probably only been in the hospital for thirty minutes or more when she heard the loud sounds of a man calling out Amy's name, his voice carrying through the aisles. She recognized Declan, either angry or desperate. Maybe both. His voice got louder as he moved closer.

"Amy! Where is she? I'm her fiancé!"

"Sir! Wait a second!" A nurse followed Declan.

"Honey, I'm okay," Amy said.

"She's *fine*," the nurse said, sounding peeved. "We're waiting for bloodwork results and the scan we took."

"What the hell *happened*?" Declan shouted.

"Some dummy was texting and rear-ended us. This is just all a precaution because I had a small headache. But honestly, I feel fine."

"A small *headache*?" Declan said, sounding as if she'd just announced she had a brain tumor. "Let me talk to the doctor. I want you thoroughly checked out, head to toe."

"I think that's what they're doing, baby."

"Take a deep breath and settle down, young man." The nurse sounded far less friendly now.

Declan seemed placated for the moment, then the voices were quiet as if they were whispering. Hushed words between two lovers.

Lying alone on her gurney, Lauren went back to the night she'd lain in this same emergency room, frightened and desperate. She'd never felt so alone in her entire life. Until Ronan.

And quite suddenly, like a movie she'd watched playing itself out in fast forward mode, she remembered.

Everything.

She'd gone to UCLA on an academic scholarship, leaving her grandparents behind in Texas. After college, she'd returned to Texas, but not San Antonio. She visited as often as she could, but life got busy. Drive and ambition drove her and there were no relationships that lasted more than a few months. Her grandparents remained that soft place to fall, and whenever she came home to visit, she spent time in the field with her grandfather, planting and weeding. No wonder she'd been drawn to Ronan's garden, practically taken it over.

Everything changed when she met Harry Poindexter, who'd held out financially rewards like a carrot stick. She worked her way up, sending money to her grandparents, paying off any loans remaining on the farm. By the time they died, they had no debt but would have probably preferred more visits from Lauren. She went back, sold the farm, and never looked back. There were conferences, parties, travel overseas.

. On the night of the party, she hadn't been pushed and hadn't jumped in. Instead, like a self-centered woman, she'd been trying to get a selfie of herself on the bow of the yacht. The music blaring, no one heard her screams when she fell in. She'd been annoyed, then desperate, then fighting like hell to stay alive. Thinking of her mother and her grandparents. She had no one in her life who loved her unconditionally.

There had been people on that boat she thought might have cared about her, even if quite honestly, she didn't much care about them. Raven wasn't a pseudo family to her, but a means to an end. Her loyalty to Harry (yes, she called him that) was conditional. There'd been no actual vacation that week. Instead, she'd taken the time off to interview with their competitor, not because she'd wanted to leave but because she'd get paid even more once they realized they could lose her.

She didn't have enough wealth, apparently. Hers seemed to be an unquenchable well of need. In her condo, she had an entire room she used as a closet, to fit all her designer clothes and shoes. There was no neighbor she'd asked to water her plants, because she had no plants. Not only that, but she also wasn't even sure of her neighbor's name and she'd lived in that condo for five years!

And Drew. Shame spiked through her, even if there were two to blame. She'd been about to sleep with a man simply because she wanted to, casual and meaningless. Worse, in the past, she'd experienced being tossed aside by a man, but she'd made plans to do it to another woman anyway.

She groaned and a nurse walking nearby rushed to her. "Are you okay?"

"Yes," Lauren squeaked out.

She wanted to scream that nothing was okay, because she'd wound up with a wonderful and selfless man who deserved the type of committed relationship and love like Declan and Amy had, and wanted that more than anything. She couldn't ever give that to him, because her obviously cold and bitter heart would wind up breaking his someday.

The curtains between them slid open and Amy had turned to her. "What's wrong?"

What's wrong? What's *wrong?*

Her entire life was wrong. Somewhere along the line she'd decided to prove to all the high school classmates who'd thought she was a dirty farm girl that she was better than them. Not the same, even though her grandparents were twenty years older than everyone else's parents. She was better than them and so were her grandparents. Even if she was repeatedly reminded she had no mother and no father, she was *better* and she'd prove it someday.

When Lauren lowered her hands from her face, even Declan was studying her, eyes filled with concern. They obviously believed she'd been injured in the accident.

"Oh, nothing."

"It's not nothing," Declan said, sitting on the side of Amy's gurney. "I'm sorry you were both in an accident. I really should have— Oh, crap. Did anyone call Ronan? Does he know?"

"I... I didn't think to call him," Lauren said.

"Leave it to me." Declan took out his cell. "I'll let him know."

In that moment, Lauren realized she wasn't going to tell Ronan she'd remembered the past ten years, not until she could find a gentle way to tell him the whole sordid truth.

The interview in Houston with the Executive Protection Agency couldn't have gone any better. They'd offered him a job on the spot, and the six-figure salary was more than he'd ever earned in his life. There were apparently going to be some attractive parts of civilian life. He'd never been one to pursue wealth, but the idea of providing for a wife and children enticed him. The job would mean some travel, of course, sometimes even overseas, depending on the assignment. Nothing he couldn't handle. The elite agency protected both celebrities and heads of state and others. He'd be starting in the new year, and they were looking at him for a job that involved protecting a celebrity who'd been plagued by a stalker. The assignment wasn't something he'd necessarily share with his aunt and uncle, but hell, they should be happy to have him out of a literal war zone.

As he pulled up, Ronan immediately noticed the luxury sedan in front of his house because it was so out of place. Similar to the one Poindexter had driven the other night, this one was cherry red. It also had body damage to the rear end.

The tow truck driver had finished unhooking it by the time Ronan parked and walked over to meet him. He was about to ask the man whether or not he was in the right place when he remembered that Lauren would be having her car delivered soon. So…this was probably her car, damaged though it appeared.

"What happened? Did you drop it on the way?"

The driver scowled. "I'm sure I have the right place. The lady told me right before they took her in the ambulance."

"Ambulance?"

"Yeah, they seemed fine but were going to get checked out at the hospital. Some dude texting rear-ended them. You know, this kind of damage is going to be expensive because it's a foreign car. I wish people would buy American, you know?" He shook his head in disgust. "The thing is…"

But Ronan wasn't listening. His body buzzed and the surge of adrenaline kicking in made him feel like a caged animal about to bust out. He jumped back in his truck and started driving toward the hospital. Why did these things always happen in threes? Near drowning, heart attack, car accident. Also, why did chaos happen around *him*? All he wanted was a quiet life, a wife, a couple of kids. Not this constant fight-or-flight syndrome.

In that moment, more than in any other, Ronan realized he'd done the right thing. He wasn't cut out for the military anymore, and what's more, he wasn't going to miss it at all. No regrets. His cell was ringing beside him and caller ID flashed Declan's name, but he didn't have time to pull over and take the call. There was no time for anything but getting to the hospital and seeing what kind of damage had been done this time.

"Has Lauren Montez been checked in?" he said viciously to the triage nurse.

She gave him a look from under hooded eyes that said she didn't appreciate his tone. "You must be Ronan. Go through the double doors. They're waiting for you."

They? *They* were waiting for him? Who? What now, a team of doctors to tell him they'd done everything they could but hadn't been able to save Lauren?

"Ronan." He was met by Declan, of all people.

"What are *you* doing here?"

"I tried to call you. Lauren and Amy were in an accident, but—"

Amy, too? This could destroy Declan, but he didn't look too upset, which had to be good news.

Ronan pushed past him. "Where is she?"

And then he saw Lauren lying on the gurney, seemingly unharmed by all outward appearances, and he was able to breathe again for the first time in several minutes.

"Hey," he said, coming close. "You okay?"

"Yes," she said, biting her lower lip. "My car came today, and I wanted to take Amy out to do some shopping and test it out. Maybe I should have waited and gone alone to get used to the car. It's far more responsive than I ever imagined."

"It's not your *fault*," Amy protested, and Ronan noticed her for the first time sitting just past the curtain that separated the two bays. "Someone rear-ended us."

"You've both been checked out?" Ronan said.

"Yes, and I'm fine, but Amy has a headache, so she got a scan, and now we're just waiting for the results. Right?" Lauren said to Amy.

"It shouldn't be much longer," Declan said. "Oh, here they come now."

The doctor slid the curtain shut again.

"Oh, Ronan." Lauren covered her face. "I'm so, *so* sorry."

"Why? It wasn't your fault. And look, Amy's going to be fine."

"I don't want to leave here until we know for sure."

"No, of course not." He sat on the edge of her bed and took her into his arms. "We'll just wait right here."

She laid her head on his chest. "Thank you for coming."

"Of course I did. You really scared me, you know. I thought this time maybe… I'd lost you. I know, I know. It's paranoid, but so much has happened in a short period of time. It feels like a run of bad luck."

Then Declan's voice came from the other side of the curtain. "Are you *kidding* me?"

Ronan froze and felt Lauren still in his arms. He couldn't take any more bad news. Ronan waited as long as he could, which was approximately five seconds. Amy sounded as though she was crying, telling the doctor that she couldn't believe this, and Declan was talking softly to her. Ronan stood, about to rip the curtain open when Declan opened it for him, standing there with a big smile.

"We just found out something that was completely unplanned."

"You know my food baby?" Amy said to Lauren, patting her stomach, crying. "Well…"

"It's a real baby," Declan said.

Those tears were happy ones, and Amy and Declan were

both smiling. Suddenly the mood took a decidedly different turn.

Ronan stood and clapped Declan on the back, shook his hand, then hugged Amy.

From between the two gurneys, Lauren stretched her arm out and reached for Amy's hand.

"Congratulations, Mama. You better hurry with that wedding, because that dress isn't going to fit much longer."

Chapter Twenty-One

"The last time I saw Declan this happy, his team went to the playoffs," Ronan said.

"Yeah, I'd say his 'team' certainly scored a home run." Lauren made air quotes.

"His swimmers got across the finish line?" Ronan chuckled.

He'd watched his cousin and fiancée practically floating on a cloud made of sugar. They'd excused themselves and gone straight home, probably to do some more of what got them into their situation in the first place. Planned pregnancy or not, they were ecstatic they'd be parents again soon.

Several hours after the hospital ordeal, Ronan and Lauren were finally relaxing in front of the TV. He would give her everything she wanted tonight, including yet another episode of *Outlander*. Even though she claimed not to be the slightest bit injured, he could tell she was holding something back from him. She'd been discharged with a clean bill of health, so he had no idea what could be bothering her, but so far she hadn't come clean.

"I suppose they'll get married sooner than planned now," Lauren said.

"That's likely." He handed her a cup of hot chocolate with a heap of the marshmallows she liked floating in it.

"Did your interview go well?"

"They offered me a job." He took a seat beside her.

She smiled and reached to lay her hand on his thigh. "Anyone would be an idiot not to hire you."

"I'll start after the holidays. Some celebrity is being harassed by a stalker and needs protection detail while performing in Houston. But the job itself actually involves some travel overseas depending on the detail."

She quirked a brow. "Heads of state?"

"Some."

"Very impressive, sir." Her brow furrowed. "I've been meaning to tell you: I think it's time for me to go back to Dallas."

"You think it will help you to remember?"

"Hmm," she said. "It's time to see my condo and everything I left behind."

That made sense, of course, even if he wasn't ready for her to leave. "Do you want me to go with you?"

She blinked in surprise. "You would come with me?"

Her shock surprised him. It was as if she still didn't realize how deep his feelings for her went. And maybe that was on him. Maybe he hadn't shown her enough, because sometimes words weren't enough.

"Only if you want me to." He took her hand in his. That's when he noticed she was shaking. "You're trembling. Are you sure you're feeling okay?"

"Yes, and... I want you to come but I don't know if it's a good idea."

"Why wouldn't it be?"

She hesitated a beat. "What if you don't like what you see?"

"I already like what I see." He tucked a stray dark hair behind her ear. "Nothing is going to change that."

"Are you sure?"

It occurred to him that she thought he might be one of those men who were intimidated by a woman who was successful in her own right. Nothing could be further from the truth.

"Lauren," he said her name slowly. "I don't care if you make more money than I do."

"I don't think *that*," she said. "But how does this work? Apparently I work a lot and haven't had a whole lot of experience with long-term relationships."

"You don't know that yet. Maybe there's someone in the past that your boss doesn't know about. A high school or college boyfriend."

"I just… I think I would know." She bit at the cuticle of her fingernail.

"You really won't know for certain until you have all your memories back."

"Right," she said. "I'll be patient."

The wall he'd noticed at the hospital went up again. Something weighed on her and she didn't feel comfortable enough to let him know. It killed him that she thought he might judge her for her past as a workaholic with few friends. He never would. All he wanted was the woman here with him now, the one he'd fallen in love with, but she obviously hadn't gotten the memo.

That only meant to him he'd have to find more ways to show her. He would be lying to say he didn't fear losing her to the world she'd come from, to all those people who were so different from him. He understood one thing they didn't. Their hearts were the same, perfectly aligned. He kissed her then, pulling her closer, and closer still. This was where everything really jelled together. In this place and in this moment, he had no questions and no doubt of what she felt for him. She was clear about her desire and need, never holding back. There were no walls between them now as she moaned into his mouth, meeting him with the eagerness he'd become addicted to. He kissed the column of her neck, her breasts, and they were off to the races.

They would talk about Dallas…later.

Lauren was in heaven. Rolling around in bed with Ronan was by far her favorite thing to do. She loved the way he moved, whether it was over her, under her, or just walking to the kitchen. He moved like a jaguar, so sure in his skin, so self-possessed. And he had such incredible faith in her, the kind she didn't even have in herself. He'd made his decision to stay. Now she had to make hers. She could go back to Dallas and her old life, and never once look back. That was impossible when she loved this man so deeply. He'd saved her life in more than one way, because he'd given her a chance. Too many people in her past, and she could summon up each one of them now, hadn't given her half of what Ronan had.

The men in her past could not stand the fact she was intelligent, educated, and made more money than they did. Ronan claimed not to care, but many of her exes started out that way, too, and after a while, it became too much for them. In the beginning, she'd lied about how much money she made, hid her many achievements, and touted theirs instead. She could still remember the day she'd given up on a relationship and decided she'd become more like the men in power she'd met. No more making herself smaller to get and keep a man. Sex and intimacy was casual and temporary, lasting until no longer useful.

Every once in a while, she'd look in the mirror and hate the woman she'd become. So she'd put on more makeup, hair extensions, and indulge in retail therapy, squashing those feelings of regret. She'd stopped taking risks with her heart long ago.

Ronan knew how much money she made. He'd seen her car and hadn't gotten weird about any of it. He was that rarest of men, not threatened by a successful woman. Her only concern now was that he never find out about Drew. Because the point was she'd like to believe that even if she hadn't fallen overboard, she wouldn't have gone home with Drew.

Almost dying had been the significant emotional event to bring her back into the woman she used to be. She told herself Ronan would understand this more than anyone.

The next morning after a very fun shower with Ronan, Lauren watered the garden, marveling at the progress in such a short time. Wonderful Texas, her favorite place in the world, where vegetables could usually grow at any time of the year. She stepped inside, and saw Ronan, shirtless, stirring eggs in a pan. She'd probably never get tired of watching him, even if it was probably dangerous to cook while half naked.

For a moment, she simply stared and appreciated the utter male beauty of him. She had two things to tell him: She remembered. And she loved him. If he could find it in his heart to forgive her for the woman she used to be, this could work. If there was anything he'd demonstrated to her it was his capacity to love.

After a couple of minutes, he turned, noticed her staring, and smirked. *"What?"*

She almost couldn't get the words out, her throat clogged with emotion.

"I love you. I think you should know that."

He dropped the spatula and closed the distance between them, pulling her into his arms. "I know."

She buried her face in his neck and prepared to tell him the rest. "And also, I remember everything."

He pulled her back, holding her by the shoulders, meeting her eyes. "Are you serious?"

She nodded, biting her lower lip. In her defense, she was a salesperson by trade and would only mention what she needed to. Emphasize the positive points, ignore the negative ones. It was the credo of every advertising person who understood how to put on a great campaign. There was no black or white but always gray. She worked in gray areas.

"You were right. It all came back to me. I have my memories of the last ten years."

Shutting off the stove, he walked them both to the kitchen table and sat her down in his lap. "Tell me everything."

Well, she'd tell him everything he wanted to know. Above all, she didn't want to hurt him and she didn't want him to stop loving her. He probably wouldn't, but given what Amy had shared, Lauren couldn't take the chance. She'd just prove to him, day by day, and year by year, that she was back to being the woman her grandparents had raised.

"It was so stupid." She shook her head. "No one pushed me overboard. I was trying to take a selfie of myself and the stars behind me, possibly pretending I was Kate Winslet, and I lost my balance and fell in."

Ronan blinked and looked to be fighting a smile. "But no one heard you yelling for help?"

"No, the music was loud. That's how I remember it. It

was all my own damn fault. I thought I looked so good in my hair extensions—"

"So that's what I saw floating away from you when my fishing line caught you."

She closed her eyes. "I was self-centered and so caught up in my own importance, in the beauty that was just skin-deep, that I nearly drowned. And I would have, if not for you."

"Look, what I want to know the most, what I've wanted to know all along…" She felt the tension in his shoulders.

She knew exactly what Ronan needed to know. He'd never cross those clear lines had he known she'd been someone else's woman first. He would have backed away and never intervened. And even though Harry had told them she was single, there was that small smidge of doubt that maybe there was someone. Someone Harry didn't know about. Like Drew.

"You didn't take me away from anyone. There *was* no one else. The last man I 'dated' was a year ago, and it didn't work out. Relationships never did for me. Most men didn't do well with my earning more money than they did or working all the time."

Most men, that is, who weren't Ronan Sheridan.

His breath came out in a whoosh. "I've been waiting to hear that and relieve my conscience. I would have never come between you and anyone else. That's wrong and the reason I waited until we could know who you were."

"Because that's the kind of man you are."

Her breath hitched, and it was more important than ever to explain something she'd learned about herself. "Babe, listen to me. Even if I remember everything about my past, I'm never going to be the same woman who fell overboard."

"No?" He rubbed her back with smooth strokes that were soothing her frazzled nerves.

"I'd turned into a woman my grandparents wouldn't even recognize. It took something like the accident to remind me of who I am. Family was always important to me, just as it is to you. But then they were gone, my only family, and I had no one."

"You will always have me."

"Oh, Ronan. Have I said how much I love you?" She ran her fingers through his thick hair. "But...how does this work?"

"How do *we* work, you mean? With you in Dallas, and me in Charming?"

"I like what I do and I'm good at it. It's not all about the money to me. Not anymore."

"Loving your career is not a crime, Lauren." He chuckled. "Look at it this way. At least I won't be half a world away. We can make this work."

"How did I get so lucky."

"I'm the lucky one."

She kissed him, knowing everything was finally right in her world. Every day she'd show him and prove to both him and herself that she wasn't the woman who'd been minutes from making a terrible mistake with Drew.

For the first time since it happened, she felt grateful for falling overboard.

Chapter Twenty-Two

Lauren had a wedding to help plan. There was less than a week left until Christmas Day, so she would have to work fast if they wanted to get married before Christmas.

When she'd announced her plans to Ronan later that day, he seemed genuinely surprised. "You really think they're going to do the wedding that fast?"

"Especially if someone else does all the work for them. Believe me, her dress isn't going to fit much longer. And it's a beautiful dress."

Ronan shrugged. "I don't know, I figured they'd just head over to city hall and get it done."

"How boring."

"Actually, it's a very nice old building with a huge staircase and cathedral ceilings." At her blank stare, he chuckled. "Don't look so surprised I know these things."

"Is that where you were going to get married?"

He nodded. "But it was also where my friend Adam Cruz and his wife were married a few years ago. Right around Christmastime, too."

"I'll have to investigate that avenue further."

"Actually, I think maybe you want to talk to Amy and Declan. You know, be sure this is what they want."

"Of course this is what they want! They're in love. And now they're having a baby."

"Again, better check with them." Ronan quirked a brow.

He wasn't wrong. Lauren might be a real go-getter in the ad agency world, but she remembered too many occasions when she went a little too far in assuming things.

Her grandmother used to remind her frequently, "Mija, despacita."

Which meant, of course, "my daughter, a little slower."

Lauren didn't really know how to slow down and she'd never been good at it. Still, Amy deserved to be in on the action. It would be her wedding, after all. So, Lauren found herself knocking on the front door once again, hoping she wasn't, ahem, *interrupting* anything celebratory.

Amy came to the door quickly, and fully dressed, too. "Hey! How are you feeling?"

"I should ask you that! Please forgive me for the accident."

She waved Lauren inside. "There's literally nothing to forgive."

"Is Declan here?"

"No, he went to see his parents before they leave, to give them the news. I'm surprised he didn't call last night, but I had his attention for a while. I won't lie, I don't mind when he treats me like I'm going to break if I'm not careful, because I have a baby inside. It's ridiculous and silly but also kind of sweet."

"Are you going to move up the wedding?"

"If I don't, I'll have to get married in maternity clothes and that would be incredibly depressing."

"Okay, so I have an idea. Hear me out." Lauren stretched her palms out. "There are a couple of things you should know. First, last night, I remembered everything."

Amy's jaw gaped, then she clapped her hands. "Was it being in the hospital again that jogged your memory? Either way, I'm so happy for you!"

"I knew you would be." She hugged Amy, delight pulsing through at having found this friend, even in the midst of all the disaster.

It was like the old days when she'd pitch to a marketing team, never sure how they'd react. Hoping beyond all hope that they would love her ideas. It was only much later, with so much success behind her, that it had all become rote and money became the true pursuit.

"What's your idea?"

"A Christmas Day wedding! Bam! The whole world is already celebrating, and it's one of those anniversaries where it's unlikely the groom will ever forget the date."

"We can't. If Mr. and Mrs. Sheridan aren't able to attend they would be heartbroken. We'll have to wait until they get back, but we'll do it soon after."

"I was worried you'd say that." Lauren steepled her fingers. "Then, you have some time. Please let me throw you the wedding of your dreams, whenever you decide to do this."

"I couldn't let you do that."

"Are you sure? I have so many connections in the advertising world, I bet I could do it for far less cost than most people."

Amy shook her head. "No, that's too much to ask of anyone."

But Lauren caught the longing in her eyes. Amy couldn't fool her. She wanted the dream ceremony with her first love. It didn't matter that she wasn't exactly virginal. Weddings were about celebrating love, no matter the age.

"I know how much you want to celebrate this second chance with Declan. And it deserves to be every bit as important of a wedding as your first. It doesn't matter less just because you've already done this once before."

That seemed to strike a chord in Amy and she straightened. "Absolutely not. It's particularly meaningful for me this time."

"Exactly."

Amy waved her hands in a surrender motion. "Okay, okay. I'll talk to Declan and let you know."

Lauren had been gone from her real life for two weeks. Even if she'd wanted to avoid this, it was time to go to Dallas and see what she'd left behind. She'd called Harry and informed him all her memories were back. He sounded ecstatic when she told him of her plans to drive to her Dallas condo. She made no promises to check in at the office, however. She'd simply phoned Katrina and asked if she'd please just have a courier drop off her work laptop with the security guard in the condo's lobby. Her plans were to do a little bit of catching up during any downtime before Christmas Day.

Due to the nearly four-hour drive, Lauren agreed with Ronan's opinion they should leave after rush hour traffic had died down. They took Ronan's truck since her sedan was still in the body shop. Even though they'd left late enough, traffic lingered on the highway as they approached the city skyline.

She had a love-hate relationship with Dallas, but there was no denying it was home. A familiar and comforting sense of recognition slid into her soul as she recalled many happy times. The city had an arts district she frequented and supported. There had been dinners and lavish parties both with the artists she supported, and with her clients. Predominantly, a sense of pride that her work and creativity was well recognized. She'd been at the top of her game before the accident. There was no doubt in her mind she could be again.

Lauren remembered her luxury executive condo, and with every mile they drew closer to it, her fear escalated. Once, she'd brought a date home and he'd left within fifteen minutes. From the moment he'd stepped inside to when she poured him a glass of wine, she sensed his mounting anxiety. She had a nicer place than he did, and that was definitely not acceptable. He was not different from most of the men she'd dated, all professionals who expected to do better than their significant others.

When they arrived, she gave Ronan the security code and he punched it in, driving them through the iron gates into her appointed parking spot.

"This is nice," Ronan said with a nod of approval. "I like the idea of you being safe in the big city."

"Maybe, but I've been thinking I should move into something a little less… I don't know, luxurious? Pretentious? I don't need all this." She made a motion with her hands.

"Why not?" Ronan turned to her, not a sound of displeasure or disdain in his tone. "You work hard and earned it."

"I can do with far less. Remember, I grew up on a farm."

"You've come a long way, baby." He chuckled.

The elevator took them up to her floor, where apparently someone had been picking up her mail even though she'd never arranged for it. She usually planned with the post office to hold her mail. There were no neighbors she talked to a regular basis, because no one had been particularly friendly. Living on the same floor with a surgeon and a criminal defense lawyer who'd both served as the condo co-op's president at different times made her reticent to form bonds. These were not "her people."

The two men hated each other with a passion, and the only time they were caught in the elevator together, no one spoke except for Lauren. She'd made a lame comment—

"How about those Cowboys?"—during the football season, and "How about those Astros?" during the baseball season. Nothing more than a grunt. She should have tried hockey. Those two disagreeable men had been immune to all of her sales tactics, and she'd never sold them on the idea that neighbors should get along, at least superficially.

She opened the door, and no sooner had Ronan walked in the door that he said, "What, no Christmas tree?"

"I never got into decorating for the holiday."

With the little time she spent here, the trouble of decorating for only one month didn't make any sense to her. She hadn't been into the holidays at all until she'd met Ronan.

"Good thing you met me. I have enough Christmas spirit for the two of us."

"Yes, you do, babe."

Her apartment was as spacious as she remembered, but now she saw it with a fresh set of eyes. The occasional splash of beige accentuated the decor in cream colors and white. She'd never loved it, but she'd used the interior designer Harry recommended and figured the man knew more about home style than Lauren ever would. At least she had some rather brilliant impressionist art on her walls by local artists. One of the paintings, a shack in the woods with a pathway filled with colorful flowers, was her favorite.

She didn't realize she'd been studying it, finding those peculiarities and strokes of the artist's brush, until Ronan came up behind her, linking his arms around her waist. "You okay?"

"Yes, this one is my favorite. The artist who drew it, funny enough, is named Jane."

"How ironic."

"It reminds me of my grandparents' farm. I was always happiest there, even if the house we lived in wasn't large.

We had land, but basically, we lived in a tiny cottage, like this one in the painting."

"Yeah, you don't need much money when you have that kind of unconditional love, do you?"

"I knew you would understand." She pointed to the picture. "This was my real home."

She'd never forget the moment she'd attended the exhibition and saw the image, which Jane had titled *Yesterday*. It seemed almost magical that Lauren had come upon the picture, with that particular title. It hadn't come cheap, but she believed in supporting artists. It hung on her wall, reminding her of where she'd come from, but somewhere along the way, she'd stopped looking at it. It became part of the background when she'd been too busy slaying ad copy and working her behind off. But if she could only walk away with one item, it would be this painting.

"Let me give you the tour." She took Ronan's hand and led him to the kitchen, where she had state-of-the-art appliances.

A refrigerator blended into the wall and matched the cupboards. A gleaming granite counter, stainless-steel range, dishwasher, and double oven. The kitchen was immaculate because she had a maid service that came weekly. Lauren didn't cook much, and the evidence had been clear enough at Ronan's house. She did, however, know how to clean. Just didn't have the time.

"I have a service who comes in every week," she explained to Ronan, lest he think of her as a neat freak.

Lauren would like to believe that Anne liked Lauren as much as she liked the housecleaner. She paid her well with bonuses, but she'd recently been reminded that money wasn't everything. Money wasn't *how* you demonstrated love. More important was caring for people and their feelings by showing them.

By the time she gave Ronan the full tour, room/closet included (for which he teased her mercilessly), they wound up on the patio, which faced the city's skyline. Building upon building of all sizes, bustling city streets below, not anything like the small-town-Charming view of the bay, dotted with sailboats and yachts. The place where her life had forever been changed.

"What do you think?" she finally dared to ask Ronan. "Could you live here?"

The words came rushing out before she could stop them. She hadn't meant to put him on the spot. He'd just accepted a position in Houston, which included international travel, and she'd never expect him to simply follow her lead. Would it be easier if he did? Yes.

He smiled, lowering his head to tug her earlobe. "I could live anywhere with you."

"But…?"

"Why don't we play it by ear? I'll come up and visit you on weekends, and whenever I'm not working."

"Or traveling? Look, let's not think about it for now. You're taking me back to Charming today. I don't plan on moving before I at least say goodbye to Amy and the kids."

"Yeah, that would not be cool. You need to give them notice. Me, too. I'll need to start interviewing roommates."

"Don't you dare."

He smiled and she returned it, knowing he was teasing her. Her heart shimmered with the knowledge that he'd miss her. This was her home, but she had another one with him. And she didn't have to leave Charming until after Christmas Day.

"I'm going to miss living with you, and watering and weeding our garden."

"You'll come visit." He brought her hand up to his lips and spoke through her fingers.

"Yes, every weekend. You're going to get tired of me."

"Never." He kissed her, his hand palming her neck, drawing her up to him.

Neither one of them wanted to talk about next steps. Weekend love affairs were for younger people. She wanted a real relationship and an almost four-hour drive would be one hell of a commute, especially with Texas traffic and the constant roadwork. For now, she refused to dwell on the negative and, like the true salesperson she was at heart, accentuate the positive. She loved this man, and he was perfect for her, and she for him. It was all that mattered.

Their mini make-out session on the balcony was interrupted by the doorbell. Lauren wasn't expecting anyone but she finger-combed her hair and pulled away from the sexiest man on earth.

"I'll just go see who that is."

"You do that." He patted her behind and gave her a slow, easy grin when she walked away. "But I need a minute."

"Of course," she said, chuckling.

Maybe it was one of the condo owners, who'd noticed activity in her apartment. It could be the proverbial snoop on the floor below her, Mrs. Sinatra (no relation, though she eagerly claimed her undying love for ol' blue eyes).

It could be Katrina from the office, bringing the business laptop Lauren wanted so she didn't have to drop by the office. Instead, she opened the door to find the last person she wanted to see.

Drew.

Chapter Twenty-Three

"Hey!" Drew tipped back on his heels. "The prodigal daughter returns. Welcome home, stranger."

Fear spiked through Lauren. She hadn't prepared for Ronan to meet Drew. Not now. Not ever. Certainly not *today*. The timing was off. She didn't want this to happen on the same day she'd introduced Ronan to her old life.

"How did you find out I was here?"

"Katrina told me." He handed her a satchel. "Your laptop. I told her I'd be the delivery guy today."

"I told her to leave it for me in the lobby."

When Lauren took the bag but stood still, barring him from entry, he said, "Are you going to let me in or what?"

"I'm not here to stay," Lauren explained. "As I said, it's Christmastime and I'm spending the rest of the holiday in Charming with the people I've been staying with all this time."

"Either way. Can I come inside?"

Seeing few options, Lauren moved aside. "I just came to Dallas to get a few things I'd been working on before I…"

"Fell overboard?" Drew chuckled. "Tell me again how that happened."

She didn't see why she should share her humiliation with Drew, except to assure him it was an accident.

"No one pushed me in. I must have, um, gotten too close to the edge and lost my balance."

"I'm glad to hear it wasn't Julie who shoved you off."

"Of course not. She had no reason to."

Drew quirked a brow and looked over her shoulder. She turned to see Ronan approaching.

Time to introduce the love of her life to the man she'd been about to settle for before everything changed. And to think she'd been attracted to Drew on some microlevel. They'd had a hot, magnetic attraction between them, and he'd never been intimidated by her. It also helped that they'd never acted on the attraction and the forbidden always seemed like a tantalizing idea. But the connection she had to Ronan couldn't compare. Drew was like a flickering matchstick to Ronan's roaring wood fire.

Even before Ronan settled his arm around her waist, it seemed Drew sensed the change in the room. He smiled as if he had a secret. She wanted to wipe the entitled smirk clean off his face and tell him some of the best moments of her life happened *after* she'd fallen overboard.

The two men shook hands, and she caught Drew sizing Ronan up.

"You're the man who saved her life. Words just can't express how grateful we all are. If only I'd known, I'd have jumped in after her myself."

Lauren had to choke back the snort she wanted to cut loose. Drew, jump into the bay wearing his Armani? He'd probably get his assistant to do it for him.

"Well, the point is you didn't." Ronan tensed beside her and his tone bordered on hostile.

He still had a quiet kind of outrage that no one had saved her, but she now understood it couldn't have been helped. Even if Ronan didn't accept it. She wasn't close enough to anyone who cared enough to track her movements that evening or care enough to find out where she'd gone. She'd been so easy for everyone to forget.

Now she had someone who would walk through fire for her and would notice the second she was missing.

"Pretty lucky break for you, I see." His eyes focused on Ronan's arm around her waist. "It would have been me, honestly, but I was a victim of domestic violence that same evening. My date figured out that Lauren and I were going to hook up later that evening. I tried to break it off with her like a gentleman, but before I knew it, she'd kicked me in the stomach, the shins, and spit on me. The police were called and so we didn't even realize Lauren was missing."

She desperately wanted Drew to stop talking, but like a runaway train off its tracks, she stood speechless, frozen to the spot, watching the disaster that would happen next.

Ronan lowered his arm from her waist. "Is that right? Sorry, but it sounds like you got what you deserved."

Drew scowled. "Maybe so, maybe so, but it takes two to tango, right? And Lauren was ready to go home with me. I'm sorry I ruined it."

"That's…just not how I remember it," Lauren stammered.

Ronan opened the door and stood. "We shouldn't keep you. Thanks for dropping by."

Oh, thank You, God. He didn't believe Drew. He wanted him to leave and stop ruining their lives.

Drew threw up his hands. "Fine, fine. I know when I'm not wanted. See you at the office, Lauren. Merry Christ—"

Ronan practically slammed the door shut and turned to her. That's when she noticed the dead eyes, the glare, the tick in his jaw. The judgement. She was in trouble.

Accentuate the positive, divert attention from the negative.

But that didn't work in life, did it? In the real world, people had questions and they wouldn't stop until they got the answers.

"Tell me it's not true," Ronan said, his jaw tight. "Tell me that jackass was just grandstanding like a damn ostrich. Circling the prey he lost. Just tell me and we'll forget everything he said."

"I would have never gotten together with him. We'll never know because of what happened. But that's what I firmly believe in my heart."

"So, you weren't going to come between him and his girl that night?"

"I... I didn't remember that for a while."

"But you eventually did, didn't you? What part of you thought it was okay to come between two people who were *together*?"

It didn't escape him that she'd been about to do what had been done to him. What had been done to so many military men while they were on the battlefield fighting and sometimes dying. It happened a lot. Affairs, temporary or otherwise. Marriages destroyed and families broken up due to zero loyalty. He didn't actually know whether Belinda had ever been faithful, as she claimed. He couldn't help thinking of Belinda and Paul. Paul, stepping into what he believed to be an empty space and filling it. Belinda, simply accepting Ronan could be replaced easily enough by his best friend.

And now the woman he'd come to know and love was also capable of this kind of betrayal.

"Drew is a womanizer and no there's no part of me that thinks that's okay." She tried to reach for him but he pulled away.

"Then, *why* were you about to do it?"

When Lauren flinched, he realized the words had come out of him with more hostility than he'd intended. And then, not surprisingly, the fighter he'd known was in her all along came out swinging.

She tipped her chin. "I don't know! Maybe because I was lonely? But can you see that you're judging me for something I *didn't do*?"

His fists clenched and unclenched. "That seems incidental at this point. Fate intervened but otherwise...it would have happened."

"I don't know that to be true. I've never done anything like it before, and I honestly don't think I would have gone through with it. I was drinking that night, and my inhibitions were lowered. Poor decision-making skills, like the one where I tried to take a selfie and fell off the yacht!"

He wanted to believe her. He didn't want to lose her, but...she was certainly not the woman he'd believed. Initially, there was all her money, which didn't bother him. The materialism disturbed him, and he'd seen that as a red flag, but one he'd chosen to ignore, which might have been a mistake.

Now this.

He didn't know if he could get past it. Yes, maybe he was too uptight about rules and ethics. This was some of the coloring outside the lines and utter chaos of civilian life. It was what he'd thought he wanted, but now he felt sick. He didn't expect the first person to send him into a tailspin to be the woman he loved.

"I understand how this is difficult for you because of what you went through with your ex and your best friend. But I'm not the kind of woman who breaks up relationships." Lauren's voice sounded shaky. "Please believe me."

"No one thinks they're that kind of person, until they are."

"You're being so unfair."

"I'm not trying to be." Ronan fought for control over his emotions, so all over the place they were beginning to worry him. "Maybe I expected too much."

"You *can* expect that I'll always be faithful and loyal to you. I love you and I'd never cheat on you."

He'd be lying not to admit the physical distance they'd now have nagged at him like a warning. Only four hours, which on paper wasn't bad. Reality was far different. They wouldn't see each other during the week and possible some weekends. With his travel and hers, they might be separated for weeks since they wouldn't be living together. He'd already seen firsthand what a relationship killer physical distance could become. Emotional distance usually followed closely behind, which meant temptation lay everywhere. He wasn't worried about himself, but Lauren was a beautiful woman who'd already made a bad judgement call due to loneliness. While he'd never expect her to quit her job and come live with him in Charming, or Houston, he no longer felt certain this relationship would work. And he just couldn't go through another huge loss again. Losing at love again would kill him.

"Ronan." Lauren spoke softly, touching him, planting her hand on his chest, reminding him of their intense connection. "Tell me what you're thinking. We've always been able to talk. Don't stop now. Please don't shut me out."

But he couldn't think with her this close. Her influence would keep him from being logical. Instead, he'd focus on the way her hair smelled like coconuts and her skin felt like silk. It was important to make a good decision when it might affect the rest of his life.

He took a step away for clarity and dared to look at her

again. She was beautiful, but that's not what drew her to him. It was the courage she'd displayed even when enduring the most unsettling situation he'd ever seen a person go through outside a war zone. She was kind, too, and he'd seen that in the way she dealt with his family. With the children. This was his problem. His burden to deal with and not pass on to her. She'd already expressed how fearful she was at the thought she hadn't been a good person before the accident. He didn't want her to believe it was true, but at this point, the ground was shifting under him while he fought to stay upright.

"Listen, I'm sorry, but I can't help what I'm feeling. Maybe I just need to time to think. This all happened so fast. We probably need some time apart. You have a life you need to get back to and I should probably let you do that."

"But...not yet. I was going back with you." She gestured at her laptop. "I can do some work from Charming, try to slowly get back in the swing of things."

"Or you can do it here and give us some time apart. To think this over carefully."

That's when the light in her eyes seemed to go out. "I have nothing to *think* about! It's almost Christmas! What about Amy and Declan and the kids? What about the wedding?"

"Don't worry, I'll explain everything. They'll understand."

"Oh, Ronan. Please don't do this. I've changed from the woman who fell overboard, and you know that more than anyone."

"You had a significant emotional event and that changed your direction. But that doesn't usually alter a person's character."

"Sure, I get it. You think my character is less than ideal.

I'm a flawed human." She glanced around her apartment, at all the spacious luxury, waving her arm. "But *this* isn't who I am. I can see you won't believe me."

"I want to believe you, but it's a big risk."

"And you don't take them with your heart anymore, do you?" She crossed her arms. "You're not willing to take *this* risk. Me, with all my complications and baggage."

He did not answer that, but instead, took a deep breath. "Will you be okay here if I go back to Charming alone?"

She studied the ground. "I'll take rideshare if I have to go anywhere, until my car gets fixed."

Moving toward the door, he dared to glance at her one last time. "Okay. You take care."

Lauren followed him and he caught the tears in her eyes. "This is it, isn't it? This is goodbye."

"I don't know." He had to get out of here where he could think and reason.

"I think I do. And I love you," she said, her voice breaking. "Bye."

He froze, hand on the doorknob. Doubt clouded his decision, when in that slice of a moment, she'd laid herself bare. But she wasn't wrong about him. Yeah, he was a damn coward when it came to love. He didn't want to go down this road again and take this kind of monumental chance with the rest of his life.

He rushed out the door before he changed his mind.

Chapter Twenty-Four

Lauren was accustomed to men leaving. This was more of the same even if it had never hurt or mattered quite this much before. Not like this. Her heart was shattered seeing the shadowing in Ronan's eyes that showed he didn't *trust* her. She'd been a dummy to get involved with a man who obviously had some of his own troubles, whether he would admit to them or not. Ronan liked to pretend to be this hero, this rescuer, but he was the one who needed rescuing. He was grieving for his mother and grieving for his military career. He was one big ball of grief, and she hadn't even seen it until this moment, too caught up in her own mess.

She wanted to kill Drew with her bare hands for bringing up that night. It wasn't important except to his ego. Ronan never had to know about a choice she'd *almost* made, which would never define her. Whether he would admit to it or not, he was punishing her for not meeting his absolutely rigid expectations. No, she wasn't perfect, and neither was he.

They'd met and fallen in love when she was a blank slate and he'd written on her heart.

Now he was gone and she didn't know what to do with herself. She wanted to call Amy but that might be viewed unfavorably by Ronan. They were his family. Not hers. He'd asked her to give him time, and she would, even if she understood what that meant. It meant goodbye.

She wandered around the apartment, searching through all the stuff she'd accumulated over the years. The bedroom closet seemed outrageous now. Nobody in the world needed this many shoes. She could have funded several charities with this collection.

"You idiot!" She picked up a designer shoe and threw it against the wall.

The next few minutes were spent pitching everything she owned against the wall and floor. But she wouldn't cry, damn it. Not a single tear would be shed, because she was stronger than that. Besides, she'd cried enough in the past two weeks. Instead, she yelled every curse word she could think of. Then she screamed in rage just for the sheer joy of it. Sometimes anger was the proper response. There were injustices in the world, and although this was not the greatest of them by far, it was unfair. If she ever saw Ronan again, she was going to judge him for something he didn't do, either, and see how he liked it!

Hey, remember that time you made fun of the way I danced, until I cried? No? Maybe because it didn't happen! But admit it, you were thinking it.

Not surprisingly, there was a knock on her door. Probably Mrs. Sinatra wanting her to "keep it down, dear," even if she'd never so much as shouted in her home. But with her apartment just below Lauren's, Mrs. Sinatra often complained she could hear Lauren walking, the tap-tap, clickety-clack of her heels giving her a headache. Too bad, because she wasn't going to stop walking and might actually try stomping around from now on for good measure. Let them kick her out of the co-op, she didn't care.

She headed toward the door, ready to give the older lady

hell. Not only was she not going to stop walking on her own floor, but she might move out of this overpriced apartment and see how Mrs. Sinatra liked it when a drummer moved in instead. But when she swung open the door, there stood Mrs. Sinatra, wearing a reindeer hat and carrying a plate of Christmas cookies. The memory now came swiftly, piercing her with a soft ache. The nurses at the hospital had sent her home with a bag of them, asking her to come back and visit when she remembered. That night she'd been so terrified, clinging to her only comforting memory. Ronan.

"Hello, dear. We had a little holiday party while you were gone, and I kept a few cookies for when you came back."

Her kind words were too much for Lauren's barely pent-up rage. Surprising herself, she burst into tears. Mrs. Sinatra set the plate down and took Lauren into her arms. God, it felt so good to get a grandmotherly hug. She hadn't even realized how much she missed them after all these years. There was nothing like a grandmother's unconditional love.

"I'm s-sorry. Thank you for the cookies."

"Never mind that, honey. Tell me what's wrong. Why are you so emotional? And where on earth have you been? This apartment has been like a tomb."

"I've been away."

"No wonder. I thought you'd really taken my advice and started walking barefoot. I was going to drop by and say thank you. I haven't had one of my migraines in weeks."

It had never occurred to Lauren that simply kicking off her heels would be enough to placate Mrs. Sinatra. Something so simple. Here she was, a brilliant woman, Summa, and she missed the small things. Lauren explained everything. The accident, the temporary amnesia, staying in a small town by the coast, and lastly, falling in love. She ended with the breakup, only a couple of hours ago. Ronan wasn't even home yet. She hoped he felt twice as bad as she did. She hoped he'd go home tonight and choke on a dinner roll.

Okay, so she didn't want him to die, but she wanted him to suffer the way she was.

"This explains everything," Mrs. Sinatra said. "Unrequited love can make you scream and cry and make a damn fool out of yourself."

Lauren winced. "So, you did hear me scream?"

Mrs. Sinatra's hand rose to her neck. "I almost called the law. Good thing I came down to check on you first, with my cookies."

Great plan. If Mrs. Sinatra couldn't fight off the imaginary robbers, she could at least feed them.

"Thanks for checking on me. I sometimes feel like the only people who know I exist are the people I work with. Even they took a long time to realize I was missing." Lauren sighed.

"And this man you fell in love with, what's he like?"

Lauren had a difficult time describing him. One could use words like *handsome* and *built like a rock* but it became far more difficult to define his heart. This was the part of him she'd fallen hard for, the compassion he had for people and the way he'd never questioned helping her, even when it must have been a huge disruption to his life. He had his own problems but had focused entirely on hers. She'd never dreamed he'd walk away so easily.

"He's strong but hurting. I didn't see it until it was too late."

Lauren had lost her mother a long time ago, but Ronan's loss was far more recent. While the hurt never went away, the years had allowed it to slide into a place where the memory only surfaced strong enough to slice with pain once a year, or when certain holidays arose and there was no family left to share them.

Mrs. Sinatra patted Lauren's hand. "Don't worry, dear. If he loves you, he will be back."

"I don't know about that. There was a finality in his words I can't shake."

"Take your mind off it by giving to others as you do every year."

"What do you mean?" Lauren sniffed, wiping tears from her eyes.

It did seem that there was something she was forgetting, but considering everything she'd been through, Lauren wouldn't be surprised if she'd dropped a few balls here and there. She reached for a tissue box, then realized she didn't have any. Not only did she never cry, she also rarely got sick. *Go, Lauren.*

"The check you write every year for Lone Star Futures. Last year, it was so big they gave you a plaque."

The plaque. It all came back to her. The organization for underprivileged teens. She'd been so embarrassed to be rewarded for something that should be expected of anyone who had much to give.

"That's right. I'd almost forgotten."

And how funny that she'd judged herself so harshly when she only recollected bits and pieces of her life. When seeing only one side, it was easy to think of herself as a dragon lady. It didn't help that Ronan almost confirmed it for her when he left, but he was wrong about her. Although she believed she could still do with less shoes and clothes, clearly she was generous. The part of her that didn't quite remember everything, yet wanted to go on a spending spree for her friends. The woman who bought her new friend a wedding dress and wanted to pay for her wedding.

"You've always been generous. Whenever my grandkids are selling Girl Scout cookies or popcorn or having a walk-a-thon, you're the only one in this building who doesn't complain about writing a check."

That was also true. She had the boxes of cookies to prove it and wondered when they might expire, since she never allowed herself a damn cookie. Another thing she was going to change about her life.

More cookies. Less drama.

Hey, that could be an advertising slogan for one of her accounts, a brand of cookies that had been part of Americana for generations but recently had wanted to up their game with the younger demographic. She could already see it in her mind's eye and would get started on sketches of promotions tonight. But nothing said that she couldn't work on this campaign from Charming. Whether or not Ronan approved, she was *going* to see Amy, Declan, and the kids on Christmas Day. She'd rent a car or take a rideshare and rent a place when she got there. Maybe one of those beach cottages, where Ronan had pointed out that Michelle and Finn lived. She would let Ronan take his time considering this decision. Going back didn't mean she had to see Ronan.

Too bad if he didn't like it.

"Mrs. Sinatra, I'm curious. How fast do you think I could find a buyer for my condo?"

She smiled. "Well, there is a long waiting list."

Just what Lauren wanted to hear.

The drive back to Charming took a lot longer than four hours on Ronan's return, mostly because he turned back twice. Then he argued with his conscience, and reminded himself he'd simply told her he needed some time. No need for dramatics. It wasn't *goodbye*. Not yet, anyway.

But she said goodbye.

Because she thinks it's goodbye and you didn't do anything to discourage that.

That was the first time he'd turned back.

He should reassure her, remind her he loved her, and explain he just needed time to think. Yeah, but if he hadn't left, he wouldn't get the clarity he needed. And he had to be away from her, because if he'd stayed...they would have wound up in bed again. That was clearly the place where rational decisions went to die.

You didn't have to leave and dump her there when she wasn't prepared for that.

That was the second time he'd turned back.

But she'd be fine. Lauren was self-sufficient, a fighter, could take care of herself, and now had her memory back. She had everything she could possibly need and enough money to hire a limo service if she had to get around. The guilt still poured through him like a monsoon, but that time he didn't turn back.

It bothered him far more than he liked to admit that Lauren had almost wound up with Drew, if even for only one night. That insufferable, bean-counter cheater, wearing wingtips and Ronan's Lauren. Whoa. Okay, not *his* Lauren. No, he wasn't *jealous*. Of course not. That idea was insane. But seriously, what could she have been thinking to get together with such a dweeb? Yeah, he guessed Drew was good-looking by most standards, but anyone could see the level of his character went no deeper than a flea's. He was ready to get rid of his date to hook up with Lauren and she was willing. Whether or not she did wasn't the issue.

By the time he got back into Charming (thank you, eternal highway work), it was dinnertime. Seeing as he didn't have to get home to anyone, he headed to the Salty Dog to get some grub and maybe a cold beer. Possibly some consolation or a little clarity if nothing else. He wasn't the type to ask for help, so if someone couldn't guess his problem, he'd simply have to figure this out on his own. If he asked Declan, that would imply Ronan was failing at something, and he couldn't have that.

This was not the fun part of their one-upmanship.

He'd told Lauren the competing was all in good fun but only when he was winning. The actual truth bomb was that Ronan was in competition with himself much of the time. And right now, he was in a dead heat for last place.

Sidling up to the bar, Ronan found an empty stool. Being this close to Christmas meant the establishment was filled with garland, a tree, and twinkling lights draped across the bar. It was stuffed with friends and coworkers having last minute get-togethers. Exchanging gifts, and probably drinking too much. He thought he recognized the guy who'd been at the same agency where Ronan had interviewed earlier this week, sitting in a booth alone. Archie? Archer? Asher? Another former military man, but if Ronan recalled right, army. He wouldn't hold that against him. When he caught eyes with Ronan, he nodded and lifted his drink. Ronan nodded back. They'd likely be working together at some point.

His friend, Adam, and a couple of other retired Navy SEALs owned this bar. It meant that Ronan felt at home here because he'd be lying to say the adjustment to civilian life was going smoothly so far. First, he'd had the distraction of trying to find a way to relax and consider his options. Next, Lauren had entered his life as one shiny, bright disruption. He should be happy Lauren had regained her memory. He was, of course, happy *for* her. But life would have been simpler if they could have stayed in their little bubble. Simple, easy, and completely unrealistic. He was selfish, thinking he could always have the woman he'd previously imagined as a woman with zero flaws because she had no memory of them.

"Hey there, frogman." This time Cole Kinsella, one of the owners, was behind the bar.

"*Former* frogman," Ronan said.

"Ah, you're one of us now. A civilian. What'll you have?"

"Can I get some food at the bar?"

"You betcha."

"Let me have a Guinness and a burger."

Cole put the order in, then came back with the Guinness. "Don't worry. It will get better."

"Huh?"

Ronan had never been accused of being particularly expressive with his face, but now he wondered if the heartache he felt inside was written all over his mug. This pain was far, far worse than when he and Belinda split up. If he thought he'd been heartbroken then, this was as if someone had ripped into his chest cavity and walked away with his heart, not bothering to stitch him up.

"You're wondering how in the world this all works when there's no real leader in charge of the team." Cole gave the bar a wipe. "Or no one to lead."

"How'd you guess?" Ronan smirked.

"It happens to all of us, but you adjust right back into this world as if you've never been gone." Cole crossed his arms. "Mostly. But if you ever need to talk, I'm here. So are Adam and Max."

It was good to know, because Ronan would need the support. Some days, he felt like he was diving in deep water without his air supply. Cole, Max, and Adam had adjusted smoothly and were thriving. All of them married with children, or ones on the way. It gave Ronan hope that he could reintegrate, too.

"Look." Cole leaned closer. "You're going to wind up reevaluating a lot of stuff in your life. Don't be too tough on yourself."

"Funny, right now I'm afraid that I'm being too tough on others. My expectations might be too high."

"That will happen, too." Cole picked up a glass and polished it. "We were all part of an elite team and had each other's six without question. We held each other to the highest of standards. But you're going to remember how fragile and flawed people are, and that includes you."

He wasn't exactly perfect nor ever claimed to be. In the desert, he'd definitely been in places he hoped never to see again. Followed orders which were, at best, morally gray. The end justified the means. He'd be lying not to say he'd followed orders that he regretted to this day.

I was lonely. You're judging me for something I didn't do.

"Lots of gray areas," Cole said as if he'd read Ronan's mind. "Go ahead and keep your high standards but don't expect everyone else around you to."

He was probably talking about Belinda and Paul, since he didn't know about Lauren and Drew. Ronan had never forgiven them, even if he was way past the heartache. He'd moved on and hadn't loved Belinda in years. Now he'd fallen for someone else entirely and still held a grudge for what Belinda had done to him. For her weakness.

Maybe it was time to let it go.

Chapter Twenty-Five

The next day, eyes pink and swollen from crying all night, Lauren went to the office. A rideshare picked her up and dropped her right at the JPMorgan Chase Tower and she took the elevator to the twenty-fifth floor. The wide glass doors were etched in white cursive letters that read Raven Advertising.

"Ms. Montez! You're back! Welcome!" The young receptionist stood to greet her, wearing a headband with reindeer ears, which jingled.

"Thank you, Priscilla." Lauren smiled, making sure to use her name, and kept walking toward her corner office. "You're always so cheerful, and I've missed you."

"Thanks!"

The door to her office was open when she reached it, and Drew sat in her chair. Not surprising he was here, as she had the better office.

He spun around. "Hey, there."

"Move."

"We didn't expect you to be back so soon." Drew stood, ambling toward her. "Had I known we could have arranged a welcome-back function."

"Too close to Christmas for that, and I'm fine." She side-stepped him and took possession of her chair. "Not fine with what you did yesterday, however."

"What *I* did?" He went hand to chest. "Tell your boy toy the truth, you mean?"

Lauren narrowed her eyes. "The truth, is it? Whose truth? Because we both know I *wouldn't* have gone home with you. If I hadn't fallen off the boat, I'm sure your date would have gone after me, too. She'd have slapped some sense into me, if nothing else."

"You're probably right."

"I *know* I'm right. The point is, Drew, nothing happened between us. Nothing ever has. Nothing ever will. Do you get that?"

Drew shrugged. "Your loss."

"Sure." Lauren snorted. "Please close the door on your way out."

He slammed it, but ask her if she cared. Lauren turned in her seat to look out her floor-to-ceiling window. Had she ever taken the time to check out the view? She had a corner office, considered a real coup here. Unlike her condo, she could see far more below this tower of a building. Below her, people were walking quickly and efficiently, as though time was of the essence. It was the pacing of the city downtown. Rush, rush, on to the next thing to check off the box. Get to your appointment, and when you arrive, find out you have to wait for something or someone. Hurry up and wait. So many years wasted hurrying through her life. She'd recently learned there was a different pace of life, and there was still plenty of time to accomplish things.

She pulled out her laptop and checked emails. Nothing urgent, because Harry and Drew had been busy putting out her fires. Fine. This was good and might make her decision easier for Harry to accept. She pulled out the notes she'd made last night for the cookie-brand campaign. Her thoughts were scenes with dramatic situations in the age of technology, like breakups over texts, which were immediately resolved with a cookie. Recurring actors viewers would grow to like featured in a series of connected commercials. The main character would bring the cookie to the argument each time, with their new slogan, More Cookies, Less Drama. The actors would increase the budget but have a huge return. It worked with insurance, and it could work with cookies.

She looked up to see Katrina outside the glass walls of her office, as if waiting to be allowed inside the sanctum.

Lauren beckoned her. "I'm only here for a little while today, trying to catch up on things."

"Let me know if I can help."

"Right now, all I want to ask is where you'd like to go to lunch. Why don't you find a place you want to go and make the reservations for us today?"

Katrina blinked. "We already had the company holiday luncheon."

"But I missed it so this one is for you and me." It was high time she showed Katrina how much she appreciated all she did around here.

"Thank you, Ms. Montez."

"Lauren."

"Okay. Lauren." The corners of her lips quirked in a hint of a smile, as if uncertain.

"And also, I need to meet with Harry. Do you know what his schedule is like today?"

"He should be free before lunch."

But just then, Harry joined them, draping his arm around Katrina in a familiar way that HR would not appreciate.

He smiled at Lauren. She glared back.

"Well, well! You're back sooner than expected. Fantastic!"

"Please come in. I wanted to check in, and I'm taking Katrina to lunch today, so there isn't much time."

Katrina shut the door and Harry took a seat in front of Lauren's desk.

"Taking Katrina to lunch?" Harry squinted. "How hard did you hit your head?"

"Things are going to be different around here."

Harry cleared his throat. "What's going on? Do you want to run an idea by me? That's something you haven't done in years. You know I trust you. Whatever it is, go for it with my full blessing and support."

"I'm glad you said that. Because I'm going to be making a few changes in my life." She clasped her hands together on her desk. "I don't want to work as much as I've been."

Harry scowled and shook his head. "Is that boyfriend of yours already complaining? Anyone who is *that* insecure about a successful woman—"

Lauren stopped him, waving her hand in a cutting motion. "He's not complaining. This is me. I want to have a life outside of work, and apparently, I didn't have one. I thought I could have it all but I'm wrong. I've wasted a lot of years working so hard with little to show for it other than things. That's going to change."

"Don't tell me you're thinking of getting *married*."

Lauren sighed. "Why is that always where a man's thoughts go? I want to remember *me*, Harry. This is not about a man but about the woman I used to be. And to get back to her, I need to work less. I'm going to take days off, make friends, and go out to lunch with them. After today, I'm heading back to Charming and taking some time off until after the holidays. I'm working on a campaign idea for Front Porch Cookies you're going to love, and I'll be in touch via email. I'm working from home, in other words."

Harry leaned back, rubbing his hands on his pants legs. "Listen, I can't have different rules for you and all my other ad executives."

"I'm not asking for the moon. I was just in a terrible accident which could have *killed* me."

"But it didn't kill you and you're back, stronger than ever. You're tougher than you know."

"I know exactly how tough I am, but I'm not indestructible. This experience taught me, more than anything, what matters to me. I lost myself for a while, but who I found inside was the woman my mother and my grandparents raised. I'm ashamed of the way I've behaved in the past and all that's going to change."

Harry's eyes narrowed. "You're starting to scare me a little bit."

She was beginning to scare herself, too. Working less would mean finding hobbies when she had none. Probably never had. The closest she'd come was the garden she'd helped start in Ronan's backyard. No wonder the idea had come so easily to her. She was a farm girl at heart. She wanted to get back to a garden, the one in her mind, even if only metaphorically. Once she sold her condo, maybe she could live in a much smaller place, and instead, buy a farm where she could retreat on weekends.

"I'm sorry to scare you and I know this may sound crazy. It doesn't to me. I'm a different person now, even with all my memories intact."

"What am I supposed to tell everyone else? That you have different rules?"

"Tell them whatever you think is best. You can fire me anytime you'd like."

"You *know* I won't. You've got me over a barrel."

"I'm not leaving you, Harry." She reached to pat his hand. "You've always been so generous and I appreciate that."

"Good, because God knows you could walk away with half of our clients."

It was tough not to smile when Harry admitted the truth. She *could* walk away, but starting her own agency would mean she'd work harder than she ever had.

"Start my own agency? I don't think so."

Harry smiled, perhaps realizing the knife had a dull side, too.

Next, lunch with Katrina. Lauren still remembered the day she'd hired her, young and enthusiastic, a recent graduate from Texas A&M. At one time, she'd expected to take Katrina under her wing and guide her through the maze of the boy's club. The memory of how she'd struggled to be viewed as an equal was heavy on her mind at the time. But it had been five years and Katrina was still Lauren's assistant. Not good. Where had the time gone?

"Tell me about yourself." Then, realizing that sounded like the start of an interview, Lauren rephrased, "What I meant is… I'm sorry, I just want to know if everything is okay with you."

"Sure! Sure, it is. I really love my job. The bonus this year was incredibly generous of you and Harry, thank you *so* much."

"You're welcome. I want you to do something for yourself with that bonus."

"Well, it's really going to help at home since we've been taking care of my mother-in-law's nursing home care. My husband is an only child so it falls to us. Things have been super tight and I didn't think we'd have much of a Christmas. I was counting on that bonus, but it was even more generous this year."

It should be, since they'd had a great year, enough to hire a yacht for the party.

Lauren wasn't even aware Katrina was married, but that was probably the dark-haired man she'd brought to the party who stuck close all night long. They were strapped with taking care of her mother-in-law. This is how little she knew about her employee. Guilt spliced through her. They didn't have to be friends, but she should still know a *little* about her personal life. Clearly, people everywhere were struggling, and Lauren had been happily oblivious long before she fell into the bay and lost her memory.

"I'm sorry, I didn't know about your mother-in-law."

"Oh, I don't talk about it at work." Katrina shook her head.

"But you never even call in sick," Lauren said, amazed by how she managed to balance her life.

"I know how much you rely on me." She smiled, not a hint of bitterness.

"How long have you been married, then?"

She prayed it hadn't happened sometime in the five years she'd worked for Lauren and she'd missed the whole thing. Surely she'd have sent a gift, but since Katrina was who Lauren used to send gifts...

"We celebrated our sixth anniversary this June." Katrina reached for her goblet of water. "I met him in college, love at first sight."

"That's the handsome man I saw you with at the party," Lauren said.

"Tony. He was a jock in college but he was injured."

Lauren remembered what Ronan had told her: *We*

don't love you because of what you can buy us. He told her there were other ways to show him how she felt aside from splurging on him. Now she realized that the bonus checks Katrina got yearly were only slapping a Band-Aid on the problem. She needed to increase her earning power. Lauren could do some good here.

"I've been meaning to ask you," Lauren said. "How would you feel about taking on more responsibilities?"

"I would love that." Katrina sat up straighter.

"I've been rather shortsighted." Lauren buttered a piece of bread. "It's been a long time since I brainstormed ideas with anyone. Harry and I used to, when I first came on board, and I learned so much from him. Now he just lets me do my own thing. It's time I pass it on and I'd like to start with you."

"Really?" Katrina's wide eyes said that it had been a long time since anyone believed in her.

"I didn't mean to turn this into a working lunch." Lauren laughed. "But as you probably know, my own private life has been lacking for years. That's going to change, and I'll rely on you more. For instance, I've got this idea for a new ad campaign for Front Porch Cookies and I want to run it by you."

And for the next few several minutes, they brainstormed on how best to bring a classic family-cookie company into the new millennium.

It didn't take long for Declan to figure out something was wrong. He was over later that evening and Ronan regretfully waved him inside.

"What's going on? Where's Lauren?" He whipped his head around as if maybe Ronan was hiding her somewhere.

"She went back to Dallas."

"For good? What *happened*?" Declan said. "What did you do?"

"Thanks for assuming it's something I did."

"Isn't it?"

Ronan scowled. "I took her back because that's where she belongs. This was all temporary. She was always going to go home and the rest of us were foolish to hope she'd stay."

Okay, so maybe it wasn't everyone who'd hoped. Maybe it was just him.

"She didn't want to say goodbye to Amy and the kids? That doesn't sound like her."

"Maybe you don't know her like you think you do." But he couldn't let Declan assume the worst. "She actually wanted to say goodbye, but I thought it best if we take a break. Think things over."

"Ah, suddenly the murky water becomes clearer."

"You're going to use water metaphors with *me*?" Ronan thumped his chest.

"Whatever, man. I hate to see you lose the best thing that's ever happened to you. She's great."

"I know, I know. And I never said it is over. I just wanted a break."

"You mean like when Ross and Rachel took 'a break'?" Declan held up air quotes. "We all know how well that worked."

Ronan did not love that comparison. Like so many millennials, he and his cousins had grown up with that show.

"I'm not going to sleep with someone else. And I'm not in a *sitcom*."

"No, this is real life, and you're going to blow it if you lose her to some jealousy and fear you have over what happened with Paul and your ex."

"This isn't about that," Ronan protested.

He told Declan about Drew, and Lauren, and what she'd nearly done that night. Would have done if she hadn't fallen overboard.

Declan's breath came out in a whooshing sound. "That's... I can see why that bothers you, but damn. If we were all held to the standards of what we *almost* did? Then, I guess I'm going to hell for sure. I'm a terrible person. I almost robbed a bank the other day."

"What are you *talking* about?"

"The money would help. We all know my life would be easier if I'd stayed playing major league baseball and made millions in commercials and endorsements."

"Then, you wouldn't have been living next door to Amy after she divorced. You would have been a spoiled athlete with five kids from five different women. In a mansion."

"Yeah, it's just one of those things. I don't regret it. It was meant to be, but how am I supposed to raise a family on my salary? So, anyway, yeah, I thought for one nanosecond about how nice it would be to rob a bank."

Ronan all but rolled his eyes out of their sockets. "But you weren't *serious*."

Declan shook his head because, of course he wasn't. "And maybe Lauren wasn't seriously going to hook up with that dude, either. Plus, you can't be jealous when she hadn't even met you."

"I'm not jealous!"

Declan made the same face he did whenever Ronan tried to bluff at the poker table. He didn't buy it.

"Sure, sure. But let me get this straight. Are you telling me you never felt anything for Lauren before you realized she was single?"

"That's not the point. I behaved myself. Never even suggested anything happen."

"Nothing at all?" Declan quirked a brow. "Because I do recall quite a lot of coziness whenever I saw the two of you together. Holding hands, gazing at each other all googly-eyed."

"We didn't even kiss."

"Right. Want to tell me what you *almost* did? What you *thought* about?"

Ronan absolutely did not want to go there. There were at least three times when he almost kissed Lauren without knowing whether she was someone's wife or mother.

He'd been caught in his own net.

"Okay, got it. *Almost* doesn't count, and I'm not perfect, either. Definitely not a candidate for sainthood."

"Imagine, two flawed human beings finding each other, coming together." Declan moved his hands apart then clapped them together. "You're perfect for *each other*."

"*She is*, maybe, but I'm certainly no catch. I'm barely hanging on here."

"I thought things were better since you decided to stay." Then Declan's eyes softened as if he understood. "Oh. This is about your mother, isn't it? You still haven't dealt with that loss."

"I wasn't there for her like I should have been."

He'd been deployed at the time and had to request an exemption which went through several channels before approved. Thankfully, he'd been with her the week before she died and taken her on that last ride to the hospital.

"Look, I can't imagine what it's like losing both parents. Last year when my father fell and was rushed to the ER, I panicked, worried so much I'd lose him when we were on bad terms. You and Aunt Diane were close and she knew how much you loved her. You were here for her when it mattered."

Ronan pictured the slamming ER doors in his face, similar to the night he'd ridden in the ambulance with Lauren, and even then, the memory had risen like a slap. His commander had allowed him to leave his duty station when it was clear his mother was dying. If not for his compassion, Ronan would not have been here in her last days. After her funeral, all arrangements taken care of by Uncle Dan and Aunt Lorna, he'd gone straight back to his duty station and finished that deployment. Little wonder that Uncle Dan had begged him not to go back. And not surprising that Ronan did feel done. It just wasn't going to be easy to ease back into this new life.

"If you need the name of a good therapist," Declan said. "I've got one."

A few years ago, Declan had been teaching and coaching at a high school in Houston when a disgruntled father came to school with a gun. All because Declan had benched his son. A tragedy had been averted, but Declan wouldn't go back to coaching for years after the event.

"Maybe I'll take that number," Ronan said, plopping down on the couch. "If I'm going to be in a serious relationship, I've got to be whole for her. She deserves it."

"I don't blame you for taking a step back. This all happened so fast, and the entire time, you felt responsible for her. The relationship was one-sided when she didn't have much to give you. It has to be tough knowing that she doesn't need you anymore. Not in the same way."

His cousin had definitely nailed it, as he always tended to do when he wasn't busy trying to beat Ronan at something. Declan took a seat and grabbed the remote, switching it to the baseball game where the San Francisco Giants were beating the Padres. Great. From bad to worse.

"I did enjoy it for a time, being able to imagine her as this perfect woman who'd been dropped into my world. We connected but couldn't do anything about it. My job was to take care of her, to—"

"*Rescue* her?" Declan gazed at Ronan from under this baseball cap.

"Maybe."

"But she doesn't need your help anymore, which has got to be killing you."

Ronan didn't want to believe that to be true, but there might be a slight, however miniscule, truth to that statement. Most of his life, he'd lived to save people. He'd made a career out of it and learned he wasn't always going to win. There had been many casualties at war, and one at home. The one which mattered the most, and he hadn't been able to save his mother from the illness that took her from him. The disease took her from ever becoming a grandmother, or ever seeing her only son find the love of his life. She'd missed a lot of Ronan's adult life, in no small part due to the fact he'd been off trying to save the world instead of being home with her.

He'd be lying to say it hadn't sliced a piece of his heart off to realize this fundamental truth.

Chapter Twenty-Six

Always skilled at networking, Lauren found negotiating deals for herself while in a position as an ad executive to a major agency was, in one word: *priceless*. She'd worked on a major real estate campaign years ago, and now had agents spinning in circles to work fast and find her a rental in Charming before Christmas. Not as impossible as one would think, considering December wasn't exactly tourist season on the coast. She offered a generous bonus to the first agent who found her a place.

Right before Christmas, she moved into her little beach cottage rental. She came bearing only a couple of suitcases, one filled with shoes (sue her, she still loved them) and the other with clothes. The cottage came fully furnished, and Jane's painting of the cottage in the woods was the only picture Lauren hung on a wall. This was all temporary. She'd contacted the co-op to start the process of selling her condo and hired a company to put everything she owned in storage. Where she'd go after this was not certain, only that she wouldn't go back to the place that had given her such little joy.

After the holidays, she'd consider a less luxurious place in Dallas or one of the suburbs. Maybe Harry would consider allowing her to start a satellite office in lieu of working from home. Or she might simply go into work a few times a week. Either way, she had pull at the agency, and Harry would work with her rather than lose her. All those years of hard work and sacrifice were finally going to deliver in a way that mattered other than financially.

On the afternoon she moved in, she was startled to receive a text message from the last person she expected to hear from.

Ronan:
How are you doing? Is Dallas everything you remembered?

How was she doing?
How was she doing?
Not well! She wanted to throw her phone at the wall. How *should* she be doing when he'd left her in Dallas like an old piece of furniture? She was still angry with him. He could have explained his feelings, kissed her and reassured her, and not simply left her on the first day she'd come back to her old life. Yes, she was fine but what he'd done wasn't very nice. Maybe he didn't think she needed him anymore, and in many ways, she didn't. But because she loved him, it was a very different kind of need.

It took her ten minutes to formulate a response.

I'm fine.

Ronan:
The garden is doing good.

He sent a photo of their little garden, and her eyes filled with tears. She missed that house so much. In just two weeks, it had become more of a home to her than any other place she'd ever lived, other than her grandparents' farm.

Looks nice.

After that followed several hours of radio silence. Lauren had just finished purchasing one of the last Christmas trees left on the lot when she had another text message.

Ronan:
I'd like to see you. We need to talk. Maybe I could come to Dallas.

Sweaty and sticky from single-handedly hauling in her tree, a thrum of outrage shot through her at his request. So, now he'd "like to see her." She didn't know what kind of game he was playing, but she wasn't just going to forgive him anytime soon. He'd been everything to her when she had nothing. Her center. Her heart. And then he'd left.

I'm busy working on an ad campaign. Sorry.

He didn't respond for several interminable seconds as she stared at her phone, the bubbles indicating he might be composing her a lengthy response. Maybe several paragraphs of an apology. A poem, perhaps. She waited, filled with stupid hope.

Ronan:
Okay.

Okay? What in the world did that mean? Did he expect her to forget about him so easily and just go back like nothing ever happened? She considered telling him she was back in town, but she'd rather let him squirm and believe she was going on with her life, without him. Maybe he'd wonder whether he'd pushed her straight into Drew's arms. A hint of completely unfounded jealousy had flared in Ronan even if he'd denied it. And yes, she understood what he'd been through before, but how about a little faith in her?

Later that night, there was another text just as she'd finished decorating the tree and was getting ready for bed.

Ronan:
I'm going to start therapy soon. Finally figured out I have a few things going on. Thought you should know.

She read the text twice to make sure she'd gotten it right. A small tingle of forgiveness for the way he'd treated her surfaced, and she pushed it back down. Good for him for getting help. She responded.

Great idea.

She added the lightbulb emoji for emphasis. Genius move on getting counseling for the grief, and possible PTSD, and, oh, maybe some abandonment issues.

Ronan:
Occasionally, I do have them. Not many lately other than the garden.

Lauren considered replying to keep the conversation going since it seemed he was reaching out. But he'd have to do a lot more than a few text messages for her forgiveness.

She went to bed with her phone beside her but received no further texts from Ronan.

Tomorrow, she'd see Amy, and the thought warmed her as she drifted off to sleep.

Ronan couldn't stop thinking about Lauren and the mess he'd made. But thinking about her, dreaming about her, that was one thing.

Now he thought he was *seeing* her everywhere.

He'd been driving by the tree lot yesterday when he'd witnessed another tall, dark-haired woman who could have been Lauren's doppelgänger hauling a tree to her vehicle. Then, the very next day, he saw what looked like the same woman at Glamtique, the place she'd been keeping in business. But that couldn't be, because she was in Dallas and stated so when he'd asked to come see her. He didn't have any right, of course, but in a moment of weakness, he'd texted her. If she'd ever loved him, she might find it in her heart to forgive him for leaving her in Dallas. But he'd been wrong. She was now too busy for him. It was nothing less than he deserved.

He'd been so damned judgmental about her very human flaws, as if he didn't have any. There were many, and he thought the best person to remind him of these was Belinda. She might also have some insight into where he went wrong in their relationship so that he could fix himself for Lauren's sake. Although he suspected that his main mistake with Belinda was his absence. And ironically, he was repeating history with Lauren.

When he'd called her, Belinda agreed to meet him at the Salty Dog for a drink. She'd said she wanted to be friends. Understanding how he'd failed her in so many ways, he was willing to forgive now, even if they'd never truly be friends.

Friendship, for him, was now forever reserved for the people who would die for him. They were few and far between.

He arrived first and found a booth on the dining side of the bar, even though he wasn't hungry. Thoughts of Belinda, of their good times, rolled through his memories, but they were few. Once, he'd loved her more than he thought possible. Now the memories of their days were slippery, like the ones Lauren had described to him. Like the thought caught in some drawer of his brain that was locked to him.

She saw him immediately and waved, walking toward him without hesitation. "Hi, Ronan."

He stood, though he gestured for her to sit on the opposite side of the booth, which thankfully, she did.

"Belinda."

"Thank you for meeting me."

"I'm the one who should say thank you. I was rude to you the last time we saw each other."

She waved it away. "Imagine meeting for the first time in so many years in the garden center. It wasn't exactly the right place to talk and I'm sorry if I pushed too hard."

The waitress arrived and took their orders. A soda for him. He didn't want to be here long.

"That was all me and I'm sorry if I was an ass."

"It's okay. It's not like I didn't deserve it."

"You didn't. I'm not in the habit of being rude to women, especially not you." Ronan fiddled with the coaster under his cold beer. "I think... I don't know exactly how to say this, and it isn't easy for me. You should know how much you hurt me. *Both* of you."

"Yes, I know." She reached and put a hand over his. "And I'm so sorry."

He pulled his hand back. "I wasn't lying when I said I've

moved on. But this bitterness toward both of you stayed with me. That probably hurt me more than it ever hurt you."

"Frankly, I was surprised you took the breakup so hard. That last time you came home… I actually thought you'd met someone else. You had no time for me."

"Belinda, my mother was *dying*." He met her gaze.

"I know, but that's when the people you love surround and support you. You allowed your family inside that inner circle, but not *me*." She pointed to herself. "You shut yourself off and wouldn't talk about any of it. Not with me."

"You're right." Ronan clasped and unclasped his hands together. "I can see now how that was a mistake."

He'd never been one to talk about his problems, and when he'd been with Lauren, her problem was big enough to take over everything. She was just what he'd needed. A distraction from his own grief and doing the hard work. His problems were miniscule in comparison to hers. He'd grown accustomed to the bubble they'd been living in and hadn't wanted it to end with the harshness of reality. She *wasn't* a blank slate. She had a past filled with experiences, pain, and mistakes.

Not unlike him.

Belinda fiddled with the silverware, not looking at him. "The problem is you're a rescuer. And while that's great for those who are in desperate need of saving, in a relationship, you've got to let yourself be rescued a little, too. It's a give-and-take."

"Yeah, well, this time I fell in love too fast. That's not like me. It takes me years to trust someone."

"I remember that about you. So, are we talking about the girl you rescued?"

"Yeah." Ronan let out a breath.

"That's not a surprise. She needed you, and you love being needed."

"But I screwed it up. All because I hadn't taken the time to forgive you, and accept the fact I made mistakes, too."

"Aren't you going to try and fix this?"

"I don't know if I can. She won't see me now." He opened his palms, studied them like they had the answer.

"Well, you need to try harder if she means that much to you."

"There are laws which frown on stalking. I'm not going where I'm not wanted."

Belinda made a face, like he was being deliberately obtuse. "I'm sure you can think of something. Is there something she really loves, I mean, besides you?"

"Shoes," Ronan said, fighting a smile. "She really loves shoes. I'm not going to buy her more shoes."

Belinda rolled her eyes.

"We *all* love shoes. Something far more personal. Meaningful. Something that would show her you were paying attention all along."

Chapter Twenty-Seven

"What a cute little cottage," Amy said, turning around in circles. "It's a bit like the one Finn and Michelle were staying in for a while."

"It came fully furnished, other than the tree I put up." Lauren walked to the only thing in this house that was truly hers. "But this is mine."

Once again, she admired the soft lines, flowers sprouting all along the country lane in bright beautiful splashes of color. It made her happy in a way she couldn't really describe.

"It's beautiful," Amy said. "I can't believe you know the artist."

Lauren had told Amy that she didn't want Ronan knowing she was back in Charming. He still owed her an apology and she hadn't received it via text, mail, or carrier pigeon. Until he apologized for being rude and judgy, she didn't want to see him.

Today, she and Amy were going to volunteer at a soup kitchen outside town.

"Christmas is day after tomorrow," Amy said as she pulled into the parking lot at Helping Hands. "This could all go a lot faster if Ronan knew you were in town. He'd come after you. I know it."

"Amy, no offense but stop trying to play matchmaker. *He's* going to have to step up."

"Okay, okay. I get it, but can I help that I love the idea of you two together?" She playfully batted her eyelashes. "You would be a dream sister-in-law. Don't get me wrong, Michelle is great, but I feel especially close to you."

"Aw, Amy." Lauren pulled Amy into a hug. She was petite, several inches shorter than Lauren, and it did feel like hugging a little sister. "You would be a dream of a sister for me, too."

She dropped the in-law part and Amy noticed. Her eyes filled. "I never had a sister."

They stood at the entrance to the soup kitchen, hugging, crying a little bit, until someone got in line behind them.

"Oh, we're not here for the food," Amy said, wiping her eyes. "Please go ahead."

The woman was young, with dark hair like Lauren's, holding a little girl's hand. They were both dressed in clearly secondhand, well-worn, and faded clothes, their shoes dirty. Lauren ached for them like she hurt for the little girl who'd been called a "dirty "farm girl." It took her years to realize she *was* a dirty farm girl and proud of it. She only hoped this little girl wouldn't have the same problems with her self-esteem.

Lauren bent down to speak to the girl. "What's your name?"

"Anna Maria," she said, flashing Lauren a toothy smile. "This is my mami, Lydia, she don't speak English too good."

The mother spoke a few words in Spanish, and Lauren, who wasn't bilingual but could certainly still recognize the language, understood that the mother wanted to know what her daughter had said to the two strangers. Anna Maria spoke rapidly, translating, looking up at her mother with adoration. She looked to be about seven.

"You and your mami come to my line," Lauren said. "And I'll give you extra just because you're so cute."

Several hours later, they'd fed close to the one hundred people who'd shown up for the soup kitchen's holiday meal of turkey, ham, stuffing, cranberry sauce, and mashed potatoes. As promised, she gave Anna Maria and Lydia extra, with a little wink.

Afterward, Lauren confessed to Amy that the mother-daughter duo had reminded her of her own mother.

"We didn't have much, but though it sounds like a total cliché, I didn't realize this for a long time. I adored her and my life was everything when she was with me. It was only later, after she died and I went to live with my grandparents, that I noticed I was poor. I had to switch schools and the kids called me a dirty farm girl because everything I owned was secondhand."

"That's horrible."

"It is, but so many of those little moments shape who we are, and it's not all bad. They certainly gave me a purpose and drive to do better, to be better than them. Lucky for me, my mother was the first person to write on my heart and I always felt loved. Just not by everyone." Lauren laughed. "I'm sorry to say I carried my desire to prove myself worthy too far. Do you realize I have a bedroom full of shoes and clothes?"

"That used to be a dream of mine." Amy sighed.

"Obviously, it was mine, too, but it's not all you might think. A bedroom for a closet gives you too much room. Then you buy things for the sake of buying them, or because they're on sale. I have dresses I've never worn. When I move, that's the first room I'll clear out. I'll find places to donate everything. I just want to make sure they don't charge people for the clothes, but just give them away."

"I'm sure I can put you in touch with some organizations."

"The people I work with act like I've gone nuts. I took my assistant to lunch before I left Dallas and she kept looking at me like she expected me to sprout wings at any moment. They think I'm a different person, but they don't realize I've simply gone back to who I used to be. True, I could have chosen to go back to the woman I was before the accident, but I didn't like her very much. She had a lot to learn, and if it took losing everything I had, I'm glad it happened."

"I'm just happy you survived."

"Me, too."

Amy dropped Lauren off at her beach rental. "You sure you don't want to come over? We could sneak you in through the back and Ronan would never have to know."

Lauren snorted at the image. "No, but I'll see you on Christmas Day."

On that day, she didn't care what Ronan did.

Later that day, she'd finished firing off her initial proposal to Front Porch Cookies since she'd been working on it in her spare time, nonstop. She signed off, explaining she would be unavailable until after the thirty-first and to please get in touch with Katrina, her assistant, who would relay any urgent messages. Then, she did something she'd never done in ten years of hard work: She set up her email automatic response that she'd be unavailable for the holidays.

And even though she'd wanted him to take the lead, Lauren missed him so much she had to text Ronan before she went to bed that evening.

I was thinking about you. How are you doing?

He replied immediately.

Funny, I was thinking about you too. Thought I saw you at the tree lot but it must have been someone who looked like you.

Curse her for initiating the conversation! Now she would either have to lie or tell him the truth. She went for the middle ground.

That is funny. Well, I'm whipped, so goodnight. Sweet dreams.

She waited a few seconds for a response, but the bubble never even came. Lauren pulled back the covers and climbed in. Ronan did seem sorry, but he'd never *said* he was. She wasn't a mind reader. He was the one to basically break them up, so if he wanted to see her again, he was going to have to grovel. Should she tell him, or just let him figure it out for himself? Was he sorry, or just trying to ease her hurt feelings and his own guilt? He'd said he'd wanted to see her, so that had to mean something.

Her thoughts were a maze of confusion, and she tossed and turned until she finally found sleep.

Ronan read Lauren's last text message twice. She hadn't even denied it. Nope, no denial. Ha. Busted.

He wasn't seeing things and he wasn't becoming unhinged with heartache. He might have let the tree lot and the boutique go, but this afternoon, he'd seen Amy and

Lauren just outside the soup kitchen. Neither one of them realized it was across the street from his gym.

He'd finally decided what he had to do to *show* Lauren he loved her. Now he wasn't taking care of her, protecting her, because that part of their relationship was over. But he had other ways of showing his love, and facts were he understood her better than most people did. For his gesture, he'd need Amy's help.

That evening, he found himself knocking on his next-door neighbor's door.

Amy opened. "Oh, hi, Ronan. Declan isn't here. He went to—"

"That's okay, I'm here to talk to you." Ronan let himself inside.

"What about?" She followed him, then pressed her hands together prayer-like. "Is it about Lauren? Because I promised her I wouldn't play matchmaker, but I didn't promise you any such thing."

"Yes, it's about Lauren. I thought I saw her at the tree lot, but since she's in Dallas… Then, funny thing. Earlier today, I saw you and her both at the soup kitchen. Time to 'fess up. Where is she?" He narrowed his eyes and crossed his arms.

"Well, she's not *here. I swear.*"

"Obviously. I'd like to think I would have noticed that."

"She's… First, let me say I know she really loves you. And she was desperately hurt when you left her."

"I didn't *leave* her. Okay, yeah, but I *said*—" He was about to explain how he'd only meant "time to think," but even he realized how it must have all sounded to her. Like he'd given up when they hit a rough patch.

It was the reason he'd almost turned back twice.

"Don't be a dopey guy. Forget what you *said*. The point

is how she feels about what you did. It was a statement. It made it look like you had judged her for something she didn't do." Amy went hand on hip, in a scolding tone.

Ronan groaned. He hated his mistakes broadcast to anyone. "She *told* you about that?"

"Listen, mister, we're besties. Of course she told me."

Ronan ran a hand down his face in exasperation. "If it helps, I regret it. It's possibly the biggest mistake I ever made."

Amy jumped up and down clapping her hands. "Oh goody, that's the first step. Admitting you were wrong. Do you love her?"

He no longer had any doubt. "More than anything."

"Then, I'm going to help you. She's coming to our house on Christmas Day, and if you happen to be here, too, there's not a thing I can do about it." She gave him a conspiratorial smile.

"Thank you, Amy."

"Don't ruin this, big guy, because I want her for a sister-in-law for Christmas!"

"Even I don't work that fast." He smirked. "But let me see what I can do about that, given a little more time."

Ronan had a short time to work his miracle. He had a plan and all he needed was twenty-four hours of hard work, and a whole lot of dirt.

On Christmas morning, Lauren wrapped the last of her packages with a pretty pink bow. This one was for Naomi, an entire set of artist's pencils in every color under the rainbow. On the tag she wrote "To Naomi: never stop seeing colors."

David was harder to buy for until Amy mentioned his interest in baseball. She'd managed to order a special collection of baseball cards of all the greats. On the tag she wrote "To David: never stop reaching for your dreams."

Lauren had worked hard to reach her dreams of financial freedom. And if she hadn't, if she'd allowed those mean kids to define her future, she'd have never been on that yacht and fallen overboard. She would have never met the love of her life. Then again, she might also not feel this raw ache inside that maybe things wouldn't work out. Maybe he couldn't get past her mistake. Maybe he was too damaged to forgive.

Later that morning, she loaded her car with presents. Two days ago, her car had been delivered to her beach rental, good as new. She now found it kind of funny that it was red, as she wanted to be a female Santa driving her sleigh. Lauren was prepared to possibly see Ronan today, as it was nearly inevitable. But she'd managed to keep her expectations dialed to zero. He'd stopped texting after their last string of messages. Either he was angry she'd lied and decided to make himself scarce on Christmas, or he would be there, wanting to talk. She didn't know what other reason he would have wanted to see her in Dallas. He might have felt guilty about the way he'd left things and wanted to break it off like a man. Or maybe this time, he'd give her time to explain.

She arrived at the appointed time Amy gave her. They'd exchange presents with the family, and then have brunch prepared by Amy and her mother. Declan and Amy would be having a family dinner later with Finn and Michelle.

Lauren did not expect the tsunami of emotion that filled her once she pulled in front of the home on Bluebird Lane. The light displays were on, the choir figurines singing "O Holy Night" on Ronan's side not synched with the ones on Declan's side. The effect was jarring, overwhelming, loud, and messy. And she loved every single bit of it. The time she'd spent at this home had changed her. On that crazy and fateful night, she'd wound up in this little enclave with the most generous people she'd ever met. She'd been so scared that night, not knowing who she was or where she belonged. Ronan had pulled her out of that dark place.

The moment she walked in the door with her bag of presents, Naomi and David ran to her.

"Look, it's Elsa. I mean, Lauren!" David laughed.

"Oh, Lauren." Naomi hugged Lauren's waist. "I missed you."

Tears welled in Lauren's eyes. "I missed you, too."

"See?" Amy went hands on hips. "I told you she'd be back. Does your mother know everything, or what?"

"Okay, kids. Let's give her some room to breathe." Declan reached for her bag. "Can I take this for you?"

Lauren handed over the sack filled with wrapped gifts, and as the kids moved away, and Amy stepped aside, it was as if the crowd parted, and there he was, standing only a few feet away from her. Seeing him again, the overwhelming surge of love for him hit her hard and fast. Her heart tugged powerfully. She loved him beyond words.

"Hi," he said.

"Hi," she parroted, and then for creativity points, added, "How are you?"

He answered with a smile and her heart swelled with hope. She couldn't stop looking at him because it seemed like far longer than a few days. In such a short time, she'd fallen so hard it would seem odd were it anyone but Ronan. But he made it easy to love him, easy to trust.

"Let's open gifts!" David yelled from the living room. "C'mon, what are we waiting for!"

"David, please," Amy said. *"Behave."*

"But Mo-om…" David whined.

"Mom, please?" Naomi asked.

"Kids, if you don't mind, can I give my present first?" Ronan said.

"Yeah! Whatever. Let's get going," David said, picking up a package and shaking it until Declan took it away from him.

"My gift for Lauren is next door," Ronan said, not breaking eye contact with her.

"Go get it, Uncle Ronan!" Naomi tugged on the sleeve of his shirt.

"No, it's…something that can't be moved." His eyes were still locked with hers. "We all have to go next door."

"Next *door?*" David whined again.

"It's not like it's far," Declan said with an eyeroll. "You could use the exercise."

Something that couldn't be moved. Lauren's mind reeled with possibilities. It obviously wasn't jewelry, or shoes, or sexy lingerie. And she understood. They'd taken a step back and that would be a leap forward. It didn't matter what he had for her. Point being, he had a *gift* for her. Like David, she could hardly wait to unwrap it. It could be anything at all and she'd be happy he'd thought of her.

Ronan held his hand out to her and she clutched it tightly. She never wanted to let go. He led the way and together they walked into the house next door. Amy, Declan, and the kids followed them like in the tale of the Pied Piper.

"It's out here," Ronan said, motioning to the backyard.

"Outside?" Naomi squealed, her range going higher with each word. "What is it? *What is it?* Is it a *puppy?*"

Naomi's over-the-top excitement echoed Lauren's sentiments exactly, but she hoped it wasn't a puppy. She wasn't ready for a puppy when she lived in a rental.

"Not a puppy," Ronan said and then he slid open the glass door.

Lauren followed him outside and her breath caught in her throat with a gasp. She blinked twice as though seeing a mirage.

This couldn't be real.

Chapter Twenty-Eight

For several moments, Lauren couldn't speak, taking it all in.

"Where is it? I still don't see anything," David said, hands over his eyes in "search" mode.

"David, sweetheart, please stop talking," Amy said.

"Did you...did you do all this?" Lauren squeezed Ronan's hand.

"Yes, he did," Declan piped up. "I tried to help, but he said this was his thing. I did, however, put up a floodlight when he was out here at midnight, working in the dark."

"There was moonlight," Ronan said. "But thanks for that."

Ronan had transformed this backyard into a virtual explosion of flowers. There were poinsettias, camellias, winter jasmine, snowdrops, and a smattering of flowers Lauren couldn't name, but all of which brought her favorite painting to life. It was her own real-life country lane, filled with color and life and love. She was so entranced with the display of flowers that she neglected to notice the vegetable garden. They'd grown, too. Ronan had added a small gate to separate them from the rest of the yard.

A wooden sign hung on the garden latch that read: Lauren's Garden.

Her heart cracked open, swelling with love. Even if she didn't already love him, this would do it. He knew her better than anyone else. She already had so much, but he'd found the one thing she didn't have. A garden like the one in her favorite drawing. He held tightly on to her hand as he led her around the path he'd made. A lot of sweat and hard labor had gone into this gift.

"This is a ton of flowers!" Naomi said, skipping along the path. "Look! It's like the Secret Garden."

"Where did you get them all?" David said.

Ronan smiled at Lauren when he answered. "I pretty much bought out the garden center. Amy's mother was more than happy to help me scout them out. This is every winter bloom we could find."

Lauren stepped closer to him and lowered her voice. "Is this what you wanted to tell me in person?"

She could see why a picture wouldn't have worked and wouldn't have nearly the impact of seeing this with her own eyes.

"No, this was a last-minute Hail Mary pass. I've told you, but I haven't shown you enough. I love you, Lauren, and I screwed up in Dallas. I should have never left you there. Can you forgive me?"

With his hand on the nape of her neck, pulling her close, she didn't even have to say yes. She simply kissed him, not caring where they were or the fact they had company. Ronan didn't seem to care, either, as his fingers threaded through her hair, holding her in place, and he took the kiss even deeper.

It was suddenly so quiet she could hear the sound of her own heartbeat thudding in her ears. Then she realized that Amy and Declan had ushered the kids out of here, giving them some privacy.

"I forgive you," she said, in case she hadn't been clear. "You're allowed to make mistakes. You're a flawed human being like we all are."

He pressed his forehead to hers. "I've made plenty of mistakes and I'm sure this won't be the last one."

"Maybe true love is forgiving each other every day. For a lifetime."

"Forgiving me once a day would be asking too much. But I'll try not to give you many reasons."

"I'll do the same because I'm so in love with you. I never thought it could be like this. But how does this work? Me in Dallas, you in Charming, or traveling all over the world?"

"We'll figure it out and I'll find a way. Whatever it takes." He motioned to the garden, and the flowers. "Obviously, you will need to come here often to enjoy the fruits of my labor."

"Every weekend." She kissed his neck, nuzzling against the stubble on his chin. "You can't keep me away."

She could stay like this for hours, him just holding her close in his arms, her leaning against him. All his strength came with a fuzzy middle, too. The softness of him that loved her, who had put her at the center of his heart. The genuine man who planted flowers for her because he wanted this place to remind her of home. If that wasn't love, she didn't know what love was.

"I've put my agency on notice that I'm no longer working all the time. I have different priorities now, and I'm going to have a rocking and robust personal life."

"Should we get started on the robust personal life now?"

She glanced up at him and found him waggling his eyebrows.

Cupping his face, she admired his shimmering blue eyes. This gorgeous man was hers and hers alone.

"I missed you, too. But what about brunch?"

"They won't care if we're late." He tugged her back inside the house.

She stopped him in the kitchen, wrapping her hands around his neck. "I want you to know something first. Even if no one had ever found me, I would have been happy to start all over with you."

There was never a "quickie" when it came to Ronan, but approximately an hour and a half later, they were both presentable again. Happy, thoroughly sated, and presentable. Holding hands, they crossed the shared lawn.

David threw open the door then stood in the doorway, arms crossed. "What *took* you so long?"

"Um," Ronan said and if Lauren didn't know any better, she'd think this big man blushed.

Declan intervened, ushering them inside. "We wouldn't open any of your gifts until you got here, so the natives are getting restless."

The living room was filled with wrapping paper, Amy slowly picking it all up. Lauren joined her to help.

"There you are." Amy beamed. "I would also ask what took so long, but I think I know the answer."

Lauren was fairly sure *she* blushed this time. "I'm sorry to keep the kids waiting for their presents."

"Oh please. David particularly needs to learn a little patience. It's good for him." She eyed the spread in the kitchen. "Are you hungry? I'll bet you worked up an appetite."

"Stop." Lauren elbowed her. "But yeah."

Lauren followed Amy to the kitchen and was introduced to her mother, who loaded up two plates with a breakfast casserole chock full of queso, bacon, chicken quesadillas, and slices of pastry. Lauren rejoined everyone in the living room and handed Ronan a plate.

"Honestly, I think we can all stop trying, because Ronan has won Christmas. He beat us all at finding the perfect gift," Amy announced.

"It's called winning." Ronan tipped back on his heels, a smile tugging at his lips.

"It's great, I admit, except for the gift Amy is giving me," Declan said, putting his arm around her belly. "I'd call that a win."

"Maybe you both won at the game of life this time," Lauren said with a smirk.

How she'd missed these two and their one-upmanship. As long as it inspired each of them to be a better man, she didn't see the problem.

"Are we ready?" Naomi held up a present and shook it.

"Yes," Lauren said. "Go ahead, and thanks for your patience."

Naomi opened the artist pencils Lauren had given her, for which she got a huge hug and kiss. "Thank you!"

"Your mom told me you love to draw," Lauren said.

David also thanked her enthusiastically for the baseball card collection. "You're the best!"

"She definitely is." Ronan slid his hand down her back.

She'd forgotten how much he loved to touch her every chance he had. Ronan's gifts were opened next. Naomi giggled when her stuffed animal dog barked as she squeezed him. Loudly. Declan narrowed his eyes at Ronan, who mouthed, "winning," and held up three fingers like a *W*. At least it wasn't a drum set for David.

The gift she'd ordered for Ronan was last, even if she didn't think it could possibly do justice to the one he'd given her. Other than her life, of course, which he'd saved.

She carried over the fishing pole and lures she'd bought from an expert.

"I don't want you to give up because your first experience wasn't stellar." She hooked a thumb to her chest. "And I'll go with you."

Ronan laughed. "*If* you promise to stay in the boat this time."

Lauren had no doubts that if she ever fell again, off a boat or otherwise, metaphorically or physically... Ronan would be there to catch her. Or find her.

He'd never give up and neither would she in finding her way home.

Epilogue

New Year's Eve

Declan and Amy's last-minute wedding was held at Ronan's house outdoors among the path of flowers he'd planted for Lauren. Ironically, Amy now proclaimed it the perfect venue for them. This home was the second place she and Declan had fallen in love, and so it made a lot of sense. It was also where he'd fallen in love with Lauren, so he liked to think of this as a lucky house.

Even with all their flowers, Lauren still placed an expedited special order of tiny little pink-and-white flowers she called baby's breath so Naomi could scatter them along the path to the makeshift altar. Apparently this was something the little girl had been dying to do. David, for his part, was officially declared Declan's faux "best man," because he'd moaned about being too old to be ring bearer, a job usually held by little kids. This made Declan's decision between Finn and Ronan as best man moot.

Lauren campaigned to pay for the wedding, but after talking to Declan, Amy had changed her mind. They both wanted something fast, small, and intimate and decided the evening of the thirty-first would be perfect, asking only to borrow their beautifully landscaped backyard. Not only would Uncle Dan and Aunt Lorna be back from their travels by the thirty-first, but it would be a great way to end the year. When Ronan picked up his aunt and uncle at the airport, at the conclusion of their Irish travels, *they* weren't the ones with the biggest news. Ronan listened patiently through the narration of their travels in Ireland, spending Christmas in a snow-capped village, and visiting long-lost relatives. Then, in quick succession, he informed them Amy and Declan were getting hitched, and Ronan and Lauren were very much together and committed to each other.

"I should go away more often!" Uncle Dan hooted. "Everything worked out."

"And without *you*, honey, imagine that," Aunt Lorna said. "See? Everything won't fall apart when we go away."

Now Ronan viewed the small crowd in his yard assembled for this small wedding. Uncle Dan and Aunt Lorna were seated together on the fold-out chairs, next to Amy's mother and stepfather. Michelle and Finn were in attendance, too, of course, as were some of Declan's buddies from his short time in the major leagues, much of the high school baseball team he currently coached, and Amy's colleagues from school, like Valerie Kinsella. She was there with her husband, Cole, part owner of the Salty Dog Bar & Grill, where Declan and Amy had worked together for a short time.

In other words, it was hardly an intimate crowd as they wanted to celebrate with everyone.

Even if Amy protested she was a grown woman with two children and didn't need anyone *giving* her away (going so far as to refer to the custom as part of the patriarchy), she was too kind to hurt anyone else's feelings. She'd invited her mother's partner, Lou, to give her away in place of her late father. When they walked down the aisle to meet Declan and the pastor at the altar, Ronan, done with his ushering duties, joined Lauren. She reached for him to squeeze his hand, but her eyes and big smile were on Amy, her new best friend. Ronan, for his part, caught Declan's eyes. He held up the *W* sign for "winning." Yeah, Ronan couldn't disagree there. It was all in good fun and he couldn't be happier for Declan, who'd regretted it almost the moment after he and Amy broke up, all those years ago, and went their separate ways.

Ronan had once envied Declan for winding up with his first love but had a different view now. As the old country song went, "sometimes God's greatest gifts are unanswered prayers." In the end, no one could ever be more perfect for him than Lauren. For the first time in his life he believed in "meant to be." He believed in dumb luck. Yes, even Irish luck. If he hadn't been fishing in the bay that night but gone to the gym as he'd originally intended, he wouldn't have been there to save Lauren.

Then she wouldn't have been able to save him.

Uncle Dan made the same Irish toast he'd made at Finn and Michelle's wedding, and Ronan hoped he'd make at his.

"'May the road rise to meet you. May the wind be always at your back. May the sun shine warm upon your face. The rains fall soft upon your fields.' May the light of friendship guide your paths together. May the laughter of children grace the halls of your home. Congratulations, Declan and Amy Sheridan!"

"You were right," Lauren said, as she danced with him to the music of Maroon 5 and Taylor Swift. Both Amy and Declan had chosen their favorite love songs from the time they were both in high school. "The DJ is perfect. An orchestra would have been too much."

"Overkill." He nodded.

She narrowed her eyes at him. "I don't think you can speak to overkill, sir. Do I need to remind you of your lights display?"

"You don't have to, but I have a feeling you will." He chuckled as he grabbed her behind.

"Hey, hey, now." She moved his hand to the more appropriate position on her waist. "Children are present."

Thanks to their display of lights, however, guests had no trouble finding the house. Particularly since they'd been written up in the *Charming Gazette* as the two cousins who'd duked it out. The jury was still deliberating on who'd officially won the battle of the Christmas lights, but Ronan wasn't holding his breath. He'd no longer cared since he'd already won the proverbial gold at the end of the rainbow.

He was, in a word, every Irish cliché of good luck and happy for it.

Ronan and Lauren were already making plans for their future. After a suitable time period of adjustment to being back at the agency and decreasing her hours, Lauren planned to broach the subject of a satellite office in Houston, or Charming itself. They both wanted children, of course, but wanted a little more time together first. Ronan had an assignment in Rome in six months and he had secret plans. He'd already asked Lauren to come with him and take some time off work. She seemed excited about the idea, as in all her travels with the agency, she'd never been to Rome. He already had the ring and hoped she'd be as excited when he asked her to marry him.

The music slowed to a ballad, and Ronan used the opportunity to pull Lauren even closer.

Hand on the nape of her neck, he tipped her face to him. "Hey, you want to know something? You have my heart, and I'll always be here for you."

Tears welled in her eyes. "I know. You've made me so happy."

"Yeah? What are the odds I can get you alone soon?"

"I'd say the forecast looks excellent. You are one lucky Irishman."

He brought her hand to his lips and kissed it. "Don't I know it, babe."

* * * * *

Get up to 4 Free Books!

We'll send you 2 free books from each series you try PLUS a free Mystery Gift.

FREE Value Over **$25**

Both the **Harlequin® Special Edition** and **Harlequin® Heartwarming™** series feature compelling novels filled with stories of love and strength where the bonds of friendship, family and community unite.

YES! Please send me 2 FREE novels from the Harlequin Special Edition or Harlequin Heartwarming series and my FREE Gift (gift is worth about $10 retail). After receiving them, if I don't wish to receive any more books, I can return the shipping statement marked "cancel." If I don't cancel, I will receive 6 brand-new Harlequin Special Edition books every month and be billed just $6.39 each in the U.S. or $7.19 each in Canada, or 4 brand-new Harlequin Heartwarming Larger-Print books every month and be billed just $7.19 each in the U.S. or $7.99 each in Canada, a savings of 20% off the cover price. It's quite a bargain! Shipping and handling is just 50¢ per book in the U.S. and $1.25 per book in Canada.* I understand that accepting the 2 free books and gift places me under no obligation to buy anything. I can always return a shipment and cancel at any time by calling the number below. The free books and gift are mine to keep no matter what I decide.

Choose one:
☐ **Harlequin Special Edition** (235/335 BPA G36Y)
☐ **Harlequin Heartwarming Larger-Print** (161/361 BPA G36Y)
☐ **Or Try Both!** (235/335 & 161/361 BPA G36Z)

Name (please print)

Address   Apt. #

City   State/Province   Zip/Postal Code

Email: Please check this box ☐ if you would like to receive newsletters and promotional emails from Harlequin Enterprises ULC and its affiliates. You can unsubscribe anytime.

Mail to the Harlequin Reader Service:
IN U.S.A.: P.O. Box 1341, Buffalo, NY 14240-8531
IN CANADA: P.O. Box 603, Fort Erie, Ontario L2A 5X3

Want to explore our other series or interested in ebooks? Visit www.ReaderService.com or call 1-800-873-8635.

---

*Terms and prices subject to change without notice. Prices do not include sales taxes, which will be charged (if applicable) based on your state or country of residence. Canadian residents will be charged applicable taxes. Offer not valid in Quebec. This offer is limited to one order per household. Books received may not be as shown. Not valid for current subscribers to the Harlequin Special Edition or Harlequin Heartwarming series. All orders subject to approval. Credit or debit balances in a customer's account(s) may be offset by any other outstanding balance owed by or to the customer. Please allow 4 to 6 weeks for delivery. Offer available while quantities last.

Your Privacy—Your information is being collected by Harlequin Enterprises ULC, operating as Harlequin Reader Service. For a complete summary of the information we collect, how we use this information and to whom it is disclosed, please visit our privacy notice located at https://corporate.harlequin.com/privacy-notice. Notice to California Residents – Under California law, you have specific rights to control and access your data. For more information on these rights and how to exercise them, visit https://corporate.harlequin.com/california-privacy. For additional information for residents of other U.S. states that provide their residents with certain rights with respect to personal data, visit https://corporate.harlequin.com/other-state-residents-privacy-rights/.

HSEHW25